Lowcountry Punch

Aloha, Rich.

Enjoy,

Boo Walker *Boo*

Also by Boo Walker

Turn or Burn
Off You Go (Novella)

This book is a work of fiction. Names, characters, places, and incidents are either the product of the author's imagination or are used fictitiously, and any resemblance to actual persons, living or dead, events, or locales is entirely coincidental.

Copyright © 2014 by Boo Walker
All rights reserved.

Published by Sandy Run Press (sandyrunpress.com)

www.sandyrunpress.com

Library of Congress Control Number: 2014903731
ISBN: 978-0-9913018-3-6

For Mom, Dad, and Ben, who made me who I am.
You are bright stars in my universe.

Lowcountry Punch

I

"Oh, God, the pride of man, broken in the dust again."

- Gordon Lightfoot

CHAPTER 1

The Miami I knew wasn't all G-strings and mojitos. We were undercover, working our way up the stairs of a parking garage in the Latin Quarter, minutes from a cocaine exchange, with no backup. We'd been trying to get to whoever was up there for two weeks and needed to make arrests. I'd be damned if we were going to let them walk away just because there hadn't been a chance to call it in.

The three of us walked in tandem, our footsteps echoing through the concrete stairwell. A crane's demolition ball banged rhythmically in the distance, the driver no doubt rushing to get some work finished before the holidays. I could empathize. I couldn't wait to get home to my fiancée, Anna. It would be our first Christmas together. I was twenty miles from our home, and I could practically smell Anna's macaroni casserole bubbling over in the oven, crisping up on the top.

Like me, Rick Quivers was a special agent in the Drug Enforcement Administration. He had combed back, greased gray hair and wore white leather shoes and linen pants. He was an inch or so taller than I, probably six foot two. His face shined like he'd shaved five minutes ago. We'd borrowed him from the Tampa field office. Rick and I had been working deep cover as muscle guys for John Latell, the other guy with us. John had no idea who we really were or that he was about to be singing "The Little Drummer Boy" from a downtown holding cell on Christmas Day.

John was in his mid-forties and slightly overweight. One of his eyes didn't work and stayed put while the other eye probed you up and down when you talked to him. He owned a couple gas stations and sold coke for extra cash, and he'd brought us along in case something went wrong. He had no reason not to trust us: we'd come highly recommended due to some preliminary work of my own, and we'd already done four of these successfully.

This time, we were meeting his main source and had to make arrests. My supervisor had a quota to meet. If it had been my decision, I would have kept working the ring for a couple months, see what kind of snakes we could shake out of the tree. But, like my bad knee, supervisors and quotas are an unpleasant part of my life I can't change.

"What kind of parking garage doesn't have an elevator?" John asked, breathing like he needed to sit down. "Two days before Christmas, it's eighty-nine degrees, and I'm sweating like hell. Santa's gonna have to climb down the damn chimney in his boxers and undershirt. Fucking Miami."

"It wouldn't hurt you to lose a few, would it?" I asked.

"Thanks, asshole. Not all of us are born looking like gladiators."

"It's all in the breeding. So what's Santa bringing you this year?"

He put the working eyeball on me. "Santa don't come to my house."

Santa Claus was most certainly coming to our house. Anna and I had been engaged for almost a year, but I'd known her since I was a boy. Her fascination with Christmas hadn't diminished since the first day I met her. We had decorated our absurdly oversized tree the morning after Thanksgiving, and, through our engagement, I had inherited her four massive Tupperware boxes of lights, and little dangly elves and nutcrackers, and all sorts of fantasy, and they were everywhere. Our home was the Graceland of Christmas, and if it wasn't for the joy it brought her, I'd throw all of it in the back of my truck and make someone at Goodwill real happy.

We reached the fourth floor. Most of the garage was empty. Not many people working late today. Only twelve cars sparsely spread between two lanes. John patted the bag swinging from his shoulder, making sure the money was still there. He'd done that five times since we'd left his car, which he'd parked on the other side of the street. A smart move, I thought. You never know, we might need a fast getaway.

"There they are," John said.

There were two ways down from the top of the garage: the steps or the ramp. The sellers were on the ramp side, standing in a corner, hidden from the lights pointing down from the ceiling. John walked between us. Rick and I both packed Beretta nines. John was carrying, too. If something went wrong, blood would be shed, and it wasn't going to be ours.

Two men stood in the darkness. One was holding a bag. They started toward us. Now they were twenty feet away. The light hit their faces. Two Cuban men. I recognized them and froze. My muscles tensed up. I slowly worked my hand toward the gun at my waist. John and Rick stopped with me, feeling my anxiety.

The Cubans recognized me at the same time. Our eyes locked, and I could tell all three of us knew things were going to hell.

The two men, Diego and Robert Vasquez, were brothers. Diego, the shorter and younger of the two brothers, had a face scarred by pockmarks. Robert, I knew well. He was a cop and a friend. Seeing me, Robert's handsome face sagged at first and then sharpened, like a dog picking up a scent. The fear in his eyes told me that he wasn't there on official duty.

I'd just caught him slinging coke. "Not good," I whispered to Rick.

Robert wasn't the first dirty cop I'd known, but he was different. He was a dear friend, and a man I owed my life to.

We began to take steps backward. Agonizing seconds melted away, all of us waiting for someone to make a move.

Diego reached for his gun. The five of us scattered like marbles. Robert and Diego slipped back into the darkness. No shots were fired. Rick and I took cover behind the nearest parked car, a Cadillac. I leaned my back up against the wheel, protecting myself. He did the same.

"I know 'em," I said to Rick.

He nodded. "What you wanna do?"

"What we came here for."

I bent down low, peering under the car. The two brothers were hidden behind a thick column that extended to the wall. There were several cars in between them and the ramp, and then a good open section where they would be exposed. It wasn't an easy escape. I fished the phone out of my pocket and called in the address.

I heard a door open back by the stairwell. John Latell was making a run for it. He had decided not to hang around. That was okay. I knew where he lived, and we'd collected piles of evidence against him. The door closed behind him.

"Lay your guns down, gentlemen," I said. "This is the end of the line."

"Let us go," Robert replied. "It's not worth it. You know how this could end."

"You're right. I do. With you and your brother in the back of a patrol car. I don't make exceptions. So there's only one way this can go down. Slide your weapons into the light and move out with your hands on your heads. We've got men on the way up."

"There's money in it for you. Give us a chance to run down

that ramp. You'll be taken care of. The other one, too."

"Not gonna happen, Robert. No way." I changed tactics. "Diego!" I yelled.

"Yeah?"

"Talk some damn sense into your brother! Or neither one of you will make it."

He didn't answer.

One of them fired at us. I jerked my arms up, making sure nothing was visible. The first shot in a gun battle is the one that triggers the "fight or flight" instinct, something I was trained to accept and work with. I could feel the tunnel vision and audio exclusion trying to taking over, but I stayed focused. Let the adrenaline work to my advantage.

Two more shots flew by. Bits of the wall rained down from above.

I could hear the mumbles of an argument.

"My brother may have doubts about killing you, but I don't!" Diego yelled. "Think about your fiancée. She seemed like a good woman when we met. You've got your whole lives ahead of you. Don't make me take them away."

I didn't like him talking about Anna at all.

More quick shots rang out from their side, plugging bullets into the Cadillac, the thunderous sound echoing out into the Miami evening. I rose to a squat, and fired over the hood. I had no problem putting one in Diego, but I didn't want to shoot Robert.

He'd saved my life the year before. That's how we met. The Miami-Dade Police Department was helping us with a raid. I took a bullet in the stomach, and Sergeant Robert Vasquez ran into the line of fire to drag me out. That was the closest I have ever come to death, and if he hadn't gotten me out of there when he did, I would have died. No doubt in my mind. Only after he had gotten me to safety did he realize he'd been shot in the forearm.

LOWCOUNTRY PUNCH

We ended up in the hospital together and got to know each other well. Anna and his wife Maria became friends. Even our extended families met. Our friendship continued after we left. Backyard barbecues, double dates, and day sails on my Catalina. Robert and his wife had even been trying to teach us to tango, but teaching T.A. Reddick to dance is like teaching yoga to a brick. It's not pretty and it's not gonna work.

Despite our history, I wasn't letting anyone go. All I have is the law. That is what I do. Make exceptions and everything breaks down. I am an enforcer.

"Damn it, Robert!" I yelled. "Control your brother. There's nothing I can do."

Sirens began to sound but they weren't close enough. This would be over long before we had help.

A shot ripped into the front tire of the Cadillac. The rubber spat air and the car dipped forward. A full minute of gunfire exchange ensued. I knew someone was going to die. Concrete powder from the missed rounds smoked up around us. Rick stood and fired with more precision, resting his forearms on the trunk, attempting to catch one of them as they peeked around the corner of the column. As I rose up to join him, a bullet snapped Rick's shoulder back and he fell.

I shuffled to him on my knees. "You alive?"

His eyes were open. "I'm all right." He tried to sit up and winced.

"You're not going anywhere. I'll take care of them. Watch my back from down here. Shoot under the car."

Movement. Footsteps.

They were trying to get out of there. Diego was moving backward, his gun pointing directly at me, rounds coming my way. I stood and pulled the trigger, aiming for center mass. He'd brought it on himself. My bullet missed and moved further into the darkness. It was only then that I saw Robert directly behind Diego, running away from me. The bullet ripped into the back of

Robert's head, and a spray of blood splatter shot up into the air as he dropped.

Diego yelled, looked at me, and then at his brother. He knelt down next to Robert. I followed him, coming around the Cadillac.

From ten feet away, I saw Robert's skull, the gray of his brain, the dark blood oozing onto the concrete.

Diego rose and charged me. Left his gun on the ground like shooting me wasn't going to satisfy his rage. He planted his shoulder into my stomach and pushed me backwards until we hit another car. My elbow cracked the driver's side window. I lost my gun but put both fists together and hammered them into his back. He dropped. Then he looked up and threw a solid punch into my stomach. I slugged him with a right hook that knocked him down. His head bounced a couple times.

But the anger inside of him, after seeing his dead brother, was hard to compete with. He wasn't feeling pain. He popped up and side-kicked me in the groin, this time making perfect contact. Like jeopardizing-my-future-kids contact. I dropped and the pain ran through me. He kicked me again, this time in the face. I lost control for a moment.

Then I heard Rick yelling, warning Diego he'd fire. Diego started running. Rick fired several rounds at him to no avail.

I collected myself and looked for my gun. Finally saw it a few feet away. I reached for it, sat up, and fired towards Diego. He'd made it too far. Jumped over the side wall. I didn't know if he could make a three story jump or not. Didn't know what was below. The sirens were much louder now. I ran to the rail. Couldn't see him in the darkness. Only a line of bushes where he'd fallen.

I dialed a number and reached my contact. "Officer down. Get an ambulance up here. I have one subject on the run. Cuban male. Early thirties. Khaki shorts with sandals. Dark shirt. He just leapt off the edge on the north side."

I turned. Rick was stumbling toward me, holding his shoulder, his gun in his left hand. The blood had colored his shirt. His face was pale.

"I'm a shitty shot with my left," he said, shaking his head. "Couldn't get him."

"How's the shoulder?"

"Hurts."

"Give me a minute, all right?"

"Yeah."

I knelt next to Robert's dead body. The friend. The brother. The cop I had killed. I took his lifeless hand in my own. "You didn't give me a choice, brother. I'll do my best to look out for Maria. See you on the other side. Merry Christmas."

I let go of his hand and his windbreaker opened, revealing his revolver. I touched it. Cold metal. He'd never drawn it. Never fired a shot.

***

I ran as fast as I could down the stairs. Three at a time. Left Rick to explain the situation, so I could get out of there before the questions came. For a lawman, firing your piece takes explaining. Killing a man takes a lawyer. But if that man happens to be a cop, you need divine intervention.

I dialed Anna for the fourth time and left another message. "Anna, call me back. Please. Something's happened. Lock the doors and go upstairs. Stay away from the windows. The police are on the way." Frustrated, I snapped the phone shut. "Damn it, where is she!" I burst out of the parking garage doors into the night. Patrol cars were coming from my left. I ran right.

Panting, running at a dead sprint, I called my supervisor. "Alex, please listen to me."

"Reddick, what the hell is going on? Where are you?"

"I'm leaving the scene."

"Your ass better turn around!" he yelled.

"I need you to listen to me. Send some people over to my house. Anna could be in trouble. I knew the buyers. We lost one of them, and he may know where I live. I killed his brother."

"I'm on it."

"Let me know if they find him."

"You know I will."

Rick and I had ridden with John Latell en route to the buy, so I had to find another way to get home. Three streets down, nearly out of breath, I saw lights and heard music. I ran that way. It was a biker bar. The neon sign high above the door read: CHAINED. The E flashed on and off, not much life left. Five men clad in leather were standing out in the lot smoking cigarettes, laughing at someone's joke. The Lynyrd Skynyrd track blaring out of the speakers must have muffled the earlier gunshots. I looked at the guy in a goatee sitting on his Harley.

"I'm a Federal Agent. I need your bike."

He blew out some smoke and smiled. "You can go—"

I didn't let him finish. Pulled out my nine and pointed it at him. "Get off your bike. Give me the keys."

"Jesus. All right." He started to get off. I pointed the gun at the group before they got involved. Their hands went up.

"Don't try anything. He'll get his bike back."

I tore out of the parking lot. *Diego isn't dumb enough to go after her*, I told myself.

I sped down the highway and made the twenty-minute drive in an agonizing twelve.

There were two patrol cars in my driveway, their lights still flashing. Anna and I lived in a brick rambler with a quarter-acre yard. The Christmas tree lit up the living room. Candlelight in every window. I ran up to the officer standing in the yard. "I'm Agent Reddick. This is my house. Did you find her?"

"Agent Reddick, you're gonna want to go inside."

"What happened?"

LOWCOUNTRY PUNCH

"Please, sir. The kitchen."

No.

Anna Tate was my first kiss. I spent many childhood summers living with my grandparents in Charleston, SC, in the house where my father grew up. Anna and her family lived next door. The summer after fourth grade, the girl I'd been digging in the sand with all those years had suddenly become beautiful. I'd never really noticed her until then. We kissed that summer and every summer after. I saw her my senior year at my father's funeral, then we both went to college and lost touch. The next time I saw her was November, just over a year ago. I'd heard she was writing a travel column for the *Miami Herald*, and when I accepted the post at the Miami field office, I looked her up.

Anna had developed into a stunning woman. She'd cut her long blonde hair and wore it just above the shoulders, and her skinny frame had filled out wonderfully. She'd spent most of her college years in Europe and had seen more of the world than me, and she talked my ear off about global politics and culture. I couldn't get enough of it. And I'll be damned if she didn't love me. Loved me from the moment we reconnected, like she'd been waiting on me all those years. After that first date, we were never apart.

I bolted up the four stairs, weaving past the ceramic elves, and into the open door. No one. I went into the kitchen. Looked on the floor, praying not to see her body.

Nothing. No sign of a disturbance.

No savory smells of Christmas cooking, either. I looked on the counter where she would have put the casserole.

Her engagement ring.

The one I'd given to her in September lay on the counter, holding down the fold of a note. My lip caved in and tears mounted. I pulled the note out from under the diamond and opened it up.

T.A.,

I'm so sorry to leave you on Christmas Eve. I couldn't start out a new year with us, knowing it was wrong. I cannot do it anymore. Please don't come after me. I'm going to find a job in L.A. and start a new life. It's over. I'll always love you. You know that.

Anna

No more of an explanation than that. We'd gotten in a couple bad fights recently, but I thought things had gotten back to normal. Guess not.

And downward I went.

SEVEN MONTHS LATER

CHAPTER 2

Charleston, SC

Last night, a dream. The same one I'd had two nights before. *I'm sipping a cold beer docked at an unfamiliar lowcountry marina, watching the afternoon go by from the console of my Catalina. High above the warm blue water and the marsh grass, a dragonfly lands on the tip of another boat's RF antenna. The flutter of its wings turns to a slow-motion wave as it works to stay put in the salty breeze. The site enthralls me. Such natural beauty. At that moment, a barefoot woman comes strolling down the dock.*

Yet again, I had woken up before I could get a good look at her face. Maybe it was Anna, making her way back to me. Maybe it wasn't. What are dreams anyway but teasing and punishment?

That dream was on my mind as Gerry Mulligan twisted metal on the car radio. I took an exit off I-26, about twenty minutes east of the downtown peninsula that everyone knows as Charleston. North Charleston, where the DEA's office was located, was home to the shopping centers, outlet malls, airport, and industrial buildings. In short, cheaper land. It also reported a higher crime rate. One of the highest murder rates in the country. Yeah, North Charleston was a long way away from the carriage rides, frozen lemonade stands, and pralines that most people associate with the Holy City.

I pulled my Jeep into the parking lot of a bland four-story building and cut the engine. Took my piece from the glove compartment, tucked it away, and headed into work. My second week with the Charleston DEA, and I was trying to make the best of it.

A jet contrail dissipated in the sky and the early morning sun cut through the dense air. I cracked a grin, the reasons behind it as complex and ineffable as the bottle of Chassagne-Montrachet I had overindulged in the night before. It was the blue sky and being back in Charleston and so many things. It was the salty remains of the ocean on my skin, left from an early morning longboarding session at Folly Beach. The waves were small but gave good, long rides. On occasion, one wave would lead into another and then another until my fin dragged in the sand, and I could step off the board into ankle-deep water. I ask nothing more of a wave.

Moments like those transported me far away from the pains of last Christmas. Of losing my love. Of killing a good friend—a man who saved my life—and destroying his family. Of becoming a cop killer. Of the downward spiral. Nearly everyone in Miami, including my supervisor, had abandoned me after I killed Robert Vasquez. They understood that I'd done the right thing, but no one wanted to fight for me. No one wanted to align himself with my quickly decaying career.

I headed toward the elevator. A short, bald man already waited, staring at the lights above the elevator as he tracked its progress. It was on the third floor and coming down. He couldn't stand the silence. "Sure is balmy out there," he said in a squeaky voice.

Sometimes you can tell immediately that someone is going to be annoying.

He rambled on. "I think it's the hottest day of the year so far.

And of course, I forgot to water my plants. I've got some hibiscus in pots in the backyard. My wife won't water them. The kids aren't going to..." He shook his head. "You on the way to work?"

I nodded, noticing the Cross pen sticking out of his shirt pocket. I bet he'd had it since college.

He said, "Me, too. Days like this, I'd much rather be on the beach under an umbrella. Watch my boys build a sandcastle. Read a book." He sighed. "Gotta take advantage of it before hurricane season. They say it's gonna be a doozy this year."

The elevator dinged and the door opened. I went through first. The short one waddled in after me. "I bet the beach is packed today," he continued. "It's probably not even worth going out there. Traffic will be backed up all the way to the bridge."

I thought about pulling my Beretta out right there, pulling the slide back and putting one in the chamber, just to see his reaction. Let him hear the steel lock into place. That would shut him up. But wasn't I in a good mood?

"Where you headed?" I asked.

"Six, please." I pressed both the fourth and sixth floor buttons. He looked up at me with a smirk and leaned his body against the far wall. "I kind of figured you were a fourth-floor guy. I can always pick y'all out."

"Is that right?"

"Oh, yeah. You got your Tony Lama boots and your blue jeans. Looks like you haven't shaved in a few days. You see what I'm wearing. Cheap suit everyday."

"I guess we need to work on our disguises."

After 9/11, our office decided not to advertise its existence any longer and removed the plaque with the DEA acronym from the sign in the lobby. Nothing but a blank space followed *4th Floor*. It lent an air of mystery to what was going on up there. Why the Charleston field office shared a building with several civilian companies was *not* a mystery to me. After you've worked with the government long enough, those types of things don't surprise you. It's hard to cram "logical" and "bureaucracy" into one sentence.

I patted him on the shoulder and exited the elevator. "Tear it up today."

"I always do," he said, with the conviction of a bad liar.

At the end of the hall, I slid a card through the reader and typed a five-digit code on the keypad. When it clicked, I pushed the door open. The reception area looked similar to a dentist's waiting room, complete with bad upholstery and a haphazard assortment of magazines on a table.

"Mornin,' " said Sharon, the receptionist, from behind the glass window. Her red hair was held in a bun, and a pair of glasses rested on the tip of her nose. I went through the next door and around the corner. Sharon had a cup of coffee for me, knowing I would be running right into the meeting. "Did you hear the news? Chad Rourke's dead."

I shook my head. "What?"

"They just found his body."

"You're kidding me. He's in Charleston, isn't he?"

"Yeah, filming a movie. He fell off his balcony at the Mazyck Hotel last night. Lots of coke in the room. It's really sad. I loved the poor guy."

"That's terrible." Chad Rourke was an up-and-coming name in Hollywood. I'd read a week earlier that he was in Charleston filming a movie with Tela Davies (pronounced *Tee-la*), another A-list Hollywood celebrity.

"Anyway, I hope everybody's treating you okay," she added.

"Like I'm their king."

"Right."

I hustled to my office, which was not much more than four white walls with some photos of bad guys on the wall above the desk. Perhaps after a few months, I would bring in my decorator.

I switched on the computer and entered the password. Scanned through my in-box and then headed off to the conference room for a 9 a.m. meeting.

A large map of Charleston County covered one wall of the conference room. A white board hung on another with various red and blue marker notes all over it. On another board were photos of the men and women we were after.

I took a seat next to my new supervisor, Steve Randall. He was barrel-chested and chiseled and had very powerful, commanding eyes. Loved to chew on toothpicks. There are two kinds of supervisors: those who go by the book and those who bend the rules a little. From what I'd heard, Steve was the latter, which I liked. He'd also taken a big chance on me, so he was okay by me.

Seven of us faced each other at the long table. Other than Steve nodding at me, no one acknowledged my presence. I had a feeling no one liked the idea of a new agent coming on board, especially since Steve introduced me on my first day as the "cocaine expert." It was true: other than Steve, I had more experience with coke than anyone. But no one wanted to hear about some hotshot from Miami coming up to show them how to deal with their escalating white powder problem.

Especially one who'd come their way after putting a cop in the ground.

Steve pulled the toothpick out of his mouth. "As you've heard, Chad Rourke died last night. They found four grams of coke up in his room. It's all over the news. Y'all know what that means. The Atlanta office, which signs all our paychecks, is going to be breathing down my neck. Dead celebrities are bad press." He looked around the room. "So get ready for it. A shitstorm is coming."

He went around the room, asking the respective agents questions about each of their ongoing investigations. MS-13 wannabes cooking and slinging meth. Some marijuana growers out in

West Ashley. Ecstasy, acid, pharmaceuticals. Just about anything one needs to get away from reality could be found within a thirty-mile radius. Then he looked at Chester Benton and me. It was our turn.

I'd met Chester when I flew up to interview a couple months before, and Steve had chosen him to get me up to speed. I had the feeling he had put up a fight when the orders first came down, but whether he liked it or not, he'd be my partner for the next few months. He was a short, stout black man with light brown skin and freckles. I guessed mid-forties. Some might have called him good looking if it wasn't for the horizontal scar reaching from his ear to his cheek. We weren't friendly enough with each other for me to ask him what had happened.

"You're not going to like this, boys," Steve said, addressing us both, "but y'all are gonna catch the bulk of this media frenzy with Chad Rourke. I want you to get your CI to give up one of Tux Clinton's crack houses. We're gonna raid it. It ain't a cocaine bust but it's close enough to buy me some time."

"You're bullshitting," Chester said. "You know he won't be there."

"His people will. I can't wait for you to build a case against Tux right now. I need results yesterday."

Chester crossed his arms. "I mapped out an insider for two months, Steve. Now, you're telling me I wasted my time?"

"I'm not sayin' that at all. I'm telling you I need to put people in jail, and it's gonna be your guys. We're gonna put some of his men behind bars, and go from there. We'll still get to the source if he doesn't back off. If he does, then we won anyway. We clear?"

"We're clear. I don't like it, but we're clear."

"I'll give y'all a chance to make a source climb, but it's not this one."

I didn't say a word. Wasn't any different from Miami or anywhere else. Short term results to make the fat asses on the top floors happy. Not even Steve could get around appeasing the brass. You can't become a supervisor without learning the tricks.

Another agent jumped in and pointed at me. "Why don't you just put Wonderboy over there undercover? He'll clean this city up in a week. We can all go sit on the beach."

I looked him in the eyes. "Thanks for the welcome, asshole."

"Anytime."

Steve said to the guy, "If you'd done your job, Baroni, we wouldn't be sitting here, would we? Keep your mouth shut. Reddick, you don't take his bait. I'm not babysitting either one of you. Goddamn five-year-olds." Steve looked back at Chester and stuck the toothpick back into his mouth. "Get everything into place. Notify the North Charleston PD. Let's take 'em down."

"All right. Give us a couple days to pull everything together. I wanna make sure my CI is safe." A CI is a confidential informant, usually someone we arrest who agrees to help us in exchange for our lenience.

"Do what you gotta do."

We finished up the meeting in less than an hour, and I spent the rest of the morning working at my desk. At 11:30, I took off to grab a bite to eat. On the way, I stopped by the Bank of South Carolina a couple miles down the road to open up a new bank account. The July heat wasn't messing around. Nothing I wasn't used to, but I didn't remember Charleston being so hot and humid. Not too different from South Florida. One minute in the midday sun and you needed a shower. I looked up at a few others entering the bank. At least I didn't have to wear a tie.

That's when I saw her. That short blonde hair. Petite frame. She was about forty feet ahead of me, walking toward the bank. Talk about a gut bomb. My heart stopped beating. A man held the door for her, and she walked in, thanking him. She had a baby in her arms, and that didn't make sense. Seven months ago, she was with me.

LOWCOUNTRY PUNCH

As inevitable as it was, nothing could have prepared me for this: seeing Anna Tate for the first time since she'd left me.

CHAPTER 3

Part of me wanted to turn around. Hell, most of me wanted me to run. Today didn't have to be the day. I knew it would happen eventually, not just because she grew up here, but also because I had moved into my grandparents' old home. Right next door to Anna's parents, Beau and Cindy Tate. *You can't run forever, Reddick. Get in there and get it over with.*

I made a lame attempt at primping and preparing myself, running a hand over my recently shaved head. Fixing the collar on my white shirt. Smoothing out my Levi's. Planning what I might say. Then, somehow, I walked in there like I couldn't even remember that she'd left me. Like I was king of the world.

I passed through the second set of doors and took a look around. To the right, civilians stood in line on the linoleum floor, waiting to make the first few deposits and withdrawals of the morning. Behind the tellers, an open vault tempted the greedy. I nonchalantly scanned the crowd and recognized the back of that blonde head of hair almost immediately. I couldn't decide what to do. Should I approach her and say something? Should I let her bump into me "accidentally?" Or should I ignore her?

Then she turned.

It was not Anna. I would have sworn it was not two minutes earlier but it definitely wasn't her. Same hair, same height, same figure. But I'd been mistaken. All that agony for nothing. I'd just proved that a few months hadn't healed much of anything.

I must have looked pretty lost, because a woman in a light blue blouse came over. "What can we do for you?" she asked.

"Hi. I'd like to open up an account. Just moved here recently."

"Sure. Please follow me upstairs."

She led me up a flight of stairs and asked me to take a seat. I got about five pages into *Coastal Living* magazine when a man in khaki pants and a seersucker jacket asked me to follow him to his office. I took a seat in front of his desk and we began to work our way through the process, him typing my information on a keyboard and me sitting back in an uncomfortable chair with one leg over the other.

Some yelling from downstairs stopped us. We listened for a moment. Nothing else. "Somebody must have a case of the Mondays," he said. "Anyway, give me your—"

A gun popped.

Out of reflex, I drew my Beretta and rushed out of his office. There were people on the floor of the hallway, screaming and crying. Near the top of the stairs, I peeked over the railing.

A black male with long dreads was running for the door, carrying the same child I had seen earlier, the one carried by the woman I'd mistaken for Anna. There was a gun in his free hand. I tore down the stairs, looking left. The mother lay on the floor, her head twisted toward me, a growing pool of blood surrounding her. Some terrified civilians were facedown on the ground in shock. Others stood and watched as the man escaped through the entrance. I took off after him.

My eyes quickly adjusted to the brightness, and I locked in on my prey. With fire under my heels, I took off in his direction. I had lost a step since my UVA soccer days, but I still had a little juice left. As long as he didn't have a car waiting, he was mine.

I didn't want him to know I was coming. Had to be clever.

Didn't want to find out what would happen if the perp dropped the child on the run. I kept thinking about the softness of the little one's skull. So I chased him through the crowded parking lot with caution. I took a parallel lane, dipping here and there to hide behind a car every time Dreads took a look behind him.

I'd cut my distance from him in half when I saw the short bald guy I'd spoken to in the elevator earlier getting out of his car. He saw me coming and took in the scene: Dreads running at him with a gun in one hand and the baby in the other. He scurried behind a car. His head popped back up a moment later. Against all odds, he dashed out from behind the car and went with both hands for the boy. I couldn't believe it. The short, fat man whose kids would've probably chosen their T-ball coach over him as their hero had decided today was his day. He caught Dreads off guard and pried the baby away without too much effort. He began to run. Dreads swung the gun around and pointed it at them.

I was on him. Like a cheetah on a gazelle. I plowed into him from behind, taking us both to the ground hard. He was bigger than me, but I was ready to go. I don't snap easily, but when it happens, you best be on my side.

Dreads was my age, fairly muscular, and filthy. His shirt and shorts were soaked in sweat. His eyes were bloodshot and lifeless, as if there was nothing behind them. He kicked hard and grunted as I pounded his face. He managed to get a couple good knees into my stomach, and I lost my breath. Gaining it back, I rolled him over. Put a fist in his eye socket and dropped several more on his nose and cheeks. He bled freely but kept kicking and swinging, getting a few shots inside. He snuck a left under my right eye, and my vision blurred. I was gone by that point, though. No pain at all. I grabbed his left shoulder and flipped him onto his stomach, then took his dreads in my hand and smashed his head into the ground.

"How's that feel?" I yelled.

I stood. I knew I should stop. But I couldn't. It had everything to do with that woman he'd shot. How it could have been Anna. How a man high on drugs could take a life so easily. A man just like him had taken my father's life, too.

I'd never known such anger. Grabbing him by the hair, I bent down low and dragged his face along the pavement, grinding it in, his nose the tip of a paintbrush dipped in red.

Someone finally threw their arms around me and pulled me to the ground. I fought for a moment and then gave up. Relaxed my arms. Sucked in oxygen. The man holding me was a cop. He pushed me onto my side and locked my right arm behind my back.

"I'm a Federal Agent," I said. "DEA. Check my pants."

He put a knee into my back, making sure I wasn't going anywhere, and then he stuck his hand in my pocket. Pulled out my credentials. He finally released my arm and let me roll onto my side.

"He's clear," the cop said, standing up. "You all right?" he asked me.

I nodded, then rolled over to my side and tried to regain control of my breathing. Of reality. My body hurt. My knuckles were raw, and my hands and rib cage ached. My head was dazed. I finally pushed myself up off the ground. The world around me came into focus. Sirens blaring. Twenty or thirty people collected on the sidewalk, their mouths open.

The man from the elevator was still holding the child in his arms and he was looking at me. We shared a moment of admiration. I have no idea what would have happened if he hadn't intervened. Looking back on it, it was really cool to see a man step outside of his comfort zone to help another. It's in times like those that true character shines through. I immediately regretted only half-acknowledging his existence earlier that morning.

I turned around. Two cops were cuffing the man I'd beaten.

They lifted him up to stand. He looked even worse than I did. As they began to march him toward the back of their patrol car, Dreads looked at me with eyes so full of hatred and evil that I knew he hadn't learned any lessons. Nothing would ever change that guy. We called them *unfixable*.

He glared at me. Spit some blood onto the ground. With a mouth full of gold teeth, he said, "I'll find you. Your family, too. You're dead."

"What was that?" I walked toward him. "I don't think I heard you right."

"You heard me right. If you only knew who I was. I'll be coming for you."

"Well, this will help you remember who I am."

Without giving the two cops escorting him time to react, I lifted my boot and kicked the side of his knee with everything I had, more strength than I'd mustered in a while. His bone snapped sideways and broke out of his flesh.

An unexpectedly violent morning, even for me.

CHAPTER 4

Steve spoke to the detective in charge, and I was out of there before the camera crews started lingering. A photo in the newspaper is a death sentence for an undercover agent. Poor guy was probably already regretting recruiting me, and I hadn't even mentioned maiming the perp. He told me to go home for the day. I climbed into my CJ7 Jeep and went out the back way.

The Jeep was originally a government car I used in Miami for some undercover work. We call them g-cars. They gave me a good deal, and I picked it up after an op a couple years ago. For some reason, unlike the rearview mirror, I was attached. She was green with big tires and a winch on the front. From the looks of the inside, the duct tape on the seats, and the worn floorboard, you would think I didn't own a top, but I had a khaki hardtop that I kept in the garage. The only work I had done was to install a marine stereo with a hardwired iPod input and some waterproof speakers. I played the Lonesome River Band loud as I rode down the highway. The wind blew, and the sound of Sammy Shelor's banjo rolled with the rhythm like a waterwheel in an old Kentucky town.

My waterfront house was at the end of a cul-de-sac that rested against the Wappoo Cut, a span of saltwater separating the Ashley and Stono Rivers. Live oaks formed canopies over the quiet street; Spanish moss hung down low from the limbs. My family had lived on that land for as long as anyone could trace back, and I'd always felt a calling to return. The Reddicks had been through three homes there. My grandparents had built the last one after Hurricane Hugo had torn theirs to the ground. It was a gorgeous light yellow with white shutters. Two palm trees rose high on either side of the front stoop. Not forty yards away stood Anna's parents' home, the place where she'd grown up. Our first kiss was on their dock reaching out over the marsh.

I unlocked the door and punched in my alarm code on the keypad just inside the front hallway. I'd had it installed when I moved in; Diego wasn't the only one who had beef with the chief. In Miami, you kill a cop and you're a cop killer. The circumstances don't matter. In short, the Miami-Dade police department had not thanked me for cleaning up their force.

I kicked my boots off at the front door. In the corner of the well-organized living room, I had a rack of some Northwest Merlots and Syrahs that I had taken an interest in lately. Above it, a photograph my grandfather had taken hung on the wall. It was a shot from the bow of a sailboat approaching the Avalon harbor on Catalina. The old Wrigley's Casino where Glenn Miller and Benny Goodman played in the 1920s and 30s stood prominently in the background.

I put on some shorts, grabbed a fishing rod off the porch, and headed out into the sweltering heat. There's not much that hooking onto a redfish won't cure. I find time alone to be powerful medicine.

At the end of my dock floated the *Pretender*, a twenty-seven-foot Catalina sailboat that I had brought up from Miami. I walked past it to the Tate's house. They let me use their seventeen-foot Key West center console, a much better companion for the rod and the reel. I hopped aboard. The Yamaha engine cranked on the first try. I steered her through the narrow channel, which opened up into the Cut. A variety of boats sped past each other, ignoring the No Wake signs that stood in people's yards along the shore.

I found Jimmy Buffett's 1974 release, *A1A*, on the iPod, skipped to number two and turned right. A west wind pushed against my back. After a half-mile, the Cut opened up into the Stono River. This was all saltwater, only miles from the ocean. The Stono ran wide but you could still see the other side, mostly marsh and trees, but further along, there was a bridge and Buzzard's Roost Marina.

Low tide approached, and the oyster beds became visible. Redfish love to hover above the beds on a rising tide. I wasn't in any hurry, so I rode along the shore scouting for places to come back and fish later. All you had to do was throw a live shrimp on a hook, float it with a bobber inches above the bed, and it was game time. I had fished these waters with my father and grandfather as a child. I had a few good spots, but it was always a great challenge and accomplishment to find another one.

Off in the distance, I noticed a ski boat with a woman on a wakeboard trailing behind. She moved along impressively, cutting across the wake, taking several feet of air on occasion. They swung around toward me. Two other women were on the boat. As they drew near, I watched the wakeboarder. She would lean forward and bend her knees, moving left, and then dip her heels and lean backward, cutting right. It was fantastic.

As she approached, she cut hard into the wake and jumped into the air, only thirty feet from me. The wind caught the face of the board and slapped her into the water. She skipped across the surface before plummeting underneath.

Popping up moments later, she looked around, disoriented. The laughter of the two women in the boat came across the water as they swung around to retrieve their friend. I motored up close.

"You almost pulled it off," I said, cutting the engine, noticing her beauty.

"I hope you enjoyed that," she replied, bobbing with one hand on the wakeboard.

"You looked great out—"

Behind me, the unmistakable sound of a hull grinding into an underwater oyster bed echoed across the water.

I jerked my head around. Her friends had been thrown to the front, and the boat was in a foot of water, stopped on a bed, probably fifty yards from us. I started to twist the key and head that way, but both of them stood and waved. "We're okay!"

I looked down at the wakeboarder. "You wanna climb in? Go get your friends?"

"If you don't mind."

"I'm happy to help."

She swam around to the ladder and handed me the wakeboard. I set it down and then helped her up. The life jacket did little to hide her unbelievably attractive body. I'd never in my life seen finer legs.

"Let me get you a towel," I said.

"That would be great, thanks."

I found a clean towel under my chair and handed it to her. God, she was gorgeous. I couldn't get over it. Gentle, brown eyes under sharp eyebrows. Rounded nose and cheeks with a touch of rose. Naturally brown skin. She surely had Native American blood running thick through her veins.

She dried off her face and then said, "I'm Liz Coles."

"I'm T.A. Reddick. Nice to meet you." I didn't bother explaining why my face looked like I'd gone three minutes in the ring with Evander Holyfield.

We looked at each other a couple seconds longer than you normally do when you meet someone. Our paths had crossed for a reason. Something deep inside me knew that we had some sort of future together, like I'd seen it through a crystal ball. We broke eye contact at the same time.

"Let's go get your friends."

"Good idea." Liz held on to the console as I sped across the water.

I pulled right up to the rail of their boat, and Liz reached over to hold the boats together. She introduced us. Jaime, the captain, wore a Nascar hat and Ray-Bans. Ashley had short black hair that looked dyed. They were both attractive. They'd hit an oyster bed. I'd hit jackpot.

Ashley sat on the cushioned seat, holding a towel to her leg.

"How bad is it?" I asked.

"I'm fine."

"I don't know," Jaime interrupted, with a thick Charleston accent. "There's so much blood." She pointed at the inside rail. "She hit that sharp corner pretty hard."

Ashley removed the towel. The cut was deep and needed some attention. I offered my opinion. They could either pay Sea-Tow to rip the boat off the bed, or wait a couple of hours until high tide lifted her off gently. They opted for the latter, so I invited them back to my place. No, not a ploy to spend more time with Liz. I really wanted to help them. Would have done the same if it were a bunch of old men. I'd like to think so, at least.

Leaving the boat anchored just in case she broke free, we headed back to La Casa de Reddick. Liz and Ashley rode on the bow, and Jaime stood next to me as I drove. She held on to her hat. "I swear I've ridden over that spot before...never seen an oyster bed."

"They pop up," I told her. We hit a bump and some spray came over the bow, beading up my sunglasses. I took a rag from under the seat, wiped them clean, and put them back on. Liz hid her brown eyes behind sunglasses of her own. I couldn't tell if she was looking my way or not.

"You must think we're idiots," Jaime continued. "How embarrassing."

"Find me ten boaters in Charleston who haven't hit a bed, and you've got nine liars. I've hit my fair share."

Inside my house, I took the first aid kit out of the bathroom and began to dress Ashley's wound. Liz and Jaime looked around the house, which bothered me a little. I'm somewhat protective of my privacy.

"Who's that with you and Chet?" Liz asked, admiring a picture on the wall of Chet Baker.

I took my eyes off Ashley's leg. "How do you know Chet?"

She shrugged her shoulders. "I've been around."

A woman who loves jazz. I was taken aback.

"Who is Chet?" Ashley asked.

I had nearly forgotten there was anyone but Liz and me in the house. Or the universe, for that matter. Maybe it's not time that heals a broken heart, but another woman. I tried to find the courage to ask for her number later.

"That's Chet Baker," I said. "The Prince of Cool. He was West Coast jazz. That's my dad with him."

I put the last piece of tape over Ashley's cut. "You're good to go." She thanked me, and the four of us sat around the table talking for a while. They asked what I did, and I lied, telling them I was a financial advisor. They asked about my face, and I told them I was a black belt. I made sure most of what I told them was the truth, though. I had found the more truths I could hold onto, the easier it was to lie. Jaime came in with one of my banjos strapped around her shoulder and pretended to pluck a tune, singing in a mock banjo sound the melody for *The Beverly Hillbillies*. Everyone laughed.

"Play us something, T.A.," Jaime said.

"Not a chance."

"Why not?"

"Not today, okay?"

We ended up sitting around the television watching the news, looking for the latest on Chad Rourke. They were showing an earlier video of the covered body being rolled under the yellow

33

tape and lifted up into the ambulance. Then back to a live feed across the street from the hotel. The newswoman stated the few facts that she knew. Behind her, a mass of solemn bystanders stood watching and waiting to find out more.

After gulping it all up, Jaime said, "I feel so bad for his wife. They were such a cute couple."

"I just don't see him being a druggie," Ashley said. "Of all the celebs, I never would have guessed. Liz, your man has met him a few times, right?"

"Yeah, but I don't think they really know each other."

So she was in a relationship. That was saddening. But not shocking. She was a catch of the highest caliber. The sudden reality check reminded me of what had happened that morning. It wasn't over by a long shot. I excused myself, walked out front, and dialed Steve.

"What's the latest?" I demanded. "I thought you were going to call."

"I was just picking up the phone. So you snapped the guy's leg after he was in cuffs? C'mon, Reddick. He'll probably have a limp the rest of his life. You're lucky the cops that saw it are going to cover for you. I can't get you out of another one of those, though. Don't make me regret bringing you up here."

"I'm sorry, Steve. You have no idea how pissed I was when I saw that little kid's mother bleeding out on the floor."

"Don't go preaching to the choir. We got bigger problems anyway. The guy whose leg you snapped—*after* he was in cuffs—he's Tux Clinton's cousin, Jesse Clinton. Tux and his sister are at the hospital with him."

I mumbled and cursed to myself. The last thing I needed was one of Charleston's biggest drug dealers looking to settle a score with me. "Is Tux asking questions? Is he looking for me?"

"Probably. Not sure if he even knows your name, but I'm not going to take a chance. I'm sending two cops your way. I want you on twenty-four-hour surveillance."

I laughed out loud. "You're kidding me! I've dealt with this before. Tux can get in line. I don't need a couple idiots holding my hand. I'll be fine."

"T.A., I'm not asking if it's okay. If he figures out who you are, he may come after you."

"Steve, Diego Vasquez and half the uniforms in Miami want me dead. I'm okay."

"Don't be an idiot. Just let the uniforms do their job. They'll stay out of your way."

"Fine." I had to pick my battles. "Any word on the mother?"

"She's in surgery. She's gonna live."

"Good to hear."

"Reddick, watch yourself. See you in the morning."

"Yes, sir."

I gave the gals a lift back. Jaime's boat had floated off the bed with the rising tide, but the anchor held it in place. I gave each one of them a hand over. As I took Liz's hand, I said, "Can I call you?"

She squeezed my hand. "If it's meant to be, we'll see each other again."

"Suit yourself." Not exactly the response I was hoping for. I waved my hand in the air. "Good to meet y'all. Keep an eye out for those oysters."

I throttled backwards and sped off across the blue. All those things I had told myself about not wanting to meet another woman anytime soon. Perhaps I was wrong. Maybe that's exactly what I needed. Something about Liz Coles intrigued me.

Back at my place, I peered out a front window and saw the unmarked police car parked up the street. I opened the closet door, pulled out my shotgun and loaded a couple shells into it. Put a few more in my pocket.

Try and get me, Tux Clinton.

CHAPTER 5

Before the sun rose, I decided to play a trick on the two cops sitting outside my front yard. Found some old Black Cat firecrackers in my garage and snuck across the street a couple hundred yards down. I cut through two lawns, moving low behind a row of azaleas.

One of the men looked like he had nodded off. The other was spitting tobacco into a cup and looking out the windshield. Now, I know this kind of game wasn't exactly professional and some might even say childish, but I couldn't help it. Besides, if I could get this close to them, so could Tux Clinton and his thugs. A lesson needed to be learned.

I lit the end of the brick and tossed it next to the driver's side door. With a huge grin on my face, I knelt down and waited. A roar of shots ripped through the quiet morning. Those two cops were out of the car quicker than you could say Dunkin' Donuts. Both of them had their guns drawn. Once the explosions stopped, the first thing they heard was my laugh.

They didn't find it as funny as I did. As they holstered their weapons, I said, "I couldn't resist."

One of them mumbled, "Asshole."

I raised my hand in the air. "Y'all are doing a great job. I'll bring cookies and lemonade out later. You take it in a sippie cup?" More mumbling. Then they both climbed back into their car and I went back home for a shower and cup of joe.

Before tackling the day, I had to get one thing out of my mind. Sitting on the couch in the living room, I Googled Liz Coles. For what it's worth, it was my first time Googling a woman. Not only did she have a website, but she had her own Wikipedia page. *Are you kidding me?* She had mentioned being an artist in New York but had certainly played it down. CBS had even done a story on her. As if that wasn't enough, Liz had also put together a foundation called The Portrait and a Dream Project that provided art lessons and supplies to children in hospitals all over New York.

I looked at the telephone number on her website. Wanted to call it. Otherwise I'd never run into her again. Charleston is small but not that small. But I couldn't. I'd already crossed the stalker line by Googling her. Some things you just have to let be.

I went up to my room, aching to play the banjo. I have three, but my go-to is my father's: a prewar Gibson with a custom-built mahogany neck. The old wood rim can bring out sounds that very few banjos can; it rings as if spirits are buried in it. Sometimes, I can feel my father's presence in those tones. I took it from the case and sat in the armless chair by the window. I rested it on my lap and put the picks on—stainless steel National NP2s for my index and middle finger and a plastic Golden Gate pick for my thumb. I started picking out Earl's version of "Sally Goodin" and focused on the sounds until everything else faded away.

***

The call came at four that afternoon. I'd been in the office most of the day. Our CI, Jared Winters, gave me an address. I crammed the last quarter of a peanut butter and jelly sandwich into my mouth and walked over to Steve's office. "We're a go," I said and handed him the address.

Steve took the yellow sticky note from me and eyeballed it. He crumpled up the paper and threw it back at me. "Things are getting busy around here."

I smiled, tasting the blood of future combat. He winked, and I knew we shared many of the same reasons for being in this business. We were both warriors until we die.

With the sun setting, Ches, myself, and two other agents pulled into an abandoned lot in the middle of flat land two miles from the address. Another car full of agents pulled in behind us. Three patrol cars were waiting.

Cinching my Kevlar vest tight, I joined the circle gathering around Steve. Seven DEA agents, eight cops. "Listen up, listen up," he was saying, again with his usual toothpick in his mouth. I wondered how often he changed 'em out.

He passed around the address. It was the first time the police officers were being told who we were looking for and where we were going. We didn't want any corrupt cops letting Tux know that one of his crack houses was about to be raided. Holding the details until the last minute is a practice we used in South America when working with hired hands, but many of us had found that using it in the States was a pretty good idea, too. I don't mean to give cops a hard time. I've worked with plenty of dirty agents.

Steve continued. "My guys are going in first. Reddick and Benton will go in the front door." He pointed at us. "I'll take a team to the back. NCPD, you will keep an eye on the windows and come in after the initial move. I want the cruisers to follow the g-cars. I know I don't need to say it but I'm saying it anyway. No fucking sirens. We're going in quiet. Any questions, gentlemen?" No one said anything. A few shook their heads.

"See you down there. Be safe."

I climbed back into the shotgun seat. As Ches drove us toward the bust, I checked my Beretta one more time. One round in the chamber. I had four extra clips, two in my belt and two in the back pockets of my jeans, just in case things took a bad turn, which wasn't rare. The agent sitting directly behind me beat on the seat a few times, charging us up. We were four blocks away.

North Charleston was a city fighting to get rid of its ugly half. Money had flooded in recently, but much was cursed by poverty and crime. We were in the middle of the worst of it tonight. We passed the last street of single bedroom homes and entered the affordable housing area, all crumbling old apartment buildings. Four stories. Brick. Dirty. Ten years from being gentrified. A/C units fighting to stay alive, dripping condensation into the dirt below. Damp clothes dangling from the lines. People congregating in white plastic chairs on their porches.

Chester eased to a stop in the middle of the road fifty yards out. A boy riding a blue bicycle on the sidewalk pedaled toward us. No shoes on. He stared for a long time, then saw the units pull up and realized what was going on. It didn't faze him. He just kept pedaling. Chester and I both pulled on balaclavas to hide our faces, a good habit to have in our profession.

I pushed open the door and stepped out onto the asphalt. Started to run. The other agents were right behind me, including one carrying an air-powered ram. The neighbors soaked up the situation, watching it go down as if this was normal afternoon entertainment. Who needed reality TV when you had this happening next door?

We were heading into a ground level unit, number 102. I ran up the four steps and took position on the right, weapon in hand. My heart roared and I embraced the adrenaline, took control of it. Chester took the left side. The bass line of some underground hip-hop music thumped inside.

The agent with the ram approached the door and waited for my signal. They'd bought two of these air-powered battering rams a month earlier and they hadn't failed us yet. As anyone who has ever stormed a house knows, surprise is all you have going for you. If you don't get a door open quickly, a bust can go

LOWCOUNTRY PUNCH

terribly wrong. Sometimes two men hauling a cement cylinder don't have the force to break down the door, and it gives the men inside a chance to arm themselves. We don't like that.

I nodded to the agent, and he pulled the trigger on his new toy. A sphere popped out, and thousands of pounds of force knocked the door wide open with ease. He stepped back quickly and I barreled in, yelling, "DEA! DEA!" You need to establish who is breaking down the door. Our hope is that the guys inside won't be as quick to shoot a Fed as they would someone else.

The front door opened up into the living room. There was a couch and a recliner, both occupied by young black males. One guy's hair was pulled back in cornrows. The other wore a do-rag. They were still holding game controllers in their hands, caught in shock by the door splitting open.

I saw a handgun on the coffee table. Cornrows eyed it.

"Get your hands way up!" I screamed, moving toward him. "Don't you do it!" I kept him and the other guy in my weapon's sights but scanned the doorways for additional danger. Ches and the two agents pushed into the hallway toward the kitchen.

Gunfire erupted.

Several bullets ripped into the wall next to me and I fell to the floor, keeping my gun aimed at my subjects. Cornrows got nervous and stood to make a run for it. I went after him with a dropkick. He fell, screaming. I pinned him to the ground with my knee and cuffed him.

More thunderous gunfire. Screams.

I yelled at the guy with the do-rag to get on the ground. He didn't move off the couch, just sat there with his hands up. I aimed my gun at his midsection. "I'll ask one more time. Get on the ground, keep your hands above your head." He got my meaning and fell knees to chest. I moved carefully toward him and cuffed him, too.

Someone yelled, "Clear!"

Ches came around the corner. I went to the stereo. Turned the volume knob to the left.

"Everyone okay?"

He nodded. "Two of them got a little trigger-happy in there. Bad shots, though. Found about a key of coke. Some cooking on the stove. Four men in cuffs."

"I hope it was worth it."

"Me, too. I have a feeling we just lost any case we'll ever build on Tux. Now he knows we're onto him."

***

That night, a woman dialed 911 and reported a body swinging from a bridge near Rivers Avenue.

I met Chester at the scene around midnight. The Police Department had closed the road and marked off the area with yellow tape. The black scrawny body of our CI, Jared Winters, swung by the neck from a rope. A CSI photographer snapped shots and, with each flash, as if I was watching an old moving picture, I saw more and more of the story.

His eyes had been cut out. They'd removed his clothes. Stabbed him. The knife still protruded from his chest. A pool of blood had collected fifteen feet below him on the pavement. I'm sure some had dripped onto several windshields as the cars passed under him before it had been reported.

They didn't need to hang a sign on him to get the point across. This was a message to the men we'd arrested earlier: don't betray Tux Clinton.

CHAPTER 6

The orders came down from the Atlanta office the next day. We had to find out where Chad Rourke's cocaine came from. Steve fed me the case on a silver platter. He told me earlier that morning, "You get whoever, whatever you need. Show me that I was right in bringing you in. Make me proud, Reddick."

I promised him I would. I was excited at the opportunity and didn't want to let him down. He was giving me another chance.

In drug enforcement, it's all about using the small-timers to get to the more important players. Then you work the more important players to get to even bigger ones, and up you go. In some cases, I've followed the supply chain all the way to the coca plants on a hillside in Bolivia. That's what it's all about. That's how you clog a leak and win the drug war. But as I was reminded yearly, the powers that be don't always let you go to the top. Steve assured me that I could take this as far as I'd like, but I took that with a grain of salt.

Chester and I rode downtown to the police station on Lockwood to get more information on Chad Rourke's death. We needed to find out where the celebrity had gotten his drugs. A Detective Rosenberg led us into his office. He probably should have spent a few minutes tidying up the clutter, but by his appearance, I didn't think he was too worried about it. Investigating death takes a toll on you. He was a heavyset guy. Gray hair. Couldn't be too far away from his pension. He wore a short-sleeved plaid button-down that looked like it came off the rack of a thrift store. His khakis might have come from the next rack over.

"Case closed," I said. "Is that the latest?"

"That's it," he said, handing over a copy of his report. "We think he was sitting on the railing, smoking a cigarette. From there, he either lost his balance or went on his own accord. No foul play. You should see the toxicology report. The guy was tweaked out of his mind. From what we were told, he had a thing for catching a buzz and then playing on penthouse balconies. It was only a matter of time. It's a shame. Some of these movie stars think they can walk on water. Good life's too much for them."

"Can you share some details? Like I said on the phone, we're supposed to find out where he got his coke. Orders from upper management. You know how it is."

"Don't get me started."

I flipped through the police report. "So where had he been all night? Who was with him? I'm assuming you've interviewed everybody and have a pretty good feel for the evening."

"Oh, yeah. Treated it like a murder. We talked to everyone. Rourke started out at a house party south of Broad. Thrown by James King, the owner of the Mazyck. Lots of the folks filming that movie with him were there. Tela Davies, too. It was one of those upper-crust shindigs. A bunch of them went back to the hotel, ended up partying at the rooftop bar. Then James King, Tela Davies, and Chad Rourke went to Rourke's penthouse. King and Davies left around 2 a.m. Got 'em both in the lobby on the video camera walking out the door. They never came back. Both have alibis. Rourke hit the pavement around two hours later."

"You spoke with King and Davies?"

"Several times."

"Did you ask about the drugs?"

"Not really. I told them to tell me the truth, that I didn't care if they were tooting some snow. Not my job."

"So King and Davies went home together?"

"No. King went home to his longtime girlfriend. Davies went over to another guy's house. I forget his name. Something Riley. It's in the report."

I searched for a minute. "Jack Riley."

"That's him. Lucky guy, right? He's got a condo over in Mt. Pleasant. He verified that Ms. Davies was with him the remainder of the night. We left it at that."

"Do you have a list of everyone at the party at King's home earlier?"

"No, I didn't bother with it."

After about five more minutes of this, we wrapped it up. On the way out of the parking lot, I called Steve and told him we wanted research and light surveillance on James King, and we agreed it wouldn't hurt to watch Jack Riley, too. It wasn't worth trying to put a tail on Tela Davies. Being one of the biggest names in Hollywood, she had enough people following her. Above all else, at this point in the investigation, we had to be stealthy.

***

King was now our focus. He'd been with Rourke the night he'd died. He owned the Mazyck Hotel where it had all gone down. And even the party earlier in the evening had been at his house. I would have bet every dime I had that he knew how to find good cocaine.

First step was searching public and private records. What did he own? Did he work with anyone else on any other investments? School records: how were his grades? What were his extracurriculars? This information was critical in prep work for a potential undercover assignment. If whoever we sent went in bad-mouthing Wake Forest—who King happened to have played basketball for—we'd already be at a disadvantage.

I wasn't ready to go under. We wanted to feel King out first, try to understand him. And although Chester's scar works wonders when he's going under for gang work, penetrating high-society Charleston wasn't his thing. So we put up a young female agent, Carly Baker, at the Mazyck for a few nights and let her work her magic. She wasn't there to ask questions; only to watch, listen, and mingle.

She ate most of her meals at the hotel, and spent hours at the bar each night. If anyone checked her out, we had put together a bulletproof backstory for her. The cast and crew of the movie, *Lonely Morning*—including Tela Davies—were all living there. Many of them had just returned from Chad Rourke's funeral in his hometown of Boise, Idaho. The bar bubbled with stories about him. Dry eyes were hard to find.

James King was always at the hotel, and he either ate dinner at the restaurant or sat at one of the two bars every night. I studied a picture of him. King didn't look like I had imagined him. He was shorter and had less hair, but he carried himself with great confidence. I could see it by the straightness of his back and the hidden grin in his eyes.

After a few days, it became very clear that he craved power and fed off the spotlight. He wanted, even needed, people to like him. We had seen that in how King treated his guests, especially those involved with the movie. If I was planning on going undercover to befriend him, I needed to be someone he would want to impress. I'd worked people like that before. I couldn't bust into his hotel selling ball bearings. James King would only help me if I could help him—if he had something to gain.

I finished up the week with good news: Steve finally called off the cops watching my house. How could Tux find out it was me who crippled his cousin? Even if he did, he wasn't dumb enough to make a move on a federal agent a week after we'd found a man who ratted on him swinging from a bridge.

Things were finally getting back to normal.

CHAPTER 7

Even I roll sevens from time to time.
The next day, luck found me at the most unlikely of places: Crosby's Seafood Market. I had vivid memories of visiting Crosby's as a kid while staying with my grandparents one summer. The store still occupied the same blue shack on Lockwood. The growth of the city had long passed it by, but they were still providing the freshest fish around. Inside, the heady aroma of the ocean brought back grand memories of my youth. Back to those days with my grandparents, and back when my father and I would drive up to the Baltimore marina to watch the fishermen unload the morning's catch.

Behind the glass, displayed on ice, was anything you wanted out of the sea: dressed flounder, mussels, scallops, shad roe, softshell crab. As I started to ask for help, the bell above the door rang and a pleasant surprise entered.

My memory had not done her justice. She was a miracle, a marvel, a maiden of the afternoon. A white and turquoise patterned sundress contrasted her tanned, stunning body. She wore several silver bangles around her wrist. Long feather earrings hung from her ears. Her hair was pulled into a tight bun, still wet from an afternoon shower. She wore no makeup, and it would have been a crime if she had.

LOWCOUNTRY PUNCH

Liz Coles came out of the gates quickly. "You couldn't catch your own fish today?"

"They don't always bite, you know?" I walked to her and put an arm around her in greeting. "I guess it's meant to be."

"What does that mean?"

"That's what you said on the water."

"I guess I did, didn't I?"

A woman behind the counter with white rubber gloves interrupted us just as we were getting into it. "You lovebirds need anything?"

"A pound of mahi," I said, "and a handful of scallops." I turned to Liz. "You like mahi?"

"You're relentless."

"I'd be honored if you'd let me cook for you. We could ride over to the harbor on the water for the bridge celebration…watch the fireworks. It's the same guys who do the Kentucky Derby every year." I could see the battle waging behind her brown eyes. I nodded toward the fish on the scale. "I can't eat all this alone."

"Sorry, I don't do pity," she said.

My heart sank.

"But you're in luck. I haven't eaten all day."

I did my best to conceal my elation.

***

Less then an hour later, we were in my kitchen. I stood at the island with tomatoes, onions, and mango in front of me, working on a salsa. Liz sat on the counter to my right, her perfectly smooth legs dangling. I had potatoes boiling in a pot, almost soft enough to mash. We drank Mexican beers and listened to the satellite jazz station and took turns naming the artist. We were off to a great evening, and I knew by the genuine smile on her face that she felt the same way.

I pretended like I hadn't Googled Liz as she gave me the rundown on her life. She grew up on Church Street, a couple doors from where Dubose Heyward wrote *Porgy*. Her mom and dad owned an art shop, and they lived above it. She graduated from the College of Charleston with a B.F.A. in studio art, got her Masters from NYU in art therapy, and had been living in New York ever since. Her alma mater had asked her to teach a summer course in Charleston and put her up in a place downtown, so she was splitting time between here and New York.

Liz talked for a while about The Portrait and a Dream Project, and I've never heard anyone speak so passionately about anything. Describing a group of terminally-ill children at New York-Presbyterian, she said, "You should see their faces when they pick up that brush and dip it into the paint for the first time." Liz hopped off the counter and came towards me. "Smearing the paints together, inventing their own colors, opening up a whole new world. Some of them have never had the chance."

"I can't imagine." She was unlike any woman I'd ever known. So damn intelligent. I had to work hard to keep up. I had so many questions for her. So many things to share.

My new crush reached in front of me, stole a sliver of mango off the cutting board, and stuck it on her tongue. She closed her eyes and enjoyed the tropical taste. I wanted to kiss her but I lost my chance.

"One of the things I'm doing here is trying to bring the project down to South Carolina," she continued. "We're starting with the Children's Hospital at MUSC."

"I'd love to help, if there's anything I can do. I'm no painter, though."

"There's always something. I'm sure they'd love to hear you play the banjo."

"I'd be happy to do it. Let me know when."

"Count on it."

We talked about art for a long time. About Jackson Pollack,

her inspiration. About her latest work. She schooled me on the modern and contemporary eras for a while, and I devoured her intellect. She explored my mind as well, poking and prodding through my memories and thoughts.

Though it was the last thing I needed, I was falling for this woman. Aside from a face that could stop wars—or start them—she was an artist, and she had a way of looking into you, right down to the depths of your being, like there was no hiding who you were. Like the great bard from Minnesota said, "She can take the dark out of the nighttime, and paint the daytime black." I didn't feel exposed when she looked into me; I felt free.

I pulled a plastic bag out of a drawer and put it around my hand.

"What's this all about?" she asked.

"You'll see." I set a jalapeño down on the cutting board. I sliced off both ends. "Have you ever chopped one up?"

"In all my years, I don't think I have ever cut up a jalapeño. I'm a takeout girl."

Her only flaw. She didn't cook.

We drank a Ribbon Ridge Pinot and dined on mahimahi with salsa, scallops, asparagus, and my famous mashed potatoes. The way to a woman's heart is mashed potatoes, I'd learned. Put 'em on a tray with eggs and some fresh-squeezed orange juice and take it to her in bed one morning. See what happens.

We finished the bottle on the porch, sharing a wicker love seat looking west toward James Island. The sun floated down past the horizon and cast resplendent colors across the sky. The clouds came alive. Off in the distance, tethered to an aging dock, a shrimp boat floated alone in the water. A ballad came on the radio, and I asked her to dance. She smiled and took my hand. We wrapped our arms around each other and danced to Nat King Cole singing *Nothing in the World,* and nothing in the world could have made me happier.

When the song ended and the sun had disappeared, we rushed

over to the harbor on the Tate's Key West. The dark outline of the new Cooper River Bridge, the longest cable-stayed bridge in the United States, appeared in the distance. I steered carefully, knowing that there were a ton of boaters out to see the fireworks and few of them knew what they were doing in the dark.

Boats were scattered like stars, hundreds of them, on both sides of the bridge, waiting to be entertained. I got as close as I could get to the bridge and tossed the anchor. It caught, the line drew tight, and the current positioned the boat so that the bow pointed at the bridge. The *Yorktown* aircraft carrier was to our right—so still and timeless—and to the left, the church steeples of downtown reached reverently toward the sky.

I joined Liz on the bow cushion just as the show began. Fireworks lit up the darkness, the booms echoed across the water, and billows of smoke began to hover like fog. I took her hand. "I'm glad you're here."

"You're a really sweet guy, T.A. Thanks for such a fun evening."

"I want more nights like these. You and I have something together."

I moved close and took her hand. Looked into those brown eyes. I went to kiss her when I noticed a tear running down her right cheek.

Her lips parted to say something, but I put my index finger to my lips. She didn't need to say anything. I knew.

We were both broken hearts, looking for some way to escape the pain. I wondered who could have possibly broken Liz's heart. What kind of fool would make her cry?

CHAPTER 8

Though I'd done what I considered to be some impressive coercing, Liz only stayed at my place for a few minutes after we returned from the boat ride. No doubt about it: she was a lady of the highest order. As much as I wanted to get to know her, I wasn't sure she was going to let me into her world.

My eyes were still following Liz's car down the road when Anna's father, Beau Tate, called out to me.

"Caught someone snoopin' in your yard earlier," he said, his feet crunching on the gravel as he approached. "Scared the heck out of me. I almost called the cops."

"What?"

"Yeah, while you were out galavantin' on the water with that good-looking chickadee, I was runnin' people out of your yard. Thought I'd wait until she left to come tell you about it."

"Who was it?" I began to scan the perimeter.

"I don't know that I'd put money on it, but it looked like that little girl, Stephanie, the one that you were seeing a while back." Beau had been my father's best friend since they were ten days old. The Charleston sun had aged his now leathery skin, and many years of drinking Coors had sculpted his belly into a nearly perfect beach ball. Since retiring from his law practice, he spent the majority of his time at the helm of his sailboat, *The Jolly*

Codger, and he gave off this kind of vibe that said he wasn't worried about anything. That life was good.

He tipped his bald head toward me. "I think you might have pissed her off."

"No doubt about that."

"Come look."

I followed him to my backyard and to the edge of the marsh, where the mud sank in some. He took out a little penlight.

"See," he said. Small footprints led out onto the grass. "Cindy and I were out on the balcony watching the fireworks when I noticed a shadow. I think she saw me looking and was holding damn still trying not to give away her position. I yelled over to her, and she just outright bolted."

I didn't want to believe it. "You didn't chase after her? I would have paid you good money to hog-tie her and swing her above the dock."

"Son, I gave up chasin' women forty years ago."

"Well, I'm real sorry you had to deal with that."

"Oh, I like a little action from time to time."

"Am I the worst neighbor on the planet?"

"Damn entertaining. That's for sure." He broke into a laugh and started to head back to his house. "Why don't you bring the new one over for dinner tomorrow night?" he asked over his shoulder.

"I might. Let me see what she's up to. I'll call you tomorrow." We bid each other good night. Beau had obviously moved on. I couldn't imagine walking into their home with any woman other than Anna on my arm, but it would have to happen eventually. After my father was murdered, he became very important to me. I smiled, thinking about how much of a hard time he'd given me when he found out I was dating his daughter in Miami.

With a shotgun leaning on the table, I climbed into the Pawley's Island hammock on my porch and let it rock me into a deep Southern dream.

***

LOWCOUNTRY PUNCH

When I woke, I rolled over to the sun sneaking up the other side of my house, its reflection shimmering along the surface of the water. I wasn't quite ready to get up yet, so I grabbed the book sitting on the table. The sound of footsteps stopped me before I found my page. I could smell danger.

I looked up. And there she was, like some porter of misfortune, some black angel from my past: Stephanie Lewis. Last night's trespasser had returned. A day after I'd moved up to Charleston, I'd spotted her car stranded on the side of the road and pulled over to help her change a tire. She was a schoolteacher. I ended up asking her out. Some kind of rebound play after Anna. We went on one date and I didn't call her again.

She still hadn't taken the hint.

She came around the side of the house. She might as well have been flying on her broom. She was wearing beige wide-legged trousers and a sleeveless shirt, not your typical witch garb. I didn't bother getting out of the hammock.

"Hey, sweets. What you reading?" she asked, her dimples showing.

"Some nonsense." I put the book behind my back. I'd like to say I'd been reading Bukowski, but the book was *Men Are From Mars, Women Are From Venus*. My mother had sent it to me shortly after my downfall.

Stephanie leaned over to kiss my lips. I turned my head away and her lips connected with my ear. "I don't get a kiss?"

"What size shoe do you wear?"

"What are you talking about?"

I looked down at the flip-flops on her feet. "I bet you have some size 9 North Face trail-running shoes with fresh mud on the soles sitting in your closet."

"Shut up, T.A."

"Don't do that again. Sneaking around my yard in the middle of the night is not a good idea. What were you thinking? You're gonna find yourself on the wrong end of my Benelli."

"Oh, don't you threaten me. God, you law types are so paranoid." There it was: exactly the reason I'd never tell another woman what I did for a living. Halfway through a beer at Salty Mike's, I'd told Stephanie my occupation, and she nearly exploded with excitement. Thought she was on a date with some kind of action hero. Drilled me with questions, her eyes blown up wide like somebody was pumping her full of air.

I hopped off the hammock and looked out over the water, my back to her. "What do you need?"

"Don't cop a tone with me. I wanted to see you."

I watched an egret fly by and didn't say a word.

"I know you miss me."

"You're mistaken. You shouldn't be here."

"What's the latest case you're working on? Maybe I could help."

"That's not even funny."

"I'm just trying to keep tabs on you. I don't see why you won't give us a chance."

I raised my hands in the air, giving up. "Look, I don't know what to tell you."

"I'm pregnant."

"We didn't have sex." I turned around and headed toward the door. "I've gotta get a shower and head into town for a meeting. Take care, Stephanie. I don't want you coming over here again."

She hesitated, then brushed past me down the stoop. "I'll call you later."

I rolled my eyes. "Good-bye."

I shut the door.

***

It never fails: when I do finally rid a woman from my head, she comes back to test me. It happened in doubles that day. When I got home from work, I found a letter from Anna in the mailbox.

LOWCOUNTRY PUNCH

From a chair on the porch, with the crickets sounding the day's end, I read her words.

T.A.,

Hi there. I just moved near a gourmet Popsicle shop in Santa Monica, and it makes me think of you when I drive by. Anyway, I hope Charleston is everything you hoped.

Love,

Anna

It wasn't even that she had much to say; but it still got to me. On Saturdays, we used to take long walks on South Beach and stop at this popsicle shop every time. There's something so personal and penetrating about a letter, and it brought me back to a place I'd almost gotten away from. Why couldn't I let her go?

I lit the tip of the letter and held it out in front of me as the paper burned. Didn't set it down until the flame extinguished. The pain in my fingertips masked my emotional pain for a moment. I wiped the tears from my eyes.

CHAPTER 9

The next day, I stopped at Ricky's Boiled Peanut Stand on the way to the office. Big Ricky parks his red trailer in the lot near the Earth Fare, which is James Island's version of a Whole Foods Market. If you can get past the folks that don't believe in deodorant or shampoo, it's a good place to fill your cart.

Ricky was pushing three hundred pounds, so as he waddled over to the back of the trailer in his overalls to fill up a plastic bag with his boiled peanuts, the trailer tilted with him. He had three choices: regular, Cajun, and ham-hock. I always asked him to layer all three in one bag. Love a good surprise. Give me a pound of Ricky's peanuts and a cup of coffee and I can go for miles. I thanked him and walked back to the Jeep, still thinking about Anna's letter.

As I put my hand on the car door handle, I heard motion behind me and started to turn. Something hit me hard on the back of the head. I dropped onto the asphalt and everything went black.

When I came to, two men were hoisting me into the back of a trunk. I thought I recognized one but my vision was hazy at best. They didn't have masks on, which was not a good thing. It meant they weren't worried about me picking them out of a lineup later. Because I would be dead. But why didn't they just shoot me and leave me in the lot? No matter the reason, I knew there was a lot of pain coming my way. Much to my chagrin, I had the day off, so no one was expecting me.

They tied my hands in front of me with a zip tie and slammed the trunk shut. I kicked and thrashed until I knew I wasn't going anywhere.

"Damn it!" I cursed. How had I been so oblivious?

The trunk was totally empty, not even a tire iron or jack. It smelled musty and old, like someone's grandfather had held onto the car for decades.

The back of my head hurt like hell. I felt around my face with my bound hands. Had a bloody gash on the right side. The pain nearly overwhelmed me. I tried to shut it out and sense where we were going, but it was hard. Much more difficult than figuring out who was behind this little joy ride. I hadn't given Tux Clinton enough credit. That's what I get for letting my guard down.

I looked at the glowing hands on the watch I inherited from my father and marked the time. Two minutes into our ride, the incline told me we were heading over a bridge. I guessed the West Ashley connector. A few more turns and another bridge confirmed it. Then the highway wasn't too hard to figure out. Smooth and fast. The engine worked harder.

Nineteen minutes later, we took an exit. It could have been one of three or four. It was impossible to tell. All I knew was that we had driven into North Charleston. The pain had faded some. I made a few more futile attempts to bust open the trunk. Then we made several turns. Finally, a big bump and we slowed down and came to a stop. A garage door squeaked open. We pulled in.

The engine shut off, then footsteps, and then the trunk door lifted. My eyes adjusted. Two of them were looking down at me. I did know one of them. Jeff Cooke. One of Tux's known associates. He had a shadow of a beard, shaved at the neck line.

A flat nose. Street tough. Detectives liked him for Jared Winter's murder and were looking for him. The other guy wore a light blue Adidas warm-up suit. His gray eyes were tucked into deep sockets.

"Did you happen to grab that bag of peanuts?" I asked. "I didn't even get one."

"Shut the fuck up."

"Seriously. That was my breakfast."

Cooke jerked me up by my elbow and dragged me out of the trunk. He had hard, calloused hands. I couldn't get my feet down in time and fell onto my back. He helped me up in a not-so-polite way.

He walked me through an empty garage and into an abandoned house. Probably for sale. The other guy followed us in and when I turned to look at him I noticed a .38 tucked into the waistband of his warm-up suit. I wasn't surprised they were carrying, and I didn't like how this was going.

Cooke threw me to the ground in the living room. I lay flat on my back and looked around. The walls were brown. Some spider webs dangled from the ceiling. Two large glass doors half-covered by a ragged blue curtain led to the backyard.

As they stood over me, the man in the Adidas made a call. "We got him…yep. A'ight." He looked at Cooke as he closed the phone and withdrew the .38 from his waist. "Change of plans."

I didn't know what that meant but I had a feeling it had to do with me dying. Was it Tux on the other end of that phone call? Had he planned on beating me up some before killing me and then thought better of it?

I started talking, just to kill the tension. Buy some time. "You gonna tell me why I'm here? I don't have all day."

No answer.

"Tux wasn't man enough to show up? Doesn't surprise me."

Cooke went to the glass doors and looked out. "Where you

wanna do it?" he asked. Obviously not speaking to me.

"The garage," the one in the track suit said as he started to pace. He stopped, dangerously close to me.

Cooke went out the doors to the backyard.

This was the only chance I had. Still on my back, I kicked my captor in the balls with my heel, hard. He nearly collapsed. I jumped up into a squat and thrust my head into his chin. His jawbone cracked and he screamed in pain, dropping to his knees as he clutched his face. You can't beat a good head butt.

Cooke ran back inside but I pivoted around and was on him before he had time to get over the shock of the action. I pulled my bound hands to my chest and ran right into him with a shoulder. His back hit the curtain and then smashed into the glass door. The curtain ripped from the wall, and the door exploded around us as we tumbled down the brick steps into the grass.

I stood quickly, knowing I wasn't even close to being free. I kicked his head with my boot just like the old UVA days, trying to knock it into the goal. I didn't score but his lights went out.

I went back up the steps. The Adidas guy was still on the ground, screaming in pain. As I reached the broken door, I started to saw the zip tie with a sharp edge of glass sticking out of the doorframe. Then Adidas looked up. With one hand still holding his face, he eyed his gun on the ground and went for it. My hands still bound, I backed away and darted toward the chain-link fence at the end of the yard. I had to get out of there.

He began firing.

The bullets whizzed by me, giving me a shot of adrenaline. I increased my speed. I reached the fence and leapt into the air. My feet grazed the top but I made it over. I tucked a shoulder and rolled. Coming back up, I didn't even look back. The bullets were flying by, tearing into the house in front of me.

As I rounded the corner, I felt one hit me in the side. A familiar feeling. Icy and hot at the same time. I could feel the warm blood dripping down my side. As long as I could run, it didn't matter. Couldn't be *that* bad of a wound or I would have been flopping around on the ground. I kept pushing with everything I had, staying close to the houses as I ran. Finally, the zip tie gave way and I got my hands back.

I spotted some signs of life in the distance and began to head that way. Breathing like I was dying, I reached the parking lot of a Piggly Wiggly. An older woman was pushing a grocery cart to her car. She was yapping away on a cell phone. I went right for her, mumbling that I'd return it as I snatched it from her hand. I ran toward the store. Didn't see Adidas behind me. "Call the cops!" I yelled to the first clerk I saw, a teenage girl.

The clerk stalled. Someone else screamed.

"I'm DEA. Call the cops. Okay?"

The clerk went for the phone.

"Is there a security guard here?"

With a phone to her ear, she shook her head. I wanted a gun. I had no idea if Adidas was still coming. I dialed Chester's number with the woman from the parking lot's cell, then walked back outside and scanned the area. No signs of trouble.

Chester picked up and I said, "I'm at the Piggly Wiggly off Rivers. I need you here now. Tux sent some guys after me."

"On it. You all right?"

"I took a bullet. I think I'm okay, though. Jeff Cooke was one of them. Black jeans and a white polo. The other one, same age, has on a blue Adidas warm-up suit. White stripes up and down. Probably in an old tan Chevy sedan. Get an APB out."

"Done. On my way."

***

After getting patched up by one of the paramedics, I climbed into Chester's g-car. The bullet had only grazed my side. Another scar to remind me of what's important.

LOWCOUNTRY PUNCH

A crime scene unit was at the house where they'd taken me. Both men were gone. Lots of good DNA, though. They hadn't had time to clean up. The whole county was looking for them.

Chester and I only knew one way to fix this problem. Something we should have done earlier. We had both logged hours dealing with gangs in L.A. and Miami, and sometimes you have to treat them like businessmen. They appreciate it and it prevents trouble. Even when we did catch my attackers, they wouldn't finger Tux. I had a feeling he already knew about the botched attempt, and that he was expecting me.

We drove to his place, only five miles away. He owned a little white house in a neighborhood that had begun its leap into gentrification. He paid the mortgage on it with income from a legitimate landscaping business that he had owned for five or six years. Tux knew how to be careful and cover his ass.

He was on the porch, looking like he was waiting for us, just like I'd thought. His feet were propped up on a table, not a worry on his mind. An older BMW sat in the driveway. I was going to let Chester do the talking, but seeing Tux there got me excited. I stepped out of the car and said, "I don't think we've been formally introduced." I slammed my door and pounded up the steps.

Tux had a well-groomed appearance complimented by some gold jewelry around his wrist and neck. No visible tats. Dark skin. He had on jeans and a white muscle shirt. Very broad shoulders. Clearly had a thing for lifting. Looked like he'd be a hell of a lot of work to beat down.

"Who are you?" he asked.

"You know exactly who I am." I pulled the table out from under him and his feet hit the floor.

"I'm guessin' you're a cop," he said, all tough and badass. "I could smell you coming 'round the corner."

"You've been looking for me. Now you got me."

"All I know is I have two pigs in my yard."

Chester came up the steps. "I'm Agent Benton. You know who my partner is. We're looking for some resolution. You don't need to admit to anything."

"You can get back in your car and ride out. I didn't do nothing wrong."

"Such eloquent speech," I said. "No Ivy League for you, huh? Very surprising."

"Don't you come into my neighborhood insulting me."

"You threatening me? Is that a good idea?" I got in his face. "That's what your cousin did." I stood back and lifted up my shirt and ripped off the bandage covering my wound. "I owe you one for this anyway."

Chester pulled me back and said, "Tux, I know you aren't gonna come clean, but I want you to hear us out. You don't fuck with us. I know you feel like you got to, but don't do it, man. We won't let up. I know Agent Reddick messed up your cousin Jesse, but I doubt you're gonna get an apology out of him."

My partner stepped towards Tux and lowered his voice. "You know he had no idea who Jesse was. He robbed a bank, took a baby hostage, and shot his mama. He had it coming. But because I want you to owe me, I can help Jesse out. We can make sure the prosecutor goes easy. That is, if you wanna back off Agent Reddick. We're still gonna track down the boys who grabbed him."

My turn. "Or you can try again. I'll dance with you every night, sunshine. We could go right here. You're the least of my worries."

Ches waved his hand, trying to shut me up. "He's a hot head. You both are. Leave this one alone, Tux. I'll look out for Jesse."

Tux thought about it and then nodded without making eye contact.

Ches started to walk back down the stairs backwards. "Then we're cool?"

"We're cool." Tux put his feet back up on the table. "Just get this muthafucka off my porch."

I threw up my middle finger and started down the steps. "You know where to find me."

As we drove away, Chester said, "You know, Reddick, I'm startin' to like you. You don't take shit from anybody, do you?"

I barely heard what Ches said. My head was still humming with fury. "I wanna know who gave him my name."

CHAPTER 10

In the early hours the next morning, a Folly Beach cop pulled over a drunk driver. The license plate was one our surveillance team had taken down while watching Jack Riley, the man who'd been with Tela the night of Chad Rourke's death. We'd circulated it through law enforcement. Because of the hit, they did a search of his vehicle and found twelve ounces of cocaine and a firearm. Finally, we were getting somewhere. We wanted to find out what this guy knew.

Folly Beach was only about a fifteen-minute drive from my house. Chester waited for me on Center Street, the main drag leading to the beach. He had two cups of coffee from The Lost Dog. I took one of them. "Thanks, podna."

"Reddick, what is this 'podna' shit?"

"I don't know where it came from. You don't like it?" I took a sip of the coffee, one of my favorite blends in the South.

He shook his head. "I hate it. How you feelin'? You look like hell."

"A little sore. Not bad." I touched my black eye.

Ches and I headed up the stairs of the government building housing the courthouse and the police department. White paint peeling from the walls. The echo of footsteps. Through a door, two officers sat at their desks. The closer one read the newspaper. His duty belt, with cuffs and holster on the side, was way too big for his skinny frame. He hadn't said a word, and I already didn't like him. I don't usually form opinions so quickly, but something about him bothered me.

"The D...E...A," he said. "You know what that stands for, don't you?" His mustache looked like a fuzzy caterpillar had crawled onto his face. I tend to judge a man by his 'stache. It bounced up and down as he spoke.

"Don't Expect Anything," he continued, "especially after five. It was real kind of you suits to come. I's needin' somebody to show me how to do my job."

"You called us," I said.

"Not by choice. Chief said we had to."

Chester is more patient than I am with numbskulls. He said, "We aren't trying to show anybody how to do their job. We appreciate you calling. It's been hard finding a lead on this uncut."

"I'm bustin' your balls. We're all professionals here." He stuck out his hand. "Name's Darby Long." We all shook and introduced ourselves. He continued, "As long as my boy stays behind bars, you can interrogate him 'til he's blue in the face. I'm sure you boys are just scrambling to cover your asses after that Chad Rourke fiasco."

Chester acknowledged his impressive assertion with a smirk. "The last thing we want is to let him go. How'd you nab him?"

"I's on late shift lookin' for DUIs. He come cross the Folly Bridge runnin' about fifty. He was swervin' like a buck with a bullet in him. I ran the plates and saw there was a watch on him, so I threw him in the backseat of my cruiser. Asked him if I could search his vehicle, and he let me. I about gave up after a few but had a feelin' in my gut he was carryin'. You know how you get that sometimes?"

Chester nodded.

"He was drivin' one of those old Ford Explorers. I noticed a

Philips screwdriver in the back on the floor, and I recalled how you can unscrew them Explorer consoles. I opened it and—" he stuck a finger in the air, "*bingo*. A loaded nine-millimeter and under that, twelve ounces of uncut, smilin' at me. Tested it soon as I got back, ninety percent pure. Found a damn Walgreen's in there, too. Xanex, Lytocaine, Valium, et cetra…"

Chester nodded, impressed. "That's good policin'—"

"It ain't my first run."

"What's his name?" Chester asked.

"George Kadopholous. I think he's a Dago."

"Must be," I said and then to Chester under my breath, "or not."

Chester asked, "The lawyer in there with him?"

"Sure is. He was here before I could finish the paperwork. Name's Frick. Big-city type. Dressed like he's going to church."

***

Officer Long walked the lanky Greek into the interrogation room. George Kadopholous, Kado for short. He had hazel eyes, thick eyebrows, and dark shaggy hair. Probably could have made it as a male model if he wanted to. Both of his eyes were swollen but the left had bruised up.

The lawyer followed him. A bent nose, like he'd injured it when he was young. Coat and tie. Briefcase. Walking in like he'd done this before. Many times.

The four of us sat down, and Officer Long stood by the door. I started with the lawyer. "You're moving early, Mr. Frick."

"I'm not a sleeper."

"Me neither. How did your relationship with Mr. Kadopholous come about? You mobilized quickly this morning."

"A lucky chain of events."

"Right." I nodded and looked up at Officer Long. "Officer,

you wanna take these cuffs off the poor guy? He's not going anywhere." Long hesitated but I gave him the eye, and he walked over and removed the cuffs. As he returned to his station against the wall, I said to him, "Can you give us a few minutes? We don't want to scare Mr. Kadopholous with too much blue." Officer Long didn't like that either, but he walked out before I had to embarrass him. As he shut the door, I said, "We'll yell if we need you."

Kado grinned, and I hoped I had him from that point forward. I touched my face. "Looks like both of us had bad nights last night." He forced a little smile. Really white teeth. I had brought a minidisc player from the Jeep, and I held it up in the air. "You mind?"

Kado looked at his lawyer. "Agent Reddick," Frick said, "My client will not go on the record until we all come to terms with exactly what we are trying to accomplish here. He may have information that would interest you, but I want to talk to the DA first."

It was Chester's turn. "I have authority to speak on behalf of Assistant United States Attorney (AUSA) Cannon on this matter. I talked with him on the way down here, and he has already spoken with the DA. I can have a signed statement here in a few minutes."

Frick nodded. "All right."

"What type of information could you provide?"

"Let's say he could share names with you."

"What kind of names?"

"For the sake of this discussion, hypothetically speaking, let's say my client could deliver the names of persons involved in the importation of cocaine into Charleston."

We did the hypothetical dance for a while, then I said, "Carrying a weapon, twelve ounces of cocaine, an array of pharmaceuticals, a DUI, and a PWID, Possession With Intent to Distribute. The officer pulled you over near a school, so we could also tag on a proximity charge no problem. I'd hate to be you right now, Mr. Kadopholous."

Kado placed his hands in his lap. Miserable, angry, afraid.

"What is your proposition?" Frick asked.

"If your client will answer our questions and deliver the names of the two men directly in charge of the drug wire, we'll drop the cocaine charge—including the PWID and proximity—leaving you with a DUI, the weapons charge, the pharmaceutical possession, and an open container."

Frick said, "The DUI and weapons charge have to go—"

"Absolutely not," Chester said. "We'll give you a few minutes." We walked out before he even tried to argue further.

Kado eventually signed the agreement, and in minutes, I was machine-gunning him with questions. Where's your family? What do your mom and dad do? Brothers and sisters? Will they care about the arrest? What do you do for a living?

His dark skin didn't give away his upbringing, but his slow Southern drawl certainly did. From Savannah. Rich family. He owned a restaurant downtown called Morph; I'd heard Beau and Cindy talk about it. It's a dangerous game trying to wedge your way into the uber-competitive Charleston culinary scene; his restaurant had been open two years, so he was obviously doing something right.

More questions. Where did you go to school? Where did you grow up? We bounced back and forth for a while, and then I got to the good stuff.

"The names you promised us," I said.

I felt like I was Kado's psychiatrist, and we had just reached a major breakthrough. He didn't even hesitate. "Jack Riley and Ronnie Downs."

Chester and I looked at each other, probably thinking the same thing. Who was in charge? Who was at the center of the circle? What did they have to do with James King from the Mazyck Hotel?

"What's your role?" I asked, sitting back and crossing my legs.

"We're all tight friends. Have been since college. But I guess you could say Ronnie and I work for Jack. We deliver coke to most of his buyers, and, in return, he gives us a deal on more quantity. Ronnie and I both have our own clientele that we work separately. Jack's got the connection, keeps it to himself. We don't know where he's getting it. I think Atlanta, but I really don't know for sure."

"Why Atlanta?"

"He mentioned I-20 one time, talking about a traffic accident. I-20 takes you right into Atlanta. He makes the drive in the morning and calls us on the way back. It takes him about ten hours, which is about right if he's going to Atlanta. He's also been talking about something new, like he's got something in the works. He wants to up the scale."

"How does he deliver the coke to you?"

"We meet at his cabin in McClellanville."

"Where does James King fit into it?"

Kado looked up, surprised. "Jack's in charge. King gets his dope directly from Jack, then he turns around and sells it to his guests." It became all too clear to Kado. "Y'all were already onto us, weren't you? Since Chad Rourke's death. Jack had a feeling. He knows you're coming."

"That's for us to worry about." Then a very important question. "You know a guy named Tux Clinton?"

"Never heard of him." That's what I was hoping for. Tux had nothing to do with this crowd. If he did, I wouldn't be able to go undercover.

I nodded. "Who gave you that black eye?"

"Jack did." I didn't say anything, waiting for more. "We were all at his place last night, all in the pool real late. Tela Davies was there."

"You were in the pool with Tela Davies last night?" Chester asked. "I don't feel sorry for you at all."

"Don't get me started. I'm not even going to say the words that come to mind when I think about her." He shook his head. "She and I were talking kind of close. Out of nowhere, she started screaming at me, saying I was trying to make a move on her, which was total bullshit. Jack came up to me in the shallow end. Told me to leave. I told him she was lying. He said I wasn't going anywhere without an apology. We ended up getting into it. The bastard got me in a headlock and held me underwater. Nearly drowned me."

"This is your friend?"

"Used to be."

We'd found my way in. Kado was the ticket. Forget James King. I wanted to go straight for Jack. I'd been using guys like Kado to go undercover for years, and if you're careful, you can make them work. The trick was figuring out what angle to use. Same questions that we'd ask about King. What did Jack need? How could I make him trust me? Keeping the details from his runners meant Jack knew what he was doing. He wasn't going to be easy to break. Kado said Jack was greedy, starting with only a few kilos but upping it nearly every month. Greed should be taken advantage of. It makes them weak. My wheels turned. I was already sculpting the perfect character.

We mentioned dropping the weapons charge and the DUI, and Kado's ratty eyes lit up like disco balls. He agreed to make an introduction and assist in building a relationship between Jack and me and testify if necessary. Chester had the AUSA fax over two more documents, one for Kado to sign and the other ordering Kado's release.

Officer Long didn't like it at all. We told him we'd mention him in our report, but he wasn't having it. "I don't give two hyenas about some dang report. You DEA fags come in here and try to pull rank. Take my damn prisoners. You can have him but you'll be sorry. Last thing you want is Darby Long on your back. I'll be on you like white on shit."

LOWCOUNTRY PUNCH

I couldn't listen to it any longer. The DEA had a long history of butting heads with local law enforcement. "Officer, once you get a few more years under your belt you'll begin to understand the meaning and value of teamwork."

"I ain't no rookie, son. You better watch your mouth."

"I know. You're gonna be on me like white on shit…or was it stink on rice? Either way, I'd like to see you try." We weren't going to fight, only exchanging pleasantries to make sure we understood each other. To be honest, I was warming up to him.

I stuffed my card in Officer Long's shirt pocket, and we walked out with Kado and his lawyer. We told him we'd be in touch. As they drove off, I said, "Ches, did I tell you about this girl I met?"

"Ten times, man. Ten times. Why don't you call her already? If you don't, someone else will."

"Yeah, you're probably right."

"Probably? I guarantee it."

***

I took Chester's advice. Liz met me at the Blind Tiger on Broad Street for a quick drink that evening. She wore this funky white top and a long, gypsy-like yellow skirt with sandals. I loved the quirkiness of her wardrobe. I kissed her on the cheek, not wanting to repeat the last time I tried to kiss her lips. We took a seat in the corner of the patio, up against a stone wall. A standing fan hooked up to a mist machine blew beads of cool water in our direction.

It was so good to see her again, and I could tell she shared in the excitement. I took her hand and we both leaned forward at the table and talked like best friends who hadn't seen each other in years.

Out of the blue, during our second beer, she said, "You can kiss me now."

"What?"

"I wasn't ready on the boat, but I am now. Don't make me beg."

"You don't have to ask twice."

I reached over and gently guided her chin towards me. At long last, our lips met. She tasted like the cool water that rushes past stones in an Appalachian stream. It was a kiss that might have been talked about in the heavens, a kiss that would never let me go.

II

"Out into the cool of the evening strolls the pretender."

- Jackson Browne

CHAPTER 11

Within a week, Security Programs at the DEA headquarters in Atlanta approved Operation Coastal Snow, a name Ches penned. I would be issued a Social Security card under my new name, Travis Workman Moody.

Our team met in the boardroom for what Steve called a pre-mortem. I walked in, admittedly, with a bit of pride. I'd finally earned a little respect. Only days after being tapped on the shoulder, I had found a way in. Of course, Kado had fallen in our lap, but still. Making headway is the goal. No one cares how you get there.

Now I just had to convince Jack Riley to let me into his world, and I didn't care how. I'd start by feeding his greed. Let him know that I could move a ton of product in a new market. Then I'd befriend him. Try to start working for him. Whatever it took to get close enough to figure out the details of his organization. Jack had kept Kado in the dark about his sources and most of his clientele. Who knew what Jack's other runner, Ronnie, knew? I needed Jack to trust me more than either one of them. To build a case, we needed all the answers.

Steve summarized what our surveillance team found on Jack, eyeing the file through his glasses as he spoke. "Jack Riley was born in Amagansett, New York. That's in the Hamptons for those of you who don't summer there. Winston and Laura Riley are his parents. The family moved down here when Jack was nine. His sister, Sarah, died that same year, hit by a car downtown. Now, they've obviously got cash. Thirty or forty million. Own land in New York, Idaho, and South Carolina."

One of the guys said, "That kind of money? What the hell's Jack doing dealing cocaine?"

"Who knows? His folks live on the Battery now," he said, referring to the most expensive span of real estate in South Carolina. Steve ran over Jack's progression from college to his father's business to his art gallery in Mt. Pleasant. Apparently one of the most respected galleries in town. Also, his involvement with the current Republican party presidential campaign. Jack's latest venture caught Steve's eye. "According to his tax records, he's claiming profits from a privately owned company, J.R. Imports, L.L.C." Steve stated the net. "Looks like he brings in everything from teak to used farm equipment."

"The guy's an entrepreneur," I said, "but no way he's bringing in coke on containers. He's not swinging globes between his legs."

Steve agreed but said, "We'll take a look anyway." He went on to explain that Jack owned a sixty-one-foot Viking sport fisher docked at Patriot's Point and lived at the Renaissance, a collection of condos that stands next to the Motley building, Ron Motley being the man who fought and won against the big tobacco companies back in the nineties.

We went on for a couple of hours, discussing surveillance, wiretaps, timelines, backstopping, that sort of thing. My focus was on backstopping, the process of building the character who'll be going undercover. I enjoy it immensely. For the next week, Chester and I would do little else. I had to become Travis Moody.

***

Ches and I made the two-hour drive down the highway toward Savannah, Georgia, my new home. Of course, it would have been a ton easier if my new character could have lived in Charleston. I wasn't particularly excited about having to spend half my summer away from home and Liz. But it made more sense: Charleston is not that big. Jack, Kado, and Ronnie already had that distribution network covered. At some point, oversaturation dilutes prices and draws attention. In other words, if I was Jack Riley, I wouldn't want to bring on another big buyer from Charleston. Not to mention that there's only so many potential buyers out there. If I was looking to move more product, I'd want to look for another market. Savannah was just far enough away to fit that niche.

Furthermore, Jack would trust me more if he knew Kado and I had some sort of history. Claiming that we'd grown up in the same town would reinforce to Jack that I wasn't the law. Sure, we could have said that I'd just moved to town and run into Kado. That we'd reconnected and I'd mentioned I was interested in buying some quantity. But it's not as bulletproof. And we wouldn't get second chances. If Jack was good, he'd check in on me in Savannah in one day, and he'd leave convinced I was legit. He wouldn't think it likely that the DEA or any law enforcement would go to the trouble of creating such an elaborate backstory.

How wrong he would be.

***

We stopped at an Exxon on the way and bought two lottery tickets and a bag of boiled peanuts. If there's not a good peanut stand on the side of the road, you have to go with the gas station type. It works out sometimes. I cracked one open, dug out the peanuts with my teeth, and tossed the shell out the window.

"Not bad for a gas station." I offered Chester the open bag.

"Hell, no," he said, pushing the bag away. "I don't eat those things."

"Why not?"

"Look at 'em. That's squirrel food, man."

"C'mon. It's like Southern edamame." I moved the bag back in front of him.

"Get that shit out of my face."

I laughed. "All right, tough guy. You keep dreaming about a Melvin's burger. I'll shut up and eat my *squirrel* food. You don't know what you're missing, though."

He changed the subject. Went for the jugular. "You gonna tell me what happened in Miami last year? I'm tired of wondering about it." Seems he thought getting my fix on boiled peanuts might have softened me up.

I laughed to myself and cracked open another peanut. "Only if you keep asking me. Maybe on the fortieth try."

"Seriously."

"You know the story."

"I know the *official* story. I know the rumors. I don't know your side of it. I don't know the truth."

"It is what it is. Leave it alone."

"Why don't you like talking about it? You didn't do anything wrong."

I raised my voice. "Don't fucking bring it up again, Ches. That's it."

He lifted his hands off the wheel for a second. "So be it."

I got all the way to the bottom of the brown bag with ease. If someone was looking for us, all they had to do was follow thirty miles of peanut shells along the side of the road headed south. I crunched up the bag and stuck it in the cup holder. Then I took out my phone and spent about twenty minutes with a woman in our Atlanta office. She would line up a new Visa card, AAA card, insurance; all the things I needed to fill my wallet.

Once we arrived, we picked up a paper and I flipped through

the classifieds while Chester drove us around and tried to be Mr. Tourguide. I had never been to Savannah. It's a gorgeous place, very much like Charleston in many ways but with its own charm. Gardens and parks on every block. Spanish moss dripping from the oaks like wax from a candle. Students with backpacks walking their dogs, old men in hats wobbling around on canes saying hello to everyone they pass.

We looked at several apartments before finding one on Broughton Street that fit the fabricated lifestyle of Travis Moody. We met the landlord after lunch. The apartment was one of two in an old colonial style home. It had high ceilings and hardwood floors, fully furnished. He agreed to keep the bills under his name, and we signed the lease on the spot. We stopped at the DMV on the way home and grabbed a Georgia Driver's license bearing my new address and then swung by Verizon for a new phone.

***

The week went by quickly. It's all about the details in undercover work, and we prepared diligently for my new role as a financial advisor. Every chance I could, I called Liz. With so much to ask her, I wanted to drown myself in her thoughts. So much to say. The sound of her voice—subtly Southern—was like candy. And her laugh made me want to leave the case behind and spend every waking moment with her, but I had to stay focused.

I spent several days with Kado. Learned everything I could about Jack Riley. How his longtime girlfriend, Kayla Martin, had caught him sleeping with Tela Davies. Now, Jack was broken-hearted and single. How he'd lost his sister. How his cocaine habit was starting to get the best of him. Kado and I also worked on our story. We were supposed to share some of the same friends, so he schooled me on the particulars.

I also talked to him about staying on the right path, making sure he didn't start regretting his decision—something I'd seen many times before. He could bring down this whole operation with a phone call, and I couldn't let that happen. I had plenty of ammo against him and didn't expect any problems, but you can't be too careful with a drug dealer. They never cease to amaze.

At the end of the week, I dialed Kado on the drive back up to Charleston. He'd been back for a couple days.

"We're ready, big guy," I said. "You're on."

"Shit."

"It's all good."

"Easy for you to say."

"All you've got to do is be yourself. Stay relaxed. Mention my name when it seems appropriate. We already know he needs me. Tell him I can take care of Savannah and tell him you trust me. That's it."

"What if he says no?"

"Don't let him."

The waiting began. Soon my life would be turned upside down. At least I hoped so. If Kado could pull it off. If Jack bit.

In the meantime, I had to see Liz.

CHAPTER 12

I'd never walked through the College of Charleston campus, and its antebellum architecture captivated me. I was in the heart of the South, the birthplace of the Southern belle, the home of hospitality. I was wandering aimlessly, looking for the Art Department, when I stumbled upon Randolph Hall, a dusty pink building with six aging columns rising in front. Old and uneven brick walkways lead from its front stairs out into the lush expanse of green grass and aging oaks that surrounded it. There was still cannon damage from the Civil War on the stucco walls. It was a war no one wanted to forget, and in this Southern city where it all began, I doubted anyone ever would.

A student pointed me in the right direction, and moments later I found my way to the Simons Center of the Arts and was looking at Liz through a glass door. She stood in front of a small class, showing slides. She wore a casual yellow dress cut right above the knees with lime green espadrilles tied around her ankles. (Don't ask me how I know what the shoes are called.) The look on her face was one I had not seen before. I realized that it was there, in the classroom—in her element, deep in the world of art—that she became who she really was.

She noticed me standing there, told the class to wait, and came outside, beaming.

"Hi there!" She kissed me, bubbling with happiness. "I was wondering when I was going to see you again."

"You missed me, didn't you?"

"Don't push it."

"Kidding. Are you free today? Let's do something."

"Will you wait on me? This is my last class. Ten more minutes."

"Of course." She kissed me again. Man, I'd forgotten all about heartache. I felt like I could fly.

When her class got out, we rode to my house. From there, we took the Tate's boat south to Buzzard's Roost Marina in John's Island. We got a table outside and sat drinking beers and eating bacon-wrapped shrimp stuffed with crab. It had to be over one hundred degrees and with the humidity, even hotter. Beau calls it the "Sauna Season." After you've lived here for a while, you get used to the sweating. Showers are a waste of time. That Charleston heat makes you appreciate the seasons, though. No doubt about it. There's nothing like the spring and fall here.

The temperature didn't seem to bother Liz. She asked, "So what else have you been doing other than chasing me around?"

"Investment advisor things. We're opening up a shop in Savannah, so that's on the plate. Other than that, boring normalcy."

"Maybe I'll bring you lunch one day this week to break up the monotony. We could eat at your desk, and I could listen to you prophesize about the next market move."

I nodded but really didn't think that would be a good idea. Time to change the subject. "Tell me about New York. What's your routine? Where do you live?"

"I live in the tiniest apartment you've ever seen on Bleecker and Charles, above a little French antique shop. It's smaller than your closet. I get coffee at this Turkish place every morning, and it takes about seven minutes to walk up Hudson to my studio on Little West 12th. It's the most wonderful walk in the world, and it always puts me where I need to be to paint. No matter what's bothering me." She made me smile. "So I did that and had a few hospital meetings and...oh, Wednesday, I touched a Van Gogh."

"What?"

"I was at the Met looking at *Corridor in the Asylum*, and I reached out and touched it with my finger."

"Isn't it behind glass?"

"No."

"Are you allowed to?"

"No...but I had to. I don't know what came over me. I feel completely awful about it. It was unprofessional and disrespectful."

"But you'll never forget it, will you?"

"Never." She told me about how Van Gogh had lost his mind in Arles, hanging out with Gauguin. That's when he cut his earlobe off. Then he committed himself to an asylum in Saint Rémy, where he painted *Corridor* to show his brother the hall where he lived. "I just couldn't help touching it. He made me do it."

"Ah, the power of Van Gogh."

"You've no idea. So can I ask you something personal?"

"Okay." I took a sip of beer, preparing myself.

"How'd your father die? Is that okay to ask?"

I thought about it. "Yeah, it is. He was murdered."

She didn't say she was sorry, which I appreciated. (Why do people do that? Did they have something to do with it? Did they shoot him?) And she did not say, *You don't have to talk about it.* I'd been hearing that one, too—all my life. You know what? I *know* I don't have to talk about it. The truth is, I rarely do. But it was time I started letting Liz into my life.

"I was eighteen," I continued. "About to graduate. I'd just accepted a scholarship to play soccer at UVA. He took me to see Michael Brecker at Blues Alley in Georgetown to celebrate. He'd been dragging me to those shows for years, and I went more for him than me." I sighed. "There was something about that night, though. The tone of Brecker's sax and the registers he used and…the soul. The way Jeff 'Tain' Watts and James Genus locked in, and then Calderazzo, the pianist. They played so far back on the beat I nearly fell out of my chair. I fell in love with jazz that night. But it ended up being the worst night of my life." Liz took my hand.

"After the show, we were walking back up toward M Street in the snow. A man stepped out from behind a trash bin with a gun. His name was Shawn Philips. He was high out of his mind. He asked for money and we both handed over our wallets. Then he asked for my dad's watch." I lifted up and turned my wrist to show her my Dad's IWC. "This is it."

"It's gorgeous," Liz whispered.

I half-smiled. "My dad started to unclasp it. Said he'd be happy to. Then the man fired into his stomach. One shot killed him."

Liz squeezed my hand.

"They found the man an hour later. He didn't remember doing it. He's doing life in Virginia now." I paused, waiting for a response from Liz. But before she could say anything, a bearded man with no shoes or shirt came running off the dock towards us.

"Hey! That your Key West out there?"

"Sure is."

"She's floatin' down the river."

"What? You're kidding me."

"No, sir."

I jumped up and ran past him and across the wooden planks to where I had left the Tate's boat tied up. She was gone. Someone had cut both lines. A foot-long piece of rope hung from each cleat. I looked out across the Stono River. The boat was floating fifty yards off, running with the current, about to pass under the John's Island Bridge. The longer ends of the lines drifted behind her.

Liz and the shoeless man caught up. "Is that her?" he asked.

"Yep," I said. "Did you see anyone around her?"

"Nope, I sure didn't. You wanna ride out there?"

"I'd appreciate it." He ran me over to the boat on his little Carolina Skiff. I hopped on board and thanked my new friend and motored back to where I had originally tied up.

Liz was waiting. "What do you think happened? Who would do this?"

I tossed her the bow line. "Maybe someone didn't like the fact that I've taken you off the market."

"Or maybe someone actually took your financial advice."

"Ouch."

She re-cleated the line. "Anyway, that's kind of brazen of you to think you've taken me off the market."

"Haven't I?"

She put her hands around my neck, drew me close, and gave me a long, soft kiss that I knew would stay with me during the lonely nights in Savannah.

"You're getting closer," she said. "I wouldn't give up now." I'm not one hundred percent sure, but I think the saltwater below us began to boil.

We went back to the restaurant and finished our meal, searching the whole time for someone's guilty eyes peeking around a corner. We were back on board thirty minutes later, zipping across the water. "Will you stay with me tonight?" I asked.

"I'm not sure."

"I don't think you should drive after drinking."

"Right. I'm sure my safety on the road is exactly what prompted your invitation."

When we got back, she asked me to play for her. We went upstairs to my bedroom and I took the banjo from its case and started to strum an open G. The low D sounded slightly flat. I turned the peg and strummed again. There it was.

I'd heard Béla Fleck do a tune one time, I think it was "John

LOWCOUNTRY PUNCH

Henry," and the whole time he kept the bass line going on the third and fourth string. He got that bass line going and then played the melody over it. It sounded like two banjos. I stole the idea and worked out the Beatles tune, "I've Got a Feeling." It had been a while, but as I started to roll, the music came out with ease.

She clapped as I finished. "I'm gonna call MUSC in the morning. You have to play for the kids." I told her I'd love to, and she asked for another tune.

I thought of one that Béla's teacher, Tony Trischka, wrote. The modal melody sounded particularly good on my banjo, especially if I kept my right hand closer to the neck, pulling out a more hollow sound. I could have played for Liz all night.

But as I was picking the last note, Liz approached me. She took the banjo from my hands and gently set it back in its case. Her eyes full of desire, she straddled me. Finally, it was happening. Her dress rode up, exposing soft flesh, which teased my skin. She brought my lips to hers and ran her tongue along them until I opened my mouth to obey. Her tongue glided in and out, exploring and caressing the inside of my mouth. The penetration made me grow hard and I felt myself pressing against my shorts.

I slid the spaghetti straps off her shoulders and reached for the zipper of her yellow dress. The top fell forward, and I touched her tan-lined breasts. I grazed my fingers across her dark nipples, feeling them harden with excitement. I would've been happy not to see or touch any other breasts for as long as I lived. Our breath deepened in unison. Her lips came up to my ear and she licked the inside of the lobe before whispering, "Oh, T.A."

"How am I so lucky to be here right now? I'm dreaming."

Ravaged and hungry for love, I lifted her up and carried her to the bed. Cradling her in my arms, we collapsed, and I stretched myself on top of her. Indulging in all of my senses, I explored every inch of her body. I was intoxicated, drunk on every part of her.

She pulled off my shirt, and the skin of our upper torsos touched for the first time. I took the waist of her dress and started to tug. I could see the soft pink lace of her panties and a clench of pure desire gripped me.

She put a hand below her waist, stopping my progress. "We don't need to rush." She ran her fingers through my hair. "We'll always wish we could recapture these moments."

"You're right." I knew exactly what she meant. I willed myself to calm down. But I couldn't help saying, "So we'll wait until the morning. Good idea."

She gave me the evil teacher eye, like I'd just tried to make a bad joke in class. "You just bought yourself another month of wishing my dress would come off."

"What! A lot can happen in a month. Hurricanes. Heart attacks. I could even get stuck at sea."

"Then you better be careful."

"A month? I feel like you're putting me in jail."

"Well, maybe you'll get out early for good behavior."

"You mean get *in*?"

"Exactly."

"Well, you won't get *off* until I do."

She hit me in the head with a pillow. "You're ridiculous. Will you please give me a ride home?"

"You're being serious?"

"Of course."

"As long as you will note my objection."

"Objection noted."

CHAPTER 13

I was sitting at my kitchen table eating some poached eggs and toast, scanning an article in the morning's paper on the Redskins' new coach. Something about looking to the future...that it wasn't quite our time yet. I live for Redskins football, and it eats me up to read about the promises of a young team. I want to read about the present. About a trip to the Super Bowl in February. As I was about to start ripping the paper into a million pieces, my cell phone rang.

"Jack wants to meet you," Kado said.

I punched a fist in the air. "Well done."

"Jesus, I thought I was going to blow it."

"You're a little shaken up. You did fine. The worst is over."

"I hope so. Jack's no fool. He asked all kinds of questions. Wants to meet you before you touch his coke to make sure you're legit."

"I don't blame him. When does he wanna get together?"

"A couple days. He said he would line up something and give me a call."

"You're doing a good thing. You'll be a hell of a CI."

"A CI?" he asked.

"Confidential Informant. You're CI 543 in the books, and you're part of my team. Trust in that. I have your back now. I will count on you and trust you with my life. You can do the same."

"He finds out, he'll kill us both, Agent Reddick. I promise you that."

"If you don't tell him, he'll never know. And Kado," I said. "My name's Travis."

I dialed Chester to tell him the good news and let him know I wouldn't be in until after lunch. Before my work ethic is judged, it should be said that agents don't work banker's hours. I might go in at lunch one day, but you can bet I'm working late. Crime doesn't follow a schedule. Besides, Liz was coming back over to take a run with me.

A lawnmower cranked up outside. Assuming it was Beau Tate, I went to say hello. The humidity hung in the air like molasses. He cut the engine, and we met where his grass abutted a grouping of shrubbery in my yard. His shirt was soaked.

"I don't know why you don't pay somebody to do your yard."

"The day I stop cutting the grass is the day Cindy'll try to move us to one of the those retirement communities. Make me play bingo. Hell, I like doing it."

"I'd rather have my front teeth pulled out with pliers," I said.

"Twenty years from now, it'll be what you do."

We were interrupted by an approaching car. It was Liz pulling into my driveway in her Mustang.

"Uh-oh," said Beau. "This one getting serious?"

"We're having a good time."

We both watched as she crossed my yard. She was dressed in yoga pants and a running bra.

"Good God, almighty," Beau said. "Jesus criminy, shepherd of Judah. My pacemaker's gonna burst out of my chest."

I laughed but I didn't have any words. Had he forgotten that I'd been engaged to his daughter less than a year ago?

"Hi, I'm Liz," she said, offering her hand.

Beau raised his in the air. "I'm all sweaty, sweetheart, but the pleasure is mine."

"Guess what T.A.'s doing tonight?" she said, like I wasn't there.

"What's that?"

"Playing banjo at the Children's Hospital."

"Oh, am I?" I replied.

She put her arm around me. "Seven o'clock. They can't wait."

"Me, neither." Did I mention my issue with ankle-biters? Still, I appreciate someone who does what they say they are going to do. Liz had said she was going to call the hospital, and I bet it was the first thing she'd done this morning.

Beau interrupted. "Isn't that Stephanie pulling up?"

I turned so quickly my head nearly spun off.

There she was, pulling into my driveway in her Honda. This was getting absurd—like restraining-order absurd. She marched over, her lips tightly pressed together, and I hesitantly introduced her.

"Be careful with this one," Stephanie said to Liz, pointing her finger at me. "He doesn't know what he wants."

"Oh, boy," Beau said. "I've gotta get this grass done. You folks have a nice day." He hopped back on his lawnmower and escaped into the backyard.

"Liz," I said, "can you please give us a few minutes?"

"Sure. It was good meeting you, Stephanie."

"And it was great meeting you, too," Stephanie replied. She could not have been more insincere.

Once I saw that Liz was safely in the house, I turned to Stephanie and demanded, "Why are you here?"

"I need to talk to you," she pleaded, her eyes filling with tears. "What did I do wrong? Why don't you want to be with me anymore?" A tear slid down her face. "Were you seeing *her* while we were together?"

"You and I were never 'together.' We went out once."

"What's so great about *her*?"

Beau made a pass on his mower, and we moved further into my yard.

"Look, Stephanie," I said, crossing my arms, "you need to get a hold of yourself. Don't make me—"

"Don't you dare threaten me! We can both play that game. Does Liz know you're a DEA agent?" It was hard to believe the mind behind those dimples was so sinister.

"Leave it alone."

Out of nowhere, she swung at me. I couldn't believe it! She was resorting to brute force.

I caught her fist with my hand. "Stephanie," I snapped, "what has gotten in to you?" She swung again. I caught that hand, too, and twisted both arms behind her back. I stood behind her and held her arms down as she struggled to get free.

"*You gotta get a hold of yourself,*" I demanded. I held her until she stopped fighting me. "Are you done? Can I let go of you?"

She nodded. I let go and she turned around. She began to cry. "It hurts so badly. I don't know what to do." She cried harder. I reluctantly let her put her arms around me.

"You have to move on," I whispered.

"You're going to come back to me, and it's gonna be too late. I've got plenty of men who would love to be in your position."

"I'm sure, and I think it would be a good idea if you explored those options."

She let go of me. She didn't like that. Beau shut off the engine, and the sudden silence overwhelmed us.

Suddenly, Stephanie surprised me with a knee to the midsection. A searing pain ran through me. I bent over and tried to yell, but couldn't. Damn, it hurt. I prayed Liz wasn't watching from a window.

"Don't patronize me!" she said, stepping away. "This isn't over."

"It sure is!"

"Or *what?*"

"Look, I'm not threatening you, Stephanie."

"This is so far from being over," she replied. "You have no idea what I know."

She strutted back toward her car and got in without another word. She sped off, spinning her wheels as she tore out of the driveway.

I stood there for a moment, thinking about her last comment. *You have no idea what I know.*

I realized I had no idea what she meant.

CHAPTER 14

You can't really understand Charleston unless you embrace its history, and I'd been doing my best to pick up on the more interesting bits since I'd moved here. Most of them came from Beau. The peninsula had many great stories to tell and you could walk through time without even knowing it. Today, I had a meeting on Broad Street. In May of 1791, President George Washington had marched up Broad Street past thousands of South Carolinians who lined the sidewalks and hung out of windows cheering their beloved leader. Dodging a horse-drawn carriage full of tourists as I crossed the street, I met Ches and Anthony Baroni, the surveillance expert, for our 1 p.m. meeting with AUSA Cannon.

Anthony Baroni hailed from Brooklyn and burned through a couple packs of Merits a day. And he had the teeth and voice and alligator skin to prove it. He was one of the guys who'd been giving me a hard time ever since I'd walked into his territory. Now, the tables were turned. He had to do what I said.

The three of us wandered into the courthouse. The man up front immediately led us into AUSA Cannon's office. Cannon came around his grandiose Cypress desk to greet us. He wore a tailor-made gray suit and expensive shoes. He was the man who would lead the prosecution against Jack Riley and any others we hauled in.

We shook hands, and he resumed his position behind the desk as we each took a seat opposite. He noticed me looking at a picture of him standing next to the bridge on the eighteenth green of St. Andrews in Scotland and asked, "You play, Agent Reddick?"

"I used to. Quit a little while back, right after a round in the wind at Wild Dunes. I left my clubs with the cart attendant."

"Really?"

"Really."

He tossed a hand up into the air. "I guess that course will do it to you. I try to play Patriot's once a week. It's a little easier to negotiate. You should pick it up again. Get some lessons. When you get my age, a round under eighty is better than a night with a hooker in Bangkok. Shot a seventy-six that day in Scotland." He tilted his head down and raised his eyebrows. "Damn wind was blowing people over, and I still shot seventy-six."

I nodded my head, trying to look impressed.

He picked up an unlit cigar and stuck it between his teeth. "I understand we're in," he said.

"Yes, sir," I said. "I believe we are. He wants to meet me."

"That's good to hear. I like the list of players. I know Jack's father. It's going to break his heart. And Tela Davies. Who-boy, I'd like to drive my cattle into her corral."

The comment disgusted me. I was already tired of hearing that kind of thing about her, and I hadn't even met her yet.

"We've got a good list," Chester agreed, "and I think we can take it far. We're confident he's picking up his shipments in Atlanta. The sooner you can get us a warrant to put a transmitter on his car, the better."

"Give me a few more days. Let's get Reddick inside, and I'll get you whatever you want. Home taps, Title III's. So how exactly are you billing yourself?"

"He wants to move a lot more cocaine than what he's doing now, so I'm going to offer him access to the buyers in Savannah. I'll build my relationship with him from there. Just need a reason to get into his life."

"Makes sense. You mentioned he might have additional sources. Any more details?"

"That's all we know," Chester said, "that he's been talking about a new project. No specifics."

"We think he's using pay phones and disposables to make his calls," I said. "He's being very careful, very smart."

Cannon agreed. "He's watching his back. Baroni, how tight you followin' him?"

"Not very. Like you said, let's get Reddick undercover."

No matter how good you are, a person can always detect if he's being followed. The thought starts to build subconsciously. That idea sounds like some sort of voodoo, but they teach it at Quantico. That's why going undercover was better than tracking Jack's moves from the outside.

We discussed wiretaps and surveillance, Baroni and Cannon doing most of the talking, and then we moved on to Jack's importing business, J.R. Imports. I handed Cannon a file folder.

"This is everything we know so far," I told him. "Mostly from public records and interviews with Kadopholous. It doesn't appear that he's importing anything illegal, but we're going to run his next couple shipments through a VACUS to be sure. We'll pull the seal if we have to."

A VACUS machine is a gamma-ray scanner similar to an X-ray machine but built to hold an entire container. Customs uses them to detect anything from drugs to weapons, and they let us use them whenever we ask. We have a much better relationship with Customs and the Coast Guard than we do with local police forces. It was that way in Miami, too. Even before I shot one of their own, Miami police didn't like me.

"He's got one coming in from Lima tomorrow," I continued.

"Shipped by a guy named Belen Merino. He owns a little place called Anduba Teak right outside of the city. We're looking into him."

"Let's follow the next two or three loads before we let it go," Cannon replied.

We talked about how we thought Jack was running his business: where he was dumping his shipments, all of his clients, how he paid, what he did with the cash; and our thoughts and the risks involved with Kado. As he thumbed through the file, Cannon said, "So he cheated on his woman with Tela Davies, and she ran out on him? Poor bastard."

That's right. Poor bastard.

***

Back at the office, I got into a little trouble. I had been scrolling through my in-box when I noticed a great e-mail had snuck past my spam filter. I couldn't resist having a little fun.

A person named Napoleon Calhoun had sent a passionate e-mail to an address that included all DEA agents in South Carolina, North Carolina, and Georgia—the three states making up our sub-sector. Mr. Calhoun's ability to track down such a mass e-mail address spoke to the DEA's impenetrable security process.

As with most of the spam that we get, the grammar was awful. The subject of the e-mail read: "Lengthen your male machine and women will love you long time." I mean, who couldn't open that and see what he had to say?

Man, I discovered very amazing thing and want to inform you about it. Before I started to use this thing my male instrument was too small so small that I feel shy to speak about length. Now my life has changed. I enlarged my jang size, women like me too much that now I am glad.

There is a part of me that can't resist sometimes. I clicked the

"Reply All" button, copying every agent in three states, and I addressed Mr. Napoleon Calhoun's offer. I thought something brief could get my point across. I wrote:

Hello, Napoleon. No shortage of dong in the DEA. Thanks for thinking of us.

Now I guess the shameful part about it is that I really didn't even have to think about whether to press Send or not. I couldn't help it. It was like I was watching my body do something I knew I'd regret, but I had no control. I sent the e-mail and just waited, like throwing a boomerang into the darkness.

I had my door open and in less than a minute, I heard the first laugh and my smile stretched. Then there were more laughs and then I was staring Steve in the face. "Love the suspenders," I said. I popped some fake ones running down my chest.

He pointed his finger at me. "Get in my office," he said.

I held up my hands. "What did I do?"

"Don't say another word. Get your ass up."

I obeyed. As soon as the door closed, he said, "What were you thinking?"

"I really couldn't help it."

"Yeah, you could. You know how many people are gonna see that?"

"A lot."

"Damn right, a lot. I'm not saying it wasn't funny as hell, but it's not worth it. You're doing some good around here. Don't ruin it. They'll suspend you in a second these days. You think they care you're going undercover tomorrow?"

"No, sir." I could tell he wasn't that mad. He was just going through the motions of being the boss. He had a smile hidden back there somewhere. "You think I could get one of those toothpicks?" I asked. "Are they the cinnamon kind? I really like those."

LOWCOUNTRY PUNCH

"Get out of here." I apologized again and went back to my desk. I could still hear laughter coming from the other agents.

CHAPTER 15

The first meeting when you are undercover is like walking out on stage. Only you have to worry about being shot.

The place was Poe's on Sullivan's Island, a Bahamian-style bar a few blocks from the beach with good burgers and cold beer. Kado and Jack sat at a table in the corner of the patio in the open air drinking Stella Artois out of gold-rimmed glasses. I could smell the ocean in the air as I stepped onto the patio. I only saw one empty chair in the place, the one between Kado and Jack. My team was in a carpet cleaning van half a block down.

All eyes on you. Make a mistake and you can lose your life.

Kado waved me over, and Jack turned his chair around to get his first glimpse of me. Right away I saw something I hadn't picked up on from the pictures. His eyes were full and bright: the eyes of ambition.

I crossed the room and offered my hand.

"Travis Moody," I said.

Jack rose. "Jack Riley," he said, shaking my hand. He was a handsome guy, about my height, six feet or so, and he had a head full of curly blonde hair. He wore a tight sky-blue polo with the collar turned up, like he had a Polo match and a Regatta to attend after this luncheon. I guess owning an art gallery tends to exacerbate your flair.

He turned my wrist. "That's a good watch. Nothing as classy as an IWC." There was still a little bit of New York in his accent, lingering from his childhood.

"I agree," I said. "My father gave it to me."

I sat down and turned to Kado, giving him a hit on the leg. "How's it going, buddy?"

"Not bad." He didn't have much to say. The nerves were eating him up. I had to make the best of it. I turned to Jack.

"Let's get to know each other," he said. "We'll talk business once we leave." Some casual conversation followed. The waitress brought me a beer and took our orders. I ordered a Black Cat, medium rare, which was a burger with homemade pimento cheese, chili, and bacon. I asked her if it came with a treadmill and a Lipitor, and it cracked her and Jack up.

Then, not thirty feet away, something right out of a bad dream happened. Stephanie came strolling onto the property, walking through the little picket fence gate. I had to conceal an explosion of panic. My jaw tightened. How the hell had this happened? I put my elbows on the table and hid my face as best as I could without being obvious. Jack was saying something about the mayor, and I was doing my best to pay attention, but my first concern was her. Had she followed me? What were her intentions?

She took the steps and grabbed a stool that someone happened to be abandoning near the bar. She spoke to the bartender for a moment and then settled in, looking around, analyzing her surroundings like a lion looking for prey. She still hadn't looked our way, at least not as far as I could tell.

The burgers came. I told Jack about my financial planning business. Kado and I ran through our spiel, how I had dated his sister in high school for a couple months and how we hadn't seen each other until only a few months earlier. I only glanced at Stephanie from time to time. She was drinking a beer and looking out toward the road, watching the beachgoers strolling by with chairs and coolers in their hands.

On our way out the door, I looked at her one last time. She quickly averted her eyes. I had a feeling she knew exactly what she was doing, and she was flirting with screwing up one of the most important operations in my career.

Jack didn't bring up the business regarding the cocaine until we were in the parking lot next to his Land Rover.

"Let's take a ride," he said. I nodded. Kado got behind the wheel and I climbed in the backseat with Jack. There was a tackle box in between us. Jack patted me down once the doors closed, and he was thorough. Exactly why I had declined wearing a wire. I wasn't there to bust him. Not yet. I was there to become his friend and find out where he was getting his powder.

"You a cop?" he asked.

I looked him in the eyes. "No. Are you?"

He ignored me. "So you've got Savannah dialed in?"

"Completely. I know who I can trust down there."

"We've never let anyone else in on this. Because Kado vouches for you, I'm gonna give you a shot. We'll start slow and see what happens. Know that if we sense something is off, we'll come after you. I might seem like a nice guy, but don't underestimate me. I don't play nice."

"Understood." I don't like threats, but I had to let it go. It wasn't easy.

"Good. You seem like you're all right."

We discussed the details, driving all the way to the end of the island and back, and then they dropped me off at my green Toyota truck, a loaner from the Columbia field office. I shook Jack's hand one last time, thinking that other than Stephanie showing up, the meeting had gone well. I could make him like me. Make him trust me. Never had the spotlight shined so bright. No way could I let a woman I barely knew destroy the progress I'd made.

I needed to talk to Stephanie.

***

Stephanie lived in a ranch-style brick three bedroom in West Ashley, about a thirty-minute drive from the island. I parked and walked up to her door. The grass hadn't been cut in a while. Nothing but dirt in the pots on the steps.

"Did you bring your handcuffs, baby?" she asked, cracking the door. She was nude. I pushed the door open and grabbed her arm. "Go put some clothes on. You're in trouble."

"Why?"

"You know damn well why. You followed me. I'm working on a case, Stephanie."

"Are you going to cuff me?" She held out her hands.

"They're on the way here to arrest you for tampering with a Federal investigation. They'll drag you out butt-ass naked if you want it that way."

"I didn't know what you were doing. I was going for a burger!"

"Bullshit."

I stormed inside. She followed me into the living room. A Tela Davies movie played on the television. I took a fleece blanket off the couch and threw it at her. "Wrap that around you." She did.

"I'll ask you one more time," I said. "You can tell me or you can tell an officer downtown. How did you end up there? Did you follow me?"

She didn't say anything. I thought of something and walked back out to my truck. I searched around looking for a transponder. I was thinking she had me marked with a real-time GPS. You can buy them anywhere these days. Didn't find anything. I stomped back inside, breathing heavier than normal.

She was crouched against the wall in the foyer, crying. "I love you. It hurts so bad."

"C'mon. You hardly know me."

"I know enough."

"What I know is that there will never be an *us*. If you will assure me that you'll stay out of my life, I will keep them from putting you in jail. If it happens again, I can't help you. You could really get hurt. This is not a joke."

We spoke for a while, and I was honest and real with her, explaining that we had no future. She admitted that she had followed me earlier. They teach us to watch our backs, and I was more than disappointed in myself for not picking up her tail. I didn't bother bringing up how my boat got untied, but after today, I was pretty sure it was her. I made it very clear to her the lengths I would have to go to keep her out of trouble for the day's debacle. She promised me I wouldn't see her again.

From there, I drove to Savannah to begin my new life as Travis Moody. But with love in the air, I couldn't totally abandon my old life. Liz and I talked for more than an hour that night, and so much of me wanted to get back on the highway and wrap my arms around her.

CHAPTER 16

The next day, I picked up a bucket of chicken and a twelve-pack of Pacifico on the way home from a meet and greet with the Savannah DEA. Good news had just come my way. They'd caught the two men who kidnapped me. A black and white had attempted to pull them over for a minor traffic violation in Fairfax, Virginia. The two men made a run for it but ended up slamming themselves into a ditch. Now, they were in a police van riding all the way back, facing charges of kidnapping and assault. It was good news, but I also knew it didn't bring us any closer to Tux Clinton. They were two of his best men, and they would certainly do time for him.

The streetlights came on as I walked down the sidewalk and took the steps up to the weathered white porch of my apartment. I fumbled for my keys, and as I stuck the key in the door, I noticed the shadow of a man leaning on a rail on the far end of the porch.

Ronnie Downs, one of Jack's runners, stepped into the light, the Clemson Tigers hat on his head casting a shadow over his eyes. Ronnie had swimmer's muscles and looked agile for his large frame. Had to be the pick of his litter.

I wasn't supposed to know what he looked like so I acted accordingly. "Can I help you?" I turned toward him, leaving the keys dangling in the door.

"I'm a friend of Jack's. You Travis Moody?"

"The hell you doing on my porch?" I put down the beer and bucket of chicken. I didn't expect a visit that early in the game, and it occurred to me that I may have left the case file on my bed. Couldn't remember putting it away. These guys weren't messing around.

"I'm told we'll be working together," he said.

"I've never heard of you."

"We can call Jack right now. I came down to check you out. I'm either coming in, or you won't be doing any business with us. You got something to hide?"

"You let people into your house you don't know?"

"I just wanna come inside and look around for a minute. No need to get defensive. We can call Jack. He asked me to come down. You think we're going into business with someone without checking 'em out?"

"How'd you find me?"

"We got ways."

I nodded. "I guess you're coming in. What'd you say your name was?"

"Ronnie Downs." He stuck out his hand but I didn't shake it. I picked up the beer and chicken and kicked open the door so it swung around and hit the inside wall. He followed me. The hardwood creaked below our feet. "I won't do this again," Ronnie promised.

I set my dinner and the keys on the tall table in the foyer. "All right."

"I tell you what, though, you try to mess with us and we'll bury you."

You don't talk to T.A. Reddick that way. I shut the door hard and the glass panes nearly shattered. I got up in his face and grabbed him where it counted. He bent over in pain, and I said calmly, "Do what you need to do and get out. Don't threaten me again." I let go of him, and standing straight again, he jerked a pistol out from his waistline and brought it toward my chest.

I deflected his up-swinging arm and simultaneously pushed the barrel of the gun up toward his face and sideways. A move I learned years ago, and if you do it just right, the gun doesn't go off. About the time I heard his trigger finger crack, he punched me in the cheek with his fist. The gun and I both hit the floor.

I bounced back up and rammed my shoulder into his waist, picking him up and slamming him against the nearest wall. A lamp fell off the table and the bulb exploded in a blue flash. I drove my right fist into his abdomen, and he gave a loud grunt. He retaliated, bringing his clenched hands down from above his head and smashing them into my back. I buckled and dropped to the floor.

Ronnie tried to stomp me with his foot. I caught it and twisted. He fell on top and for the next several seconds, I showed him how to wrestle. I'm good on the ground. I put him in an armlock and threatened to snap.

"All right, all right!" he yelled. "Don't break my arm, man. You've made your damn point."

I let go and stood over him. "You didn't give me much of a choice."

"Jesus…what's wrong with you?" he asked me.

"You're the one who pulled the gun."

"I was trying to protect myself."

"You can't come into my house threatening me. You need to understand that."

"I came down here for business." He was holding the hand with the broken finger.

"Now you know how I handle my business." I pointed at his injured hand. "You want me to fix that finger?"

He didn't know whether to accept or not.

"Like you said, it's just business. Get up and I'll fix your finger. I've had plenty of those."

He took my hand with his good one, and I helped him up. I

picked the gun up off the floor and took the bucket of chicken off the table, and we went into the kitchen. I made sure the chamber was empty and then removed the clip from the Colt, sticking it in my pocket. I set the gun on the counter.

I took his hand and examined the break. It wasn't bad enough to need surgery. Without warning him, I pressed the broken finger between both palms and snapped it back into place. He took it well. Using the handle of a spoon and masking tape, I created a splint. I happened to have one ice pack in the freezer. "I guess you get this," I said, handing it to him. I touched my cheek where he had hit me. "You've got a nice right, though. I can vouch for that."

He was in utter shock. I don't think he had ever had his ass beaten before. I started to feel bad, so I took the bucket of chicken off the table and lifted the lid. "Hungry?" I offered.

At a loss, Ronnie reached in with his good hand and pulled out a drumstick. The little boy who got his pants pulled down at recess took a bite.

"There you go," I said. "It's good poultry." I nearly patted him on the head like a puppy dog. I pulled out a wing myself and set the bucket back on the table. Before I took a bite, I said, "I apologize for that. I went a bit overboard. After tonight, we're friends."

We went into the living room, and he picked up a framed picture of my family and me from a trip to Disney when I was sixteen. When you first go deep, it's strange to include your personal life, like the true stories and pictures of your family, but you have to get used to it. I would never use the pictures if there was any danger posed to my mother or brother, Will. I'd brought a few things from home, so the house was properly stocked. If he'd looked in the refrigerator, he would have found jars half full of artichoke relish and pickles. Under the bathroom sink, used cleaning products.

Ronnie started to ask me things, going through some of the

same questions Jack had at Poe's, and I answered them accurately. We moved into the next room, a room I had set up to be my home office. Our backstopping diligence was paying off by the second. He sat in the swivel chair at the desk and opened the file drawer, thumbing through the phony files we had created.

He picked up a stack of mutual fund brochures and flipped through them. The brochures were Baroni's idea—he had called some funds he found online and they mailed them to us. If Ronnie had looked further, he would have found false tax documents, more client files on the computer, and false e-mail communications with my bogus clients. He picked up a business card off the stack that read *Moody Investments, LLC*. "You mind?"

"Go for it."

He stuck the card in the pocket of his linen shirt. "How about upstairs?"

"Sure. Follow me." We were about to find out if my good habits were better than my memory. If that file was on the bed—game over.

It was all good, though. I'd hidden it behind books on the shelf. Good habits are vital to this business. Satisfied with the bedroom, he skipped the bathroom and we were through in less than ten minutes.

We didn't shake hands as he left. I gave him his gun back without the bullets and told him I'd see him in a few days back north. Then I watched him disappear down the sidewalk into the dark cloak of the Savannah night. Despite a few challenges, I was on my way to breaking through.

CHAPTER 17

Later that night, I was watching ESPN with my feet propped up on the coffee table when Kado called. I'd gone through four Pacifico's since Ronnie left.

"Jack's bringing some in tomorrow," Kado told me.

"How's it going down?"

"He doesn't want you coming to the cabin. Not yet. He said he'd pay me a delivery fee to take you your share. I didn't push. Once he trusts you, things will change. With as much weight as you're buying, he'd rather sell to you directly. Cut me out. You'll be his third runner."

"That's exactly what I want. I want to work for him." Jack continued to impress me with his cautious moves. "What time are you meeting him?"

"Four. We'll spend about two hours cutting and then I'll head your way."

"Did he mention Ronnie coming to see me?"

"What? Ronnie went down to Savannah?"

"Yeah, not too long ago. No big deal."

"Jack did say he checked you out. Said it all looks good. I told you he'd be careful."

"Nothing I haven't seen before."

"He invited you to go fishing with him Saturday. That's a

start. He said the boat leaves at 4:30 a.m., if you're interested."

"You going?"

"No. He understands. I'll be up at the restaurant until two or three cleaning up from the night before. I never go fishing with him. Ronnie will be there, though. I don't know who else."

"Got it. I'll be there."

I shot Baroni a text letting him know that Jack was making some sort of move between now and then. If we were correct, he'd be driving to Atlanta first thing in the morning, picking up the powder, and then going straight to the cabin. We'd installed a GPS transmitter near the engine of his Land Rover, so following him wouldn't be a problem.

But, as I found out around noon the next day, finding Jack's source wasn't going to be that easy. Jack did go to Atlanta, but parked his car in the crowded Lenox Square parking lot, then disappeared with a backpack into the mall. Our team, working with agents from the Atlanta office, lost him. He showed up back at the car an hour later with two bags and drove straight to his cabin in McClellanville. We were no more the wiser, save the confirmation that he was picking up his coke in Atlanta.

Later that day, I drove up to Charleston to meet Kado in a Wal-Mart parking lot. He climbed into my truck with a grocery bag and pulled out two kilos. In exchange, I gave him sixty grand in clean bills, which he would have to give to Jack. Hopefully, we would recoup it at the end of the operation. After a little encouragement and praise, I drove away, knowing Kado still had his share of the coke. We had a GPS transmitter in his car, and part of Baroni's surveillance team would follow him as he delivered. Kado had already given us the names of his buyers, so we just needed audio and visual evidence to support his testimony. Teams were following Jack and Ronnie as well. We'd have a big fat list of buyers soon.

I met Chester a mile away. He took the cocaine to book into evidence at the police station. He did his best to convince me that going fishing with Jack wasn't safe. I told him the only way we were going to get anywhere was if Jack and I became friends. I needed to spend time with him. If Jack kept using Kado as a middleman, we'd never find the sources.

Then, despite the voice telling me it wasn't a good idea, I went downtown to meet Liz.

***

I pushed open an ancient iron gate, clearing a path through lush flora obstructing the walkway in front of me. Two blocks from the Market in downtown Charleston, and I was in the middle of nowhere, only the moon lighting my way. After thirty feet, the garden opened up, revealing four small apartments overlooking a saltwater pool fortified by a tall stone wall. Flowers and plants hung from their hooks and patio furniture was scattered about.

Liz's head rose out of the water. She was alone. I kicked off my flip-flops, peeled off my shirt, and stepped down into the warm water. She met me on the last step and wrapped her arms and legs around me. "You finally came to see me."

"I missed you."

"Me, too." We kissed and drifted in silence a while, holding each other, basking in our reunion.

"What time are you fishing in the morning?"

"I have to be at Patriot's Point at 4:30 a.m."

"Who are you going with?"

"Just some clients. Can I ask you something?"

"Depends."

"Something I've been thinking about. What makes you so good? I mean, of all the artists out there, how did you become so famous? How do you stand out?"

"You don't think I have some talent?" she asked jokingly.

"You know what I mean. How does any artist compete these days?"

LOWCOUNTRY PUNCH

"My second year at NYU, a few of us had a show at the Rosenberg Gallery at NYU. A really big critic happened to see one of my paintings, and it made her cry. She wrote about it the next day in the *Times*."

"And that was it?"

"That was it."

After drying off, we took a long walk through downtown. With each step, I fell deeper and deeper under her spell. I wasn't sure I could ever leave Liz or Charleston.

We came across an entrance to a park, its open gate beckoning. Several monuments stood among the thick grass and proud oaks. We held hands and walked up to each one. One paid tribute to Andrew Jackson's mother, Elizabeth. She died in Charleston from cholera, a disease she contracted while nursing Continental soldiers on a prison ship during the Revolutionary War.

A stone pillar standing at the far side of the park displayed a bust of a man bearing a bushy mustache. I was drawn to him. I read his name and blurted out, "Hey, I know this guy...Henry Timrod, the poet."

Liz tuned in, smiling. "You just like the 'stache."

"No...I really do know him." I told her how I'd recently read an article discussing Bob Dylan's fascination with Henry Timrod. In his album *Modern Times*, Dylan sampled some of Timrod's poems in the lyrics. Some critics accused him of plagiarism, but it wasn't that at all. Dylan had always taken ideas from people, from F. Scott Fitzgerald to the Bible. He called it "conjuring:" having conversations with the dead and sharing with the artists of another time. Liz knew exactly what I meant.

***

Later that night, after we'd returned from our walk and climbed back into the pool, all the lies finally got to me. I felt compelled to confess.

"There's something I have to tell you," I said, "and I don't know how you're gonna take it."

Liz met me in the center of the pool. Only the two bulbs in the floor of the pool lit the water and the darkness.

"You sound so serious," she said.

"I am. I've been debating this for a while."

"No turning back now."

"I Googled you a couple days after we met."

"That's your secret?" She bonked me on the head.

"Yes, and I'm completely embarrassed about it. I needed your number."

She kissed me. I think she liked that I'd Googled her. "That's so sweet."

"Did you know you have your own Wikipedia page?"

"Yes." She made fun of me for a while, and we talked about the day we met. I brought up Andy Warhol, and her eyes lit up.

"He's a genius," she said. "He did a series of screen prints that I love...all endangered animals. I wish I could show you a picture right now. There's one of an orangutan. He has a big purple and white beard—you know, classic Warhol—and he has these round, sad, blue eyes and if you really look at him, it's almost like he's saying good-bye, the last of his species signing off." She talked more about Warhol and others she loved: Jackson Pollack, Larry Poons, and Julian Schnabel, and then her time spent with Hedda Stern, the woman who had mastered so many mediums.

We held each other in the cool water under the moon. Then we went inside. Liz put on Neil Diamond and we danced our way to the bedroom.

A sudden rap on the door stopped us short.

"Who could that be?" I asked, amazed at the timing.

"I have no idea."

"Let's pretend like we don't hear it."

She kissed me. "Okay."

Another knock, this time louder. More followed. Then, "Liz! Liz! I need to talk to you." It was the muffled voice of a man. He beat on the door again.

"Oooooh, God."

"Who is it?"

"You don't wanna know."

We both hopped out of bed. "I'll take care of him," I said. This guy had done enough. I could tell he scared her. I decided to make it perfectly clear how he fit into her life: not at all. I pulled on my shorts and headed to the door. I was happy to put him in his place.

More knocks and yelling.

"T.A.," she whispered. "Stop."

I did and turned to look at her. My fists were clenched.

"Let me take care of it." She began buttoning her shirt. "I'll send him home."

He beat on the door again, five times in rapid succession. Liz kissed me. "He's drunk. I'll deal with it. I don't want him to know you're here. It will just make it worse. He's dangerous. You don't understand." For a second, I thought she was going to cry.

"Then let me take care of him."

"No." She wasn't going to argue.

"All right. I'll be right here. Say my name and I'll be there."

"I know you will." She squeezed my arm and went to answer the door.

I looked around for good weapons. Not that I would need one, but it's good to survey the area. Not only to know what I can put my hands on, but also to know what *he* can. If paintbrushes and paint and canvases were weapons, I could have stormed Normandy. Apart from those, there wasn't much to work with. My heart thumped. I was ready to go, ready to defend my lady's honor. This guy had no idea what was coming.

Through the kitchen, I watched her open the door and slip

out. They began to talk, but I couldn't make out what they were saying. I could hear anger in the man's voice. After a couple minutes, I went into the living room. Still couldn't understand anything.

I put my ear to the door.

I heard Liz say, "One more word and I'll call the cops. I'll take out a restraining order against you. You're hammered. You're not going to accomplish anything right now except make me hate you. Go away."

Then there was silence. Was she okay? I started twisting the doorknob just as Liz came back inside. "He's gone."

We went back into the bedroom. I was too wired to fall asleep after that. I asked her what she'd ever seen in a guy like that, and she told me he'd changed, that she'd cared for a different man. She didn't seem eager to talk about him, and I didn't press. We stopped talking and I lay down alongside her. I didn't sleep much, and I don't think she did, either. I held her through the night.

It wasn't easy leaving her side a few minutes before four in the morning. She was on her stomach with her arms under the pillow, and the sheets were pulled just above her waist. Her back was soft, and it rose gently as she breathed. I wanted to meet her in her dream and love her there as well. I slipped out of bed quietly, leaving her with a kiss. She mumbled good-bye.

CHAPTER 18

You can't wear a wire every time. Seventy miles offshore is one of those times. Jack steered the Viking into the shipping channel, and we raced the other vessels out to sea. I fell back in time, remembering the pirate stories my grandfather used to tell. Edward Teach, a.k.a. Blackbeard, sailed this harbor back in 1718. Teach and his men picked up syphilis after a visit to the brothels in Port Royal, Jamaica, and on their way up the East Coast, they blockaded the Charleston harbor until their demands for medicine were met. Now, years later, I had some plundering of my own to do.

The *Taggin' Wagon* was named after the practice of tagging and releasing blue marlins, but of course, you could take it a couple ways. She was a good-looking yacht, a sixty-one-foot sleek sport fisher with an open fly bridge, a tuna tower, and a baby blue hull. Jack or his old man had definitely dropped several million on it. The yacht's infamous name was printed on the back with its logo, a blue marlin jumping into the back of an old western wagon.

When I got to the marina, which wasn't more than a mile from Jack's condo, he gave me a tour of the inside. The salon had a wraparound ostrich-skin couch and a flat-screen on the wall; all the upgrades. The galley wasn't large, but Martha Stewart wouldn't have bitched. Through the companionway, there were three staterooms, all very comfortable.

I once heard someone say that the Charleston breeze blew like an Egyptian princess blowing an eyelash off her lover's cheek. Cheesy, I know, but there on the fly bridge I was reminded of what they meant; I inhaled her sweet breath. A Maersk Sea Liner container ship passed our port side, its size dwarfing ours. Ronnie was below in the salon with two women, both of whom he had allegedly slept with the evening before.

I could tell Jack was hungover. "I understand you and Ron had a little go at it in Savannah."

I nodded slowly. "I hope he's not going to hold that against me for too long."

"You never know with him. That's impressive work, though. He's a big guy. I might be able to use you sometime. You be up for that?"

"I'll do anything for a price."

"Where'd you learn how to fight?"

"With a temper like mine, you get tons of practice."

Once we hit the open ocean, I felt seasickness coming on. I never get it on a sailboat, but sometimes powerboats do it to me if I get out too far. If you're not familiar with seasickness, imagine having the worst hangover of all time and multiply it by ten. It usually sets in slowly, like it did that day, and you try to position yourself somewhere on the boat to fight it off, somewhere with less motion, but you know it's coming. Sometimes staring at the horizon can help. That or jumping overboard, turning around and going home, or lying on the closest cushion and closing your eyes. I did the latter.

An experienced mariner knows the moment the seasickness gets someone. I waddled over to one of the cushions on the fly bridge and lay flat on my back, eyes closed. Jack knew immediately and asked if I had taken some medicine. I told him I had, and he yelled down to the cockpit for a bottle of water and a towel with ice. I drifted off into some state between sickness and sleep and came back to the feeling of ice on my forehead. I opened my eyes a little, and one of the girls was sitting next to me. Her face looked fuzzy. She held an icy hand towel to my forehead and was squeezing it slowly, letting the cold water drip down my neck. It helped for a while.

I like to think that I'm a man of the sea, but from time to time, the sea likes to remind me otherwise. I thought of Captain Bruce from my days on the *Bahama Star*, when I worked for him over a few summers as a teenager. When we crossed from Miami to Bimini so many times in a storm—when half the people on board were balled into fetal positions in the cockpit throwing up into buckets, the ride too rough for them to even hug the rail— Bruce would sit on the bow rail with his legs hanging over the edge, holding on with one hand, a smile on his face, screaming for more, screaming into the night. That is a man of the sea.

Apart from a visit aft to get rid of the biscuit I had eaten, the remainder of my day involved me laying flat on that cushion with my eyes closed, drifting in and out of consciousness, waking several times to people yelling, "Fish on!" and then again to some conversation in the distance. And, hours later, the same girl waking me with fresh tuna, dipping small pieces into soy sauce and wasabi and feeding them to me. Food entering my belly felt good, and the sickness would go away for a moment, but as soon as I sat up it would all come back. I wasn't doing a great job at making these guys like me. In fact, I was wasting people's time, and I needed to do better.

There's nothing like being hungry for hours and hours and finally taking a bite. Or the feeling of a Friday after a long week. Or driving to work on a bitter winter morning and waiting those first few miles of the drive for the car to warm up, and you're frozen, teeth chattering, fingers aching, and then the warm air starts to come out of the vents, and you're hot in no time. The moment I stepped onto land that late afternoon, my seasickness disappeared as quickly as a dusty thirst goes away with an icy glass of water.

***

We went back to Jack's place to clean up for dinner, and he appeared to be warming up to me some. I think my bout with seasickness made him feel superior to me, which is important to guys like him. He showed me around his condo. Told me *Architectural Digest* had done an article on his place right before he moved in. I wasn't surprised. The keypad-controlled elevator opened into a marble-floored vestibule, which led to the open living area. Extremely expensive, over-the-top taste. Large window views of the new bridge and the harbor and downtown. Opposite the wraparound black leather couch, a canvas about six feet tall hung on the wall. Prominent streaks of yellow looked like they had been violently cast across a background of black ripples and pure white. In the middle of the painting were twenty small heads—female and male—all staring in different directions. I was oddly attracted to its uniqueness, and I wanted to take it back to my house and study it for hours.

We went into his bedroom, where he had most likely slept with Tela Davies. A blue duvet lay bunched up at the end of a king-size Tempur-Pedic bed. A large corner cupboard held a collection of artist biographies and autobiographies. I noticed a framed photograph of a young girl on the shelf above the books.

"That's my sister," Jack said, as if reading my mind. "She died a long time ago."

I nodded. "And this?" I asked, picking up a heavy, charcoal-colored rectangular object resting on a stand next to the picture.

"Remember Ava Gardner?"

"Sure."

"That's the paperweight that she threw at her husband, Howard Hughes. Knocked him unconscious. My mom gave it to me for Christmas. Found it at some Sotheby's auction." He dumped a line of cocaine on the bedside table. "You want some?"

"I'm all right."

He cut what they call a hog leg and took it up his nose with a one hundred dollar bill.

***

Later, we headed to a wine bar downtown—a dimly lit, brick-walled, modern sort of place called McCrady's. Antique mirrors and wine racks with dusty bottles hung from the walls. In an hour, we would be on our way to meet Tela, and I would get to see firsthand how much trouble she could be. We sat at a booth and got into some new world wines, starting out with a sparkling. I'm supposed to watch my drinking, and I tried to, but it was getting tough. I had on a light cream summer jacket that Jack had lent me, and I had really taken a liking to it. I was feeling good.

Ronnie made a run to the bathroom with a bag of coke and when he returned, he set the bag on my lap. "All yours," he said.

"No, thanks."

"You don't want a little punch? What's wrong with you?"

Unless it's a life-or-death situation, agents aren't allowed to do coke. "I haven't done it in a while," I said. They both looked apprehensive, and I continued, "I found out a couple years ago I've got a congenital heart defect. Haven't done any since."

"Bullshit," Jack charged.

I looked him in the eyes. "Think what you want. I started having abnormal murmur episodes. My mitral valve doesn't close all the way, and blood flows back into my left atrium. I keep a diuretic on my bedside table." This last bit was true. I don't have any heart issues, but I do have a few prescriptions I've carried over the years for this exact reason: a diuretic, an antiarrhythmic, anticoagulants. No one is going to tell me I don't have a heart problem. "It's only business for me now."

Jack looked convinced, for the most part.

Three young women walked in the door, changing the subject. Jack stood. "You guys are late," he said.

"Do we know you?" the one in front asked. She had a 1950s kind of look about her, bouncy hair, bright red lipstick.

"Not yet. We can change that quickly. Can we buy you some drinks?"

In seconds, they were sitting with us, and I could see Jack was good at that kind of thing. After another couple of rounds, we left to go find Tela at the Mazyck Hotel.

CHAPTER 19

I do fall in love a lot. But I am faithful. If anything, I am faithful.

Of course I can tell if a woman is beautiful and Tela was, but I didn't entertain further thoughts. Liz was my woman. So, contrary to my team's belief, I did not fall in love with Tela that night.

Leaving the white gloves, fresh flowers, and marble floors of the lobby, we rode to the top floor of the Mazyck Hotel. Passing the doors leading to the penthouses, we proceeded to a rooftop bar overlooking the city. It was fairly crowded at the bar and all the tables were taken. There was a pool carved out in the center, but no one was swimming. Tela was standing to the left of the pool, by the railing. We approached.

Her figure caught my eye first, her white dress hugging her large breasts, skinny waist, and curved hips. The dress stopped at her knees, and she had fine legs and a tiger's prowl. She wore a strand of pearls around her neck. She was a brunette Marilyn Monroe. I'd seen several of her movies over the years, and she was every bit as beautiful in person as she was on screen.

She was a touchy one, and I don't mean sensitive. After we all said hello, she took my hand in hers, focusing her blue eyes on me. "It's a pleasure to meet you, Travis," she said with a clean English accent. I smiled, and she put her hand on my arm and felt the material of the coat. "This looks wonderful on you. I really like it."

"It's actually Jack's."

"He should give it to you," she said, winking at me. Tela was one of those full-court press kind of women. She didn't let go of my hand for a full thirty seconds, and I felt like Jack and Ronnie were watching us, wondering what the hell was going on, maybe even asking themselves if Tela and I knew each other.

We joined the rest of her group. It was my first time meeting James King, the owner of the hotel and the man we'd originally pursued. As I'd remembered from our earlier work, he had played basketball at Wake. I had a hard time picturing such a short man on the court. There were rumors that he might try a run at the mayor's office soon. King led the conversation and told some very funny stories. The man was quick as a whip and listened very intently when others spoke. I couldn't wait to put cuffs on his wrists.

We stood there talking, Tela next to me. She was quite close. Out of nowhere, she stepped on my foot with her six-inch heels. I knew it was deliberate, but she didn't look at me or apologize. She only kept listening to King. He carried on, "Jack, I don't think you know the first thing about Chinese economics, yet you're standing here telling us that you know what they're thinking. I would call it presumptuous. I don't suppose for a moment that they are looking to—"

"Where on earth do you get your facts?" Jack interrupted. "Right out of the lips of your
father—"

"'The lips of my father?' You would be amazed, sir, at the depth of my knowledge in such matters. A childhood spent in a hotel sponging up the banter of the world's travelers is well on par with any Ivy League education."

All their bullshit made me thirsty, and I disappeared toward the bar and ordered another Pyrat and soda. As the barely-legal bartender turned around to make my drink, I felt a hand on my back and turned around to face Tela. Her dangerous eyes were all over me.

"Travis," she said to me, "do I make you uncomfortable?"

I turned toward her and put a hand on the bar behind me, leaning against it. "Maybe a little."

"Any reason why?"

"Not really. I think I'm starstruck."

"I've seen starstruck, and you're not starstruck."

I almost said I didn't want to fall off a balcony but that wouldn't have been very charming. Instead, I offered, "Maybe I'm trying to stay out of trouble."

"That one is easier to believe. But we've only just met, and you're worried about getting into trouble."

"Am I off base?"

"I'm as innocent as a lamb, and I think you're charming."

"I'm best from a distance. Believe me. And I'm scared of lambs."

My eyes left her as Jack came from behind. She turned around, saying, "Hi, Jack. Your friend is rather intriguing."

"Good-looking, too, isn't he? Trav, you'll have to watch yourself."

"Thanks for the advice."

Jack took out his phone. "You guys get together." I put my arm around Tela's waist and Jack snapped a photo. The flash lit up the night.

The evening took on wings, and the next thing I knew, a group of us snuck out the back to avoid any paparazzi and piled into a limo. Several miles and many bridges south, we reached Folly Beach and drove along the coast. A row of beach houses separated us from the water. Eventually, the houses disappeared, leaving only the sand between the road and the moonlit sea. The limo driver pulled over on the shoulder at the Washout, the public beach where I surfed on occasion. The wheels sank into the sand.

As everyone piled out of the limo, Jack grabbed me by the arm. "Don't get any ideas with Tela. I don't want you chasing her."

"What are you talking about?"

"You know what I'm talking about. You'd be smart to leave that one alone."

There were those threats again, but I slapped him on the leg. "Don't worry about it. She's not my type." With that, I climbed out onto the sand. I wanted to rip his face off.

We all dashed into the sea in our underwear. The water was as warm as a bath, and we floated on our backs and let the waves lull us into relaxation. I lost count of the shooting stars that fell like waterfalls from the sky.

After a while, Tela was at it again. I was in waist deep water, talking with Tela and Jason Corey—her new costar and Chad Rourke's replacement—when she let the waves push her toward me. Jason took the hint. He drifted away and left us alone. We were only dark shadows in the gentle waves. Another wave brought her closer, and I felt her leg against mine.

"You can't do this all night," she said.

"You aren't having fun?"

"Not really. Somehow I've given you the upper hand. You Southern men are tough."

I licked my lips. "You Brits are easy."

One of her hands came out of the water, and she slapped me hard. We had floated far enough away where no one saw it.

I touched my left cheek where she had struck it. "I didn't realize there was a line."

"There was, and you bloody crossed it."

"I bloody did, did I? You're a hot little pistol! I told you I'm best from a distance. I think we both are."

She reached out under the water and touched me. I jumped, thinking she was going to hit me again. It was a light touch, though, and she ran her hand along my stomach, saying, "Let's not jump to conclusions." I shook my head and looked over toward Jack. I couldn't tell if he was watching us or not. She asked, "Are you scared of him?"

"Who?"

"Who do you think? Jack, of course."

"Not scared of him. I don't want him to get the wrong idea."

"What does he have to do with anything?"

"I'm not looking for a love triangle."

"What are you looking for?"

"If I knew, I'd tell you." I glided my hand across the water's surface, and a trail of phosphorous sparkled like lost stars.

CHAPTER 20

Back in the limo, wet and wrapped in towels, we headed back toward downtown. Somehow, I ended up next to Tela in the far end near the driver. With the lights down low, no one noticed her hand rubbing my thigh. I didn't think anyone but Jack cared anyway. I removed her hands only for her to giggle and snuggle closer to me. "I'm cold," she whispered into my ear. She rested her head on my lap. Boy, was I in trouble.

Blue lights lit up behind us, and a siren sounded. Jack jerked his head around, then pulled a bag of coke from his pocket. Without even thinking, he stood up and dumped the contents out of the open moon roof. Hopefully before the cops were close enough to see what he was doing. Then he crumbled the plastic bag in his hand and stuck it in his mouth. He'd swallowed it by the time we stopped.

I didn't know what had caused the violation, but it wasn't that big of a deal for any of them. Everyone had their late night buzz on and didn't care a bit.

Everyone but me. I didn't feel like dealing with it.

I looked out the window. Officer Darby Long—the redneck cop who'd arrested Kado—walked past the tinted glass. Thank the Gods he couldn't see inside. There are not that many cops on Folly Beach, but I hadn't considered that I'd run into this guy again. Oh yes, I had a big problem. In that limo, my name was Travis Moody. He knew me as Special Agent T.A. Reddick, and we hadn't gotten off to the greatest start anyway.

He tapped on the driver's window with a flashlight and the driver complied, rolling down his window. But the partition separating the front and back was raised and we couldn't make out the conversation. I ran through several scenarios in my head. Obviously, if Long didn't look in the back, I was good. But I had to prepare for the worst. If he recognized me, I could be done. We had not informed the Charleston County Police Department about my insertion. The less people who knew, the better—except for times like these.

Being the good, thorough, obnoxiously curious, and clairvoyant police officer that he was, Officer Long had to come see what was going on inside the limo. The driver lowered the privacy window and said, "He wants to come check y'all out. Sorry about this."

Each step Officer Long took toward the door tested me. I wished I'd let my team follow me out there. They could have radioed in and pulled Long out. But being the rogue idiot that I am, I was on my own. He opened the side door and stuck his head in, his two-foot-long Mag-Lite shining brightly. As he shined it in the eyes of Jack and another girl, I had a clear shot at Officer Long's face. There was that mustache, just thicker than a No. 2 pencil and perfectly groomed.

"You know you're not allowed on the beach past hours, don't ya?" he said.

Jack put up his hands. "You wanna get that light out of my face, Officer? We're trying to get home and get some sleep."

I wanted to tell Jack that speaking to this particular officer that way was not a great idea, but Officer Long made that clear instantaneously. He shined the light square in Jack's face. "Now, look here…boy. You will not speak to an officer of the law in that tone. If I have to, I'll jerk you out of here, put your head in the dirt and step on it. I'll hold you there for three weeks, 'til you're licking Australia."

Right next to me, Tela burst into a loud laugh. "You can't be serious." I turned to quiet her but it was too late.

Officer Darby Long handled his job with the pride of the Secretary of Defense. Mocking him wasn't wise. He turned his light and attention directly to Tela. "What did you just say?"

I separated myself away from her and the light. She answered, "I said you can't be serious. We're out having a bit of fun, not breaking the law. Now you should run along before we have to speak with your superiors, you little troll."

"Oh, boy, sister. You just did it," said Long. "I want you all out. Let's go."

No one moved and Tela decided she wasn't done. "You bloody wanker. You'll have to pull me out of here."

I hit her on the leg. "Shut up, Tela."

Officer Long drew his weapon. "I'm gonna count to twenty. Whoever isn't standing out here in a straight line, I will come and get. And I will put you behind bars. That little lady with the mouth in there's gonna be first in line."

Jack said, "Officer, I apologize. She's hotheaded. We've all had too much to drink. If you could please just—"

"Get the heck out of the vehicle!" Long screamed. "You got 'til twenty. One, two, three…" He paused and let us drink the fear. "Seven, eight…and I can't wait to shoot somebody." He turned the gun back and forth in his hand, teasing us. "Eleven, twelve…"

The two girls closest to the door got out first. Then Jack and Jason. The rest of us followed. I still hadn't decided how to handle it. All I knew was that he would recognize me if he got a good look. There was almost no way around it. Despite his appearance as a country boy from the woods, his skills as an officer couldn't be denied.

Being the gentleman that I was, I let Tela shuffle out first. She grabbed my hand and pulled, saying, "I'll protect you, baby." Now, I do have to admit that even though I wasn't intending on committing any sort of sin, it was a wee bit of a confidence boost to have a famous actress all over me. I had no intentions of giving her the pleasure of a conquest and that made me feel even better.

The immediate issue at hand required my trained and focused attention. As I put a foot onto the shoulder of the two-lane road and stood, my first inclination was to run. What other options did I have? I could attack Long, but that would be hard to explain—especially later, when Jack would discover I wasn't going to spend a year in the slammer for attacking an officer. If I stood in line next to the others, he would peg me, say he knew me, and maybe even say my real name. One other idea came to mind. I could go hop into his cruiser and see what happened. I needed some way to speak to him without the others hearing. Just a moment to explain the situation.

I decided to run. The best plan was to cross the street and hit the closest boardwalk, then get lost on the beach. He'd have to shoot me to catch me. Just as I was about to make my move, Tela made one of her own. She stepped toward Long.

He shined his light in her face. She raised her hand to shield herself from the light and started with the damn sexiest talk I'd heard in a while.

"Officer," she started, "we're just out having fun. I'm so sorry I spoke to you that way."

Then, something magical happened. And the possibility of it hadn't even occurred to me.

"Are you—" he started. He looked like he'd just seen Jesus Christ walk out of a UFO. "Are you Tela Davies?"

"You're exactly correct, officer."

I stepped back and hung close to the open door of the limo, hiding in the darkness of the night. Before me, I watched Officer Darby Long enter a new world, one where no one existed except him and the great princess of Hollywood, Tela Davies. *Starstruck* would be an understatement. His world began to revolve and orbit on a plane of ecstasy, and a smile wide enough to hold the *Yorktown* aircraft carrier stretched across his face.

"I cannot believe it," Officer Long said, his eyes glazing over. I could have drawn his gun and pointed it at him and he wouldn't have noticed. He finally got a few words out. "I just don't know what to say. My girlfriend and sister would have a heart attack. I'm about to, too! Gee whiz, you're making me shake. Please excuse me."

She took his hand and looked into his eyes and said, "I'm just a girl from Liverpool. Nothing special. Believe me." Officer Long nearly fell backwards in enchantment. She rubbed her thumb over his knuckles, pushing him even further. It would not have surprised me if his head spontaneously combusted right there. I've never seen anything like it.

She stepped a little closer and asked, "Is there any reason you pulled us over? We're dreadfully tired. I just want to go to bed."

"I won't keep you a minute longer. The least I could do is show you some Southern hospitality." He looked at the others and then his gaze moved over to me. I turned my head quickly, avoiding eye contact. But Long was blind to everyone except Tela.

Still holding her hand, he said to Tela, "I know everybody probably asks for your autograph and all that stuff, so I won't do that, but…"

"What is it, sweetheart?"

"Can I just get a hug from ya?"

She smiled and let go of his hand. "That's so cute." She slipped her arms around him like she'd loved him for years, and his eyes rolled into the back of his head as he melted.

CHAPTER 21

I got back to my Charleston house about 7 a.m. and slept until after lunch. I had every intention of heading to Savannah afterwards, but Liz called and changed my mind. She said she'd be over later, and I couldn't resist.

Before she arrived, I made a phone call that I'd made every month since the night I shot Robert Vasquez. The US Marshall in charge of tracking down Diego picked up quickly.

"Agent Reddick, you're like clockwork. I don't blame you, though. I would be, too."

"How are things going?"

"I'm afraid nothing new to report."

"Well, it helps to know that someone still remembers he's out there."

"I haven't given up. We're still looking."

"Thank you." Given that Liz was coming over, the lack of progress in finding Vasquez didn't bother me as much as usual.

I hadn't stayed up that late in a long time, and my morning nap didn't help much. I went down to the water and swam for a while. It helped. I sipped a cup of coffee, waiting on Liz.

We tore each other's clothes off the minute she came in the door, and we ended up in my tub drinking champagne shortly after. With her back nestled against my chest, she fit perfectly between my legs. I held her there for a long time, hoping there would be many more times like this.

Anna came to mind, but only for a second. I thought about how it didn't hurt anymore, and how I didn't ache for her. For the first time, I knew that I just wanted her to be happy. Liz was all that mattered.

She leaned back against the other end of the tub, resting her feet on the tops of my thighs. I took them in my hands and massaged them while we softly spoke to each other.

Unable to wait any longer, I pulled her toward me. She stood in the water and bending down, kissed me. "Not so fast." She took my hand and led me out of the tub.

I followed her into the shower. We pressed against each other, letting the hot water splash on top of us. I soaped her with shower gel, my hands following her curves like the hands of a sculptor. She knelt and bathed my legs and feet, kissing me and loving me as the citrus smell of lemon filled my head. My knees became weak. I stepped out of the shower and left Liz to finish pampering herself.

I dried myself off and went into the bedroom with the bottle of champagne. Lying naked and erect, as it were, I waited on Liz, marking time with the patience of a gladiator awaiting battle. Finally, Liz turned off the shower.

A minute later, she poked her head around. She was wearing my Shady Brady cowboy hat, and nothing else. She winked below the brim.

I patted the bed.

She came around the corner wearing nothing but the hat and those tan lines and the confidence that was such a part of her beauty. I knew I would forever compare all women and moments to Liz and the way I saw her that night. The way she moved toward me. The way she moved me. The way she looked right down to the core of my being. Standing there before me, she was the absolute definition of sensuality. The Thievery

Corporation's "Un Simple Histoire" played in the background with LouLou's French vocals laced over a beat that might have been written for that night.

"What do you think? Is this a good look?" She turned around slowly.

I nearly found a new religion. "I think you can pull it off."

Liz lifted her arms in the air and, with her eyes inside of me, she moved to the sounds, her legs slowly bending as she danced, the round curves of her feminine figure casting a moving shadow across the wall behind her. She finally climbed onto the bed and kissed me with wet, pouty lips.

My memory of that night is almost too special to put into words. Let's just say the first time I made love to Liz was what the first astronaut felt entering space. I didn't know that depth of feeling existed.

Afterwards, as I drifted off to sleep, I knew it was time for me to tell her who I really was. I loved her.

***

The team met the next day for a surveillance recap in a suite at a Comfort Inn in West Ashley. All I could really think about was Liz cooking me dinner later. Couldn't wait to see her. Steve would have killed me if he knew I wasn't going back to Savannah tonight, but I had to see her again and tell her the truth. I couldn't lie any longer.

And I had to tell her I loved her.

Baroni had nearly blown the op earlier in the day and was suicidal about it. From what Steve had told me on the phone, he'd been following Jack and a girlfriend on King Street, taking pictures. Jack saw Baroni and confronted him. Baroni barely got out of it, saying he was taking pictures for a new photography book.

I fired one off the bow the second we began. "How's that

book coming along, Ms. Leibovitz? What's it called?" A round of laughter.

Baroni glared at me and with his scratchy voice, said, "That's hysterical, Reddick. Are you done?"

"I'm done, sweetie."

"You're the one who hasn't delivered a damn thing. I got news for you. You're not impressing anybody right now."

"Well, that makes two of us, doesn't it?"

Baroni stood. "You want to get beat?"

"You wanna die?"

"Both of you shut the fuck up!" Steve shouted.

I shook my head and kept quiet.

After he'd cooled off, Baroni stood up and plugged his camera into the TV to show us the latest images. There were shots of Ronnie and Jack with various friends, most of whom we knew. One of Jack walking on King Street, going into Half Moon Outfitters; another of Jack turning his head as a good-looking girl passed him.

Then I saw the shot that changed everything. It was a photo of Jack talking to Liz—my Liz—on the sidewalk. They stood underneath a palm tree outside of Williams-Sonoma. Two bags sat at her feet. Probably something for the meal she was cooking for me later. *What the hell?* Did they know each other?

"This is Elizabeth Coles," Baroni said. "I ran her 'Stang's tags. The College is renting it. I gave them a call. She's in town teaching a summer art class, and they're putting her up. Gave her a car. I'm not sure how she knows Jack. We need to do some digging." He flipped to the next shot. Jack was walking behind her. "It looked like she was trying to get away from him. I couldn't hear anything, but I could tell she wasn't happy. Some kind of a lover's quarrel." Then a shot of them at her car. Jack was closing her door.

My gut seized, and a swarm of emotions erupted inside of me. Suddenly it all made sense. I knew how she knew Jack.

CHAPTER 22

The pieces fit. Liz had been extremely reluctant to talk about her past relationship but I had pried a few facts out of her. She said he came from a lot of money. She also said he cheated on her. And, of course, he owned a damn art gallery.

How obvious could it have been, you fool!

Jack hadn't talked much about his past, either, but I did know some of it from Kado. I knew about Kayla Martin, the girl from Charlotte, and how he'd cheated on her with Tela. But what did Liz have to do with it? Why hadn't Kado mentioned her? Had he lied to me?

I came out of my shock to hear Baroni talking to me. Something about how good-looking Liz was. I mumbled something and excused myself. Pushing open the bathroom door, I stumbled in. I lowered my head over the sink and splashed water onto my face. Deep down, I knew the truth. This was going to be one nasty mess for AUSA Cannon, and it was hell of embarrassing for me, but what hurt most was the two of them together. I hated that he had touched her. That they had probably slept together.

On the road twenty minutes later, I dialed Kado's number. Rain had begun to fall.

"Can you talk right now?" I could hear the sounds of

Morph's busy kitchen in the background.

"Let me walk outside. It's loud in here." A few seconds later, he came back to the phone.

Remembering how fragile Kado was, I spoke softly. "You lied to me."

"What are you talking about?"

"I'm talking about Kayla Martin. Liz Coles. Tell me what the hell is going on."

His silence said it all.

"Why?" I asked. I sped up, changing lanes. "Tell me why you lied to me. You've caused some big problems."

Nothing.

"Words need to start flowing out of your mouth, Kado, or I will come to your restaurant and beat the shit out of you in front of your customers. *Who is Kayla Martin?*"

"Jack's ex. He dated her before Liz."

"Why didn't you mention Liz? You held back. Why?"

"I saw the two of you."

"What are you talking about?"

"The day y'all got me out of jail."

"Keep talking."

"We'd run out of Jagermeister, so I went over to see if I could borrow some from the Blind Tiger. I saw you and Liz together. Saw you kissing."

"And?"

"And I kept thinking about it, trying to make sense of it. At first, I wondered if somehow my whole arrest had been a set up."

"Like I was the one who stuffed a bunch of coke up your nose and a bottle of whiskey down your throat."

"No, but that you'd been watching me. Maybe you had known Liz for a while, and you were trying to get Jack back for cheating on her. I don't know. Nothing made sense." He words were caked in desperation and fear. He knew I had his future in my hands. "Then I realized how much of a hole it could put in the case," he admitted. "When you asked me about his dating life that day in Savannah, I came so close to saying something. But I held back. I thought I had a way to save my friends and destroy the case built against them." He paused. "So I told you that Kayla Martin was the last girl he dated. You would have done the same thing."

"I wouldn't be in this position! You think those people are your friends? Are you nuts? When have I tried to screw you? I never did, did I? Not once. You have put me in a shitty situation, Kado. I hope you realize that."

"I know. I'm sorry. I almost told you—"

"*Almost told me.* We are working together. I'm trying to keep you alive, and you go behind my back and lie to me."

"I know."

"What else do I need to know? Come clean *now*. I don't want any more surprises. Maybe, just maybe, I won't throw you in jail and bring every damn charge back on the table."

I was flying past the other cars. I looked down at the speedometer. Over ninety. The Jeep didn't like it at all, especially in the rain. I pulled my foot off the pedal, and it stopped shaking. Not that I'd really care if I slid off the side of the road and rolled into the woods.

"There's nothing else," Kado answered.

"You better hope not. Be around tomorrow. I want to know everything you held back about Liz." I hung up on him.

My testimony would be the key to taking down Jack and any other sources. Now it was compromised. A DEA agent's testimony is gold unless the defense can dig up some dirt. My relationship with Liz had the potential to destroy every bit of my credibility and would be priceless to a defense lawyer. Just like Kado thought, they could say that I had personal motivations to bring Jack Riley down. They could even talk about entrapment.

I had to tell my team, but it wasn't going to be tonight. I had to see her first.

CHAPTER 23

When I got home Liz's Mustang was parked in my driveway. I was definitely not in a completely sane state of mind, and I thought for a moment of not pulling in, of calling her and telling her I had to work late, giving her some kind of excuse.

Instead I walked slowly through the downpour to the front door. I didn't bother wiping my shoes off on the mat as I entered. Tom Waits was coming out of the speakers loud, his ghostly voice layered on top of a thick stand-up bass line. My mood was wild—and I don't mean a crazy, drunken college kid out on the town kind of wild. I mean Lord of the fucking Flies, swinging from the goddamn trees wild.

Liz was in the kitchen. She stood in front of the oven in her underwear, her back to me, an apron tied around her waist. I smelled soy. She swayed to the slow swinging beat of the music, her elbow moving back and forth as she tended to whatever was in the pan in front of her.

I wanted her, but I was so angry, too. Not at her, but at the situation. At myself. Waits sang about diamonds on his windshield, and I crept toward her. She had no idea I was there. I wrapped my right arm around her waist and touched her stomach.

She flung the spatula into the air. "You scared me—"

LOWCOUNTRY PUNCH

I reached around with my left hand and covered her mouth, quieting her. The spatula hit the ground. As her warm breath blew against my hand, I could sense her fear. I didn't know what I was doing. I was scared, too.

The need took hold of me, and I reached between her legs with my right hand, pressing my body against hers. She opened her mouth behind my fingers and I began kissing her neck, pulling her lower body into mine. I took my hand away from her mouth and pulled her underwear down. Felt her warmth as her back arched and our bodies convulsed.

I spun her around, taking the apron off her neck, removing her bra, finally kissing her lips. She was with me, on the same page somehow. She pulled me to the floor and ripped the buttons off my shirt, pulling it off me. Then she unbuckled my belt and unzipped my jeans.

The contents of the pan kept cooking as we made love on the tile below. Dense, dangerous love. If it was love at all. I might say it was beyond love.

Or maybe it was far less. Maybe it was two people stuck between worlds, one where they belonged together, and one where it wasn't meant to be.

***

Later, we ate overcooked stir-fry, laughing about it. Liz went to shower, and I took a seat in one of the two rocking chairs near the screen. Rain battered the roof and splashed from the downspouts.

A friend had left an unopened pack of Marlboros when he visited a month earlier, and for some reason I'd kept them. I pulled off the cellophane and took out a cigarette. I lit it with a match and drew the smoke into my lungs. I hadn't touched one in years, although there had been times when I'd wanted one. It was every bit as good as it used to be.

I pulled a drag and thought of my father. What a good man. Such grand memories. He worked later than most, but he always came home for dinner. When my brother Will and I were in early grade school, we would hide in the bushes near the front stoop or some more creative spot and wait for him. When he got close, we would jump out and scare him. He always carried his briefcase in one hand and a stack of papers in the other. Whenever we popped out, he would sling the papers high in the air, and, depending on the quality of our specific hiding place, he might even fall to the ground. He humored us for a long time with that one.

Could I ever be like that? I really didn't know. Sure, I could see myself marrying Liz and having kids, coaching soccer, all that. It would be a fine life. But it wasn't me. Not in the near future. As selfish as it sounds, I still had things to do. I needed to leave my footprint on the world before I settled down. I definitely didn't want to be one of those fathers who had too much going on to deal with his children. Putting the little ankle-biters aside, I couldn't be with anyone. It would only complicate things. As it already had.

I was trying to talk myself into doing what had to be done.

Liz came out, kissed me on the neck from behind, and took a seat in the other rocking chair. "I didn't know you smoked."

"Once a year, maybe. It's been a long day."

We talked about trivial things for a while, and I finally got the guts. "I'm worried about what we're doing to each other, what's gonna happen."

"What do you mean?"

I chose my words carefully. "I think we're getting too close. We're going to hurt each other."

Her smile went away, and she stopped rocking and looked at me. "You're serious, aren't you?"

I met her eyes. "Completely. I think we're fools to let this last much longer. You're going back to New York...for good. I'm not moving up there. I couldn't talk you into staying."

She leaned back in her chair and began to rock again. "You made this decision before you came home? Before what happened earlier? Before dinner?"

She had me there. Looking back out over the marsh, I said, "More and more I realize how much I love you, and I can't allow it. It's not the right time."

"You're right…I'm not ready to settle down, either. Maybe it's not the right time." She took a breath and our eyes met again. "But the idea of us walking away from each other doesn't really make sense. There's something between us."

"Of course there is. Something great…but—"

"But you're scared."

"Yes, I am."

Her eyes began to water. "Okay," she said, standing. "If that's all you have, I'll walk away, too."

"I don't have a choice." I really didn't. I wanted to tell her the truth, but I couldn't. The case would rely on the fact that I had ended the relationship promptly once I'd become aware of Liz's relationship with Jack. And I had no idea what their relationship was now. How could I be absolutely positive she wouldn't say anything? It was best to leave her out of it.

And I wanted to tell her I loved her, but I couldn't do that, either.

"You *always* have a choice," she said. "I think you're a fucking idiot." It was the only time I'd ever heard her say that word.

"I'm sorry, Liz."

"Don't be." With that, she left, her head held high.

III

"Stop this world. Let me off. There's just too many pigs in the same trough."

- Mose Allison

CHAPTER 24

You put it behind you.

How do you get past putting an op in jeopardy because of your own damn needs? How do you go undercover to befriend a man you would rather beat with a Louisville Slugger? How do you face the people you've let down? You put it behind you. If there are people who believe in you and demand greatness from you, and if you believe in yourself, you put it behind you and carry on. I mean: *quit feeling sorry for yourself, Reddick.*

Everyone but me had pretty much gotten past my relationship with Liz. It had been two excruciatingly painful weeks. We all knew that it was a potential problem in court, but we couldn't call off the op now. AUSA Cannon's concern was whether the information was exculpatory, meaning information favorable to the defendant that the prosecution *must* share. Forget the defense finding out; we might *have* to tell them. As I had guessed, the fact that I severed the relationship immediately would be the greatest argument against its exculpatory nature.

The message had been sent down, though. Time to make some progress. That or make arrests. I needed to make something happen or go back to Florida.

I had an old friend who I'd been writing music with since my college days by the name of Scott Simontacchi. He'd been in

Nashville for years and had become a well-known musician in the circles that mattered. I gave him a ring, and he got his hands on two backstage passes to see Bruce Springsteen at the North Charleston Coliseum. I invited Jack, knowing he wouldn't turn it down. It was that night that our friendship began. A good old-fashioned bromance. I buried my feelings and opened my heart, allowing myself to not only like the man, but to connect with him.

My supervisors over the years always said I was one of the best in the business at making friends. We spent a good bit of time together, fishing, drinking, surfing, philosophizing. We got to know each other well. Or, I should say, he got to know Travis Moody. He even started calling me Trav. That's when I knew I had him. I made it clear that I wanted to work for him—in any way that he needed—from pushing coke to muscle work. And I'd already proven myself in both arenas.

As hard as it was to admit, I could see what Liz saw in the man. Behind the layer of cocaine that had put a shadow on his spirit, he was charming and quite entertaining. He was one of those people who had something to contribute. I wasn't growing fond of him, but I did understand his appeal.

Speaking of Liz, I was in pain. Though losing Anna had battle-hardened my heart, I definitely wasn't bulletproof. Tears were shed. Weight was lost. Drinks were downed. I hoped that after this was all over, I could find her and tell her everything and that she'd forgive me. But I didn't count on it. Optimism can often set you up for pain.

***

The call finally came. Jack asked me to accompany him to Atlanta. He needed some protection. Steve was ecstatic. Chalk one up for Agent Reddick.

Jack and I made the four-and-a-half-hour drive on a Thursday morning, parking outside Atlanta's subway system, the Marta.

"Leave your phone," he said. "They won't let you in with it." Luckily, I had a GPS micro-transmitter hidden in my shoe. The Atlanta DEA knew exactly where I was, and they'd be able to track whoever we were going to meet. That's how we would open up this circle, how we'd blow this case wide open.

We hopped on the Marta and took it two stops down, where a Lexus waited on us outside the station. We climbed in the back. The pineapple air freshener swinging from the rearview mirror did nothing to mask the smell of stale cigarette smoke buried deep inside the cloth seats. The driver was white and appeared to be in his mid-twenties. From his apparel, I guessed he was quite the Atlanta Hawks fan. He wore his hat tilted to the side and spoke gangsta English.

"Whaz up, Jack?" he said, turning around to greet us. He had a gap in his teeth.

"What's goin' on, brother? This is a friend of mine. Travis. He's straight. I told your boy I might bring somebody. Travis, meet Joe." Amazing. Jack was like a chameleon. I didn't know he spoke gangsta.

"I'm cool. You guys carryin'?" Jack shook his head, and Joe reached into the backseat and patted us down.

He got a little too friendly, and I said, "All right, buddy. That's not the gun you're looking for and those aren't grenades."

He ignored me.

Joe drove evasively, making sure no one was following us. Across town, under an overpass, he swung the wheel hard left and cut in front of oncoming traffic. I took hold of the door handle as the wheels screeched, and we were thrown forward. Seconds later, we went out the way we came in, and Joe had a smile on his face, satisfied. Ten minutes and many turns later, we pulled into a parking garage out near the airport. Joe parked the Lexus on the second floor, and we switched vehicles. We exited the garage in a shabby Toyota Corolla. As long as my transmitter hadn't died, Joe had just needlessly wasted gas and given me a hell of a headache.

We eventually pulled into a sketchy motel right off the interstate. It was a two-story brick building called the Rose View. What looked like two meth-heads were arguing with each other closer to the road. A sleazy businessman looked down on us from the railing. We followed Joe up the stairs. Jack had the backpack and seemed calm, like he had done this many times before. I'd done it a few times myself, but I had to tip my hat to their vigilance. No one could have possibly followed us.

Joe knocked twice. A moment later, a thug opened the door and let us in. Thick gold chain around his neck. Might have had a rap album under his belt.

He stuck his hand out to Jack. "How's it going?" A tattoo of a dragon breathing flames wrapped around his arm and disappeared behind his sleeve.

"All right," Jack replied.

"You sure your friend's cool, eh?"

"Yeah, I'm sure." Jack didn't bother introducing me. I didn't think we had much of a future, so I wasn't offended. We followed him into the room. The curtains were drawn. The lamps near the two beds and the blaring television were the only source of light. Two other thugs were watching cartoons. One of them sat on the edge of the bed with a TEC-9 semiautomatic with at least a 36-round magazine in his hand, which wasn't exactly a welcome mat. The other sat on the noisy air conditioning unit and didn't say a word.

"So what you got for me?" the first thug asked.

Jack handed him the backpack, and the man began to flip through the twenties. I kept my eyes on Speedy Gonzalez, who was gracing the tube. I had seen that show a lot when I was younger, but I couldn't remember Speedy's cousin's name. It started bothering me.

The dragon man stabbed a knife into the side of a kilo and

dished out a couple lines onto a plate before handing it over. Jack rolled up a bill and took one down.

"It's good," Jack said, smiling. "You got eight?"

Dragon man nodded and stacked them in front of Jack, who shoved them into his backpack, stood, and thanked him. Jack said, "This is it for me, at least for a while. I wanted to tell you to your face, out of respect. I want no hard feelings. Nothing personal, but I'm trying to calm down. I think we've done well."

"You found something better, Jack?"

"Nah, man. I'm just tryin' to look out for myself. I hope you understand."

"I guess I got to. I hope you're not leaving me for somebody else. You take care of yourself."

"Not at all, buddy. Just cleanin' up." Jack's a good liar, but I wasn't buying it. I knew he had found a safer way to bring in better coke; I just didn't have all the answers yet. Could it have something to do with the containers of teak he brought in from time to time? For Jack's sake, I hope the dragon man didn't figure that out. He didn't seem like the understanding type. They bumped fists and we got out of there. I didn't bother saying good-bye.

Crossing the parking lot, I asked Joe and Jack, "Y'all know who Speedy Gonzalez's cousin is? It's killing me."

"Slowpoke," Jack said, climbing into the Lexus.

"That's right!" I slapped my leg. "Slowpoke Rodriguez." I got in the other side, behind Joe. Speedy was my guy back in the old days. I remember pretending to be sick when I was a kid, and the minute my mom would leave to go run errands, I would run downstairs and catch an episode. *Shirt Tales* was another one I loved, but apparently no one else had ever heard of it.

We said good-bye to Joe and went on our way. If my counterparts had done their job as I had expected, they would have teams following Joe and the thugs we met at the hotel. We were making progress. Next stop: Jack's cabin.

CHAPTER 25

Back on the highway, Jack brought Liz up.

"I haven't even told you about her, have I?" he asked, his eyes focused on the highway.

"No. I mean, I've heard you mention that someone screwed you up."

"Yeah. She screwed me up. First girl to ever do it, too. You ever had your heart broken, Trav?"

"Once or twice."

"Nothing like it, is there? To be honest, I'm still hurting. She'll come around though, I think. Just needs some time. We had a great thing."

"They come back sometimes."

"Yeah, they do. But I think she's seeing someone. That's something I will deal with if it doesn't end soon. I can't bear thinking about her and some other asshole."

If he only knew. "She must be a good woman. Tell me about her. How'd you meet?"

"Last year during the Spoleto festival, she came to town to accept the Menotti award, which is a big deal in the art world. CBS was even doing a piece on her. Being the Director of the Arts, I introduced her and that's how we met. I asked her out after her acceptance speech. The cameras got it on tape and ended up including it in their piece. Honestly, I've watched it way too many times lately."

I nodded.

"I knew knowing her could put me on the map. And it did. Within a couple months, she had given me exclusive rights to sell her paintings in the state. It was huge for me. Not that I didn't want to bed her, too. But I had my priorities." He took a key bump from a bag of coke in his pocket. I hated that sound.

Suppressing my anger, I said, "I can understand that."

"Then she caught me sleeping with Tela Davies."

"How'd she do that?"

"Believe it or not, it was the day Chad Rourke died. You know Tela was with him that night. Up at his place. It was in the papers. She called me as she was leaving his place and said she wanted to come over. We'd only met a few times but really hit it off at King's place earlier that night." Jack looked at me. "How the hell could I say no to her?"

I nodded in agreement though I didn't agree at all. How do you say no? With the word, *no*. You show some respect for yourself and Liz and your relationship, and you say *no*.

With his eyes back on the road, he said, "I'd had a ton of vodka and wasn't thinking straight. Liz was coming in from New York the next afternoon, so it wasn't the smartest move, but…what do you do?" He paused for a moment, shaking his head. "So Tela came over and we had a good time. It's kind of fun screwing a girl you've been watching in movies for years. Like I knew her before I knew her. The next morning, I was ripping a line in my bedroom and Tela was in my shower when Liz walked in."

"You're kidding me," I said. I wanted to punch Jack in the face, bury his cockiness behind black eyes and broken bones.

"I swear. I heard Liz say my name and I ran into the bathroom and locked the door. Opened the shower door to warn Tela. She's butt-ass naked, fine as hell, running her little fingers through her hair, shampooing. At first she thought I was joining her. Until I shut off the water. I had to beg her to stay in there, soaking wet, and not say a word. I'm telling you, Trav, not my finest moment. She never really said she'd stay in there, but I closed the door on her. Had no time. I went back into the bedroom. Liz was waiting on me. She jumped into my arms."

He stopped talking to concentrate on weaving by a patch of slow traffic. I couldn't stop feeling sorry for Liz. How was the world so unfair to allow Liz to get caught up in all this evil?

"This is getting bad," I said, hoping the story would end soon.

"It gets worse. Liz took my robe off and then dropped her clothes onto the floor. The girl had missed me. Tela's ten feet and two walls behind me. Liz asked if I was getting ready to take a shower, you know, since she heard the water running. I said yes and she said she wanted to take one with me, that she felt dirty from the plane."

I fought the images forcing themselves into my mind's eye.

"I knew I was busted. She pulled me into the bathroom and I'm not kidding you, put her hand on the shower door. Started to pull it open. I was dying inside. Had to listen to that little peel of the black rubber strip slowly pulling away." Jack laughed. "Then just as the door cracked, her phone rang. She let go of the handle and went back into the bedroom. I opened up the shower door. Tela was in the corner with her hands covering her tits. She mouthed to me that she wanted a towel and I just held up my finger, telling her to wait."

He passed another group of cars with a heavy foot and then kept going with the story. "It was one of her friends here in town, asking her to go wakeboarding. Liz asked me if I minded. Of course I didn't. I thought I was off the hook, but she ended up back in the bathroom in her bikini getting ready for another twenty minutes. I was sitting on the lip of the tub talking to her about trivial *blah*, and Tela was a couple feet away behind the wall of the shower. I can't tell you how miserable I was. Then Liz saw the remnants of some cocaine, and I had to listen to her bitch for ten minutes. She ended up leaving without finding Tela, though."

That was the day I met her. I couldn't believe I hadn't figured this out. To put this man in jail would only begin to satisfy the rage that was building up inside of me.

"That afternoon," Jack continued, his speech quickening, "I went straight to the diamond display at Geiss and Sons. I needed to get a ring on her finger. Lock her down. I spent a fortune and went back home to propose to her after she'd finished wakeboarding. She was waiting on me." He hit the steering wheel. "Dropped one of Tela's earrings on the counter. A little dream catcher. That was it. I couldn't even lie anymore. She wouldn't let me. Saw right through me. Said the only reason she was still there was to make it very clear to me that we were over. I started backpedaling, telling her whatever she needed to hear, but she wasn't buying it.

"In some kind of desperate plea, I pulled out the ring and offered it to her. I opened the box. Asked her to marry me. Completely pathetic and absurd, I know, but I was throwing out anything I could. She took the box and ring and walked out to the balcony. Threw it as far as she could into the marsh. Poof. Then she turned around, walked up to me, and slapped me. As she started to walk to the elevator, I jerked her back around and slung her against the wall. Hard. Almost punched her."

I fought hard in that passenger seat not to swing at him at that moment. I clenched my fists, but tried to tame the beast inside. I cracked the window, hoping it would help. If I messed up now, everything would have been a waste of time.

He laughed again. "Liz is not the kind of girl that takes that shit. Came back swinging. I locked her arms up. Thought about playing the famous actress card, telling her it was Tela who I'd slept with. As if that might make some kind of difference. I never did tell her, though. Let her go and watched her walk out of my life.

"She had all her paintings taken out of my shop the next day. Ruined me. Really hurt the gallery. Hurt my reputation. I didn't see her for a long time. Until I ran into her on King Street a couple weeks back. She still wasn't happy with me." He shook his head. "It really pisses me off that she's with someone else. Soon as I find out who, I'll kill him. Or have him killed. Seriously." He reached for his bag of poison again.

"How'd you leave it the last time?"

"She's done. Wouldn't even really look me in the eyes. Doesn't give a shit about me anymore. Fuck her, you know. Just another drop in the bucket."

I'd never hated someone so much in my life. Not even the man who'd murdered my father. No matter what he said, though, I still needed to see her again. I had to believe she'd never really loved him. After all, I'd learned the hard way. We can all be fooled. One word: Stephanie.

I knew I'd see Liz again. But would she care?

Would Liz ever forgive me?

CHAPTER 26

Jack's cabin stood in the woods, about five miles from the ocean and down a half-mile long driveway. If something went wrong, I was on my own.

A huge raised deck with rocking chairs and two grills looked out over his property. Inside, deer and elk heads hung on the walls, staring back at you, and a bearskin rug covered the living room floor. After tearing into some Melvin's barbecue sandwiches that Ronnie had brought, we cut the cocaine, mixing it with a concoction of Vitamin C powder and some local anesthetic. Then we bagged it. Powder covered the table and our clothes.

A newscaster on television spoke about a Hugoesque hurricane season, something about high temperatures and low pressure. There was already one called Henrietta working its way north.

I was sitting next to Kado. We'd worked out our problems, and I'd forgiven him. Not that I had a choice. As he weighed out an ounce, he said to Jack, "Hope you've got some good insurance, Riles, 'cause between your boat and the condo, you'd lose your ass. You know we're due for one. It's been more than fifteen years since Hugo."

"Bring it on. I've got plenty. It's costing me, though."

"Costing your dad," Ronnie challenged, trying to draw a laugh.

Jack stopped what he was doing and glared at Ronnie. "Not true. The old man's cut me off. The prick's gonna make me wait until he dies before I see another dime." He reached over the table to grab a baggie, and a drop of blood fell from his nose onto the powder below him.

Ronnie pointed. "Shit, Riles, you just Jap-flagged a kilo!"

He wiped his nose and looked at the blood. "It's been happening lately."

"That could be a sign of a problem, no? Maybe you should take a few weeks off."

"I'm fine." He stood and took a paper towel off the roll and cleaned himself up. He sat back down and scooped the tainted powder into the trash can, saying, "You guys need to get off my back."

"C'mon," Ronnie said, "don't let that hag ride ya." This was something Jack and his crew always said, and one of the guys back at the office had told me what it meant. Gullahs are a group of African-Americans in South Carolina that have deep African roots and a nearly Creole culture. According to Gullah legend, Boo Hags are creatures similar to vampires, but instead of sucking your blood, they suck your breath. The Gullahs call it ridin.' *Don't let the hag ride ya.* Jack and his crew had taken on the phrase and used it in their own way.

We finished our business and then sat in rocking chairs on the porch passing around a pitcher of margaritas and an elk rifle. The tin roof shielded us from the blistering sun, but I was still sweating. Kado had set up metal squares down the driveway at increments beyond 250 yards, and Jack and I put down money on who was a better shot. We were shooting his Weatherby .300 Win. Mag., something he used for big game in Africa. He had skills. We both passed 350 yards before he finally missed. With confidence, I took the gun from him and hit the target.

LOWCOUNTRY PUNCH

"You're good," he said to me, eyeing my damage with binoculars. Fury cooked his being.

I shucked the shell and smiled.

***

Jack let me stay the night in one of the guest rooms back at his condo. He left early the next morning to get some work done at his gallery, telling me I could stick around his place for a while. I couldn't turn that down. I invited Baroni over, thinking it was an opportune time to wire the place.

While I waited, I took in the last of the sunrise from a chair on the balcony. It was the kind of vision that makes your eyes water. Downtown Charleston stood across the water and, down below, a group of thirty or forty Lasers sailed in a tight swarm near the *Yorktown*. A harbor pilot led a container ship under the bridge and out to sea.

Much like my love for a woman, my love for the place I live usually dwindles after a while. It had happened in D.C. and Charlottesville and Miami, but it had not happened with Charleston. I thought about all the ghosts who hid in the daylight and danced around at night, spirits who had seen their city rise and burn and rise again. People who had loved Charleston so much so that they couldn't leave even after they died. I wondered if my great-grandfather was among them. Would I be? Though I hadn't grown up in this city, somehow I knew I would leave my bones in the dirt there, if nothing else.

Baroni and a rook named Spock showed up in civilian clothes wearing backpacks. Spock was only a couple years out of school and had just gotten married that April with a baby on the way. He had that rookie strut in his step, the one you have for a few years before realizing that fighting the drug war isn't always what it's cracked up to be. He kept his blonde hair shaved short, and his ears stuck out more than usual. That's where he got his name.

Spock was the tallest guy in our office but couldn't have weighed more than 170.

Taking off his backpack, he said, "Stay away from Baroni this morning. I wouldn't stop at Starbucks, and he's like a little girl when he doesn't get his way. It's bad enough I gotta put up with him sucking down Merits all day."

Baroni shook his head. "You wanna get to work, rookie? Don't forget I'm your boss. Don't get too comfortable with that little mouth of yours."

"What happened with Atlanta?" I interrupted.

Baroni shook his head in disgust at Spock, then said to me, "Not bad work, Reddick. Maybe your shit don't stink." He gave me the details on the thugs Jack and I had met. The Atlanta DEA would take it from there and see if they could climb a little further up the tree. No matter how far they got, those men would most likely be arrested the same day as Jack and Ronnie in a nationwide roundup.

They moved from the kitchen to the living room, installing the audio equipment. As they finished each mic, they would call down to an agent across the street with their Motorola push-to-talks to confirm that they were functional.

Baroni climbed onto a chair and began to put a mic in the vent over the living room. Chester's voice came over the Motorola. "Boys, Ronnie's on his way up. Came in the back way. He just pushed the button."

Baroni pulled the phone off his belt and said into it, "Today's not a good day to kid around, Chester."

"No joke. It looks like he parked up the road. I didn't see him."

As Baroni put the phone back in its holster, the vent cover fell onto the hardwood floor with a clash. I grabbed it and handed it to him. He pushed it back in and began to twist one of the screws.

"Get the first one in," I said. "That will hold it. I'll finish it later. Y'all need to get in that bedroom." I shook my head. "I can't believe this."

Baroni tightened the one screw and hopped off the chair. "We're going off the balcony…into the pool. I'm not taking any risks." He handed me the screwdriver and nails.

Spock was not into Baroni's idea and said, "Risks? I'm not jumping off the balcony! You crazy?"

"You bet your ass we are, boy. We're not blowing this investigation now. We can make it. I'm not gonna hide under a mattress all day."

Chester's voice came back over the phone. "He's in the elevator."

Baroni hopped off the couch and stuck a finger at Spock. "You're jumping with me. Don't give me any lip."

"Somebody's going to see us."

"What did I just say?" Spock and I followed him out onto the balcony. No one was down there. It was a little early for the frozen drink crowd.

I had an idea. "Let me tell 'em you are friends of mine. We can pull it off."

"Not going to happen." I liked how Baroni had taken control of the situation, and I decided to go with it. We had no time for arguments. Baroni dropped his backpack off the side of the balcony, and I peeked over and watched it fall four stories and hit the grass. It was a long way down. Spock dropped his on top of it. Baroni climbed over the railing. "Piece of cake."

"You're not going to make it," I said, suddenly panicking. "You need to go hide under the bed."

I think I could have made it, but Baroni was older and with that spare tire around his waist, it worried me. But Baroni wasn't listening.

He bent his knees and pushed off the railing. I held my breath. I'm sure Spock did, too. I could barely watch. Baroni needed to make it about ten yards away from the building, or he would land right on the pool deck and break bones. He drew his legs in toward his chest and splashed into the water, clearing by a foot.

Spock climbed over and I said, "You don't have to do this. It's absurd."

"If he can do it, I can do it."

I wasn't sure that was true. "Then get on with it. Let's see what you got." I saw Ronnie come around the corner. I looked back at Spock. "There he is. You gotta go."

He looked at me; his eyes were watering. Poor guy wasn't going to make it. He bent his legs and pushed off. Oh, God, it was going to be painful. I heard the balcony door slide open behind me and turned around. I can't imagine what my face looked like as I said hello to Ronnie. Probably the opposite of what it would look like if I had won the lottery. I waited for Spock's scream as he hit the deck. I didn't hear a splash. I thought I heard a grunt and a thud.

"Where's Jack?" Ronnie asked, stepping out onto the balcony.

"Good to see you, too. He's working. I'm trying to get the motivation to drive back to Georgia. What you doin'?"

"I'm getting ready to run the bridge. Came by to see if he wanted to."

"He headed into work. Can I join you?"

"That's fine." This guy needed to relax. I put out my hand. "Look, I'm sorry about Savannah. I really am."

"That's all right." We shook. He approached the rail. I waited for him to say, "Hey, there's a dead Vulcan splattered on the deck below," but he didn't say anything. I took a peek over the edge. I couldn't believe it. No blood. No body.

Everything was under control. For now.

CHAPTER 27

I decided to stay in Chucktown another night. When Steve called and asked how things were going, I said, "Real good. I think Ronnie's warming up to me."

"Good, good. I want you back in Savannah for the next few, all right?"

"Yes, sir."

The last thing I wanted to do was drive to Georgia. Since when did I do what I was supposed to do, anyway? Steve just says stuff; he doesn't really mean it.

A few minutes into relaxing in a chair and chasing Nirvana, my friend from Nashville called. "Reddick, Simontacchi here." He's the one who found me the backstage tickets. "How goes it?"

"Man, you wouldn't believe half of it."

"That's what you always say."

"It's always true."

"I bet. You got time for a beer?"

"Sure." I walked to the fridge. Every few weeks, Scott Simontacchi and I drank a beer together while we spoke on the phone. An odd yet fitting ritual, one that kept our souls and songwriting spirits strumming the same rhythms. I cracked into a Sol and plopped down on the rocking chair out back. The wind that pushed through was as comforting as a woman's arms. I lay back and let the rocker put me in a good place.

"So how's Nashville treating you?"

"Nashvegas is treating you and me like kings. RCA bought 'Smokin.'"

"What!" I popped up to my feet. Occasionally, our creative muses would lead us into the realm of writing catchy country tunes, and when we did, they weren't half bad. I'd catch myself singing them even months later:

> *She left me smokin' in the rain,*
> *With nothin' but my hat and boots on*
> *Now all I feel is pain*
> *The only one I love is long gone*

That January, I had written the first couple lines of the verse and sent it to Scott by way of e-mail. He returned an MP3 with his ideas for the chords and a few more lines. We went back and forth like that for two days, and when we were done, we knew it was a special tune. That didn't always guarantee a deal, though.

"No lie. RCA bought it. Don't even know who is going to sing it yet."

"Papers signed?"

"Not yet, but it's a done deal. Trust me." Scott went on to tell me the details. We reveled in glory for a while, and then I let him go.

A little phrase and melody popped into my head. *Many miles, many women, and many moons.* What did that mean? No, not a testimony to the many conquests I've had along the way. Sure, I've been accused of being a pompous ass, but it's not really something that I'm known for.

So what did these words mean to me? Many miles, many women, and many moons. They were what it took for me to get over the women who'd broken my heart. It's not just time that heals all wounds. It's time and distance and women. The three components to healing. My recipe.

Many miles, many women, and many moons later,
I'm still thinking about you, baby, like it was yesterday.

Ah, my tragic love life. Though it was tragic, it fed my writing muse, and without all these mostly wonderful women in my life, my instruments would be lonely and silent pieces of wood. I went back into the living room and took my guitar off its stand. I sang a little of my tune and settled on G minor. I don't have the range of Sting, so the old Martin has to work with my voice.

She and I worked together until the last word had been written, late into the night. The Sol had somehow turned to wine and then to rum, and the next thing I knew, the clock had nearly ticked off the wall, and I was seeing elephants. I left the Martin on the couch and made my way to bed, this little tune stuck in my head.

I took my phone and found Liz's number. Nearly called her but somehow found enough logic to change my mind.

***

Songwriting is cathartic for me, but it also digs up some bad memories. They wouldn't let me sleep.

For years after my father was murdered, I was angry. Depressed, enraged, hateful. Despite the support of my friends and family, I couldn't see past what had happened. I couldn't shake the memory. I became something uncontrollable. I would lose my temper—great episodes where I just snapped, whether it would be at my mother or brother or my first serious girlfriend, Julia. That was ultimately what had done us in, two high school lovebirds trying to pretend that death hadn't destroyed our path together.

I remember the night she left me. She'd finally had enough. I was a third year at UVA and despite the rest of my life being in shambles, I was still playing some good soccer. My father, I knew, continued to watch over me. We were in Maryland at Byrd stadium playing the Terrapins, and they had fallen behind us by one in the ACC standings; it promised to be one hell of a game. I remember Julia and my mom wrapped up in blankets in the second row of the visitor's seats.

We were a few minutes into the second half and tied with two each. Both teams were on edge, and there was a good bit of talking, cheap shots, and jersey pulling going on. They had a corner kick and knocked the ball into the air. Our keeper, Nate, my roommate at the time, went up for it. He got his hands around the ball, but their striker clipped him in the back of the legs and flipped him upside down. Nate landed on his head and went unconscious. It was a cheap hit, and I lost it. Way beyond what I'd ever felt before.

I swung the striker into the goal post, and started pummeling him on the ground. In minutes, both teams were going at it, and then the fans joined the fray. I put one guy in the hospital. It was the last game of my life. I was kicked off the team that night.

I found Julia in the parking lot after the fight, and I remember the look of horror on her face. She told me I had something wrong with me and that it was over, and she got back in her car and drove home. She'd had enough. I'd been a selfish, insensitive bastard for way too long and that night had been the breaking point. Now, years later, we still haven't spoken.

And now I'd lost Liz, and it was nobody's fault but mine.

I sat up to reach for some water. That's when I noticed the picture of Stephanie and me on my bedside table. I blinked my eyes. Was I really that drunk? I was one hundred percent sure I didn't own a picture of the two of us.

I put my hands on it, though, and it was real. I shook my

head. "What am I gonna do with you?" I tossed it to the floor and huffed and puffed for a little while.

She'd tricked me that day when I was changing her tire, and she may have had accomplices. I'm no pushover. She'd been the exact opposite. So cool, laid-back. Smart. She could have fooled anyone. She would have fooled you.

CHAPTER 28

The next morning, with one beast of a hangover, I threw on some shorts and my Washington Redskins T-shirt and went out into the heat. Started a nice jog. Ran through a nearby neighborhood along the water. Nearly felt normal again.

I was thinking about the rest of the day when I felt something. A little stir in the natural order of things.

Someone was staring at me. Watching me. Something.

I turned my head just in time. Behind me, fifty yards off, a rifle and scope were pointing directly at me. The metal of the scope shined brightly in the sunlight. The person was in a blue sedan, sitting in the driver's seat, getting ready to take a cheap shot at me from behind. I dropped to the ground just as I heard the first report. He missed.

I stood, instincts taking over. The houses near me had tall chain-link fences on either side, so I didn't want to explore that route. There was a bridge not too far off. I sprinted in zigzags down the road, heading in that direction. He took two more shots but missed. Then I heard his car engine roaring. He was coming for me. Trying to run me over. I ran onto the sidewalk. He sped up. The bridge wasn't much further. I ran for it. He pulled up onto the sidewalk. Got closer and closer to me. I turned and caught a glimpse of the driver. He wore a mask. He was twenty feet away and gaining.

LOWCOUNTRY PUNCH

I tripped over a piece of broken sidewalk and skidded onto my left side. The cement tore at my skin but I knew that I had to keep moving. I could almost feel his bumper on my back.

I didn't have time to stand, so I scurried on all fours toward a tree planted in a square of dirt next to the sidewalk. Right as I got my legs behind the trunk, he hit it. The tree split two feet up from the roots but it stopped the momentum of the car. He backed up as I returned to my feet. Ran like hell. By the time he was moving toward me again, I had reached the bridge. I jumped over the rail. Dropped fifteen feet into the river. I popped back up and saw the car door opening. I dove under. The first bullet hit the water. Fizzled past me. I kicked as hard as I could and went deeper. Then changed direction. Opened my eyes. The saltwater burned. I couldn't see much more than a foot or two in front of me. I began to move along the bottom. Ten seconds. Twenty seconds. Thirty seconds. A minute.

I didn't want to pop up to grab a breath. That's what he was waiting for. A little potshot, like an arcade game. If he could guess which way I was moving. But I couldn't hold my breath much longer. I started pawing at the mud below me, moving as fast as I could. Rays of sunlight showed the bottom as it became shallower. I put my feet into the mud. They sank some. But I began to run as I reached three feet of water. Didn't look back once.

Ran out of the water and dove into the marsh grass, which was several feet high. Landed right on an oyster bed, and the shells cut my legs and arms. I didn't feel it, though. I carefully pushed myself off the shells and got to my feet in a crouched position. I looked back and didn't see him on the bridge. Didn't see his car either. I'd swum about sixty yards. I moved forward into someone's yard, trudging through the grass and mud, stepping in the places that looked like they wouldn't swallow my shoes.

I started running again once I hit solid ground. Mud, water, and blood dripped down my legs. My lungs burned but I didn't stop for two miles.

Finally made it back to my house. I burst into the door, no energy left. Locked the doors. I couldn't have made it much further. First I found my Benelli and my nine. Checked the house. It was empty. Then dialed Chester. He didn't answer his phone. I went upstairs. Put some jeans and a T-shirt on. My cuts were still bleeding but I wasn't too worried about it. The adrenaline in my body had begun to ebb and I started getting pissed off.

I wanted to know who was behind it. And I didn't want people getting in the way. So I didn't call the police. I like to clean up my own messes.

I've got a few enemies and I decided to call one of them. Just putting some feelers out.

"How's it going?" Jack asked, very nonchalantly, from his newest disposable phone. "You on a clean line?"

"Yeah," I said. "Just checking in."

"I was about to call you. You in town?"

"No, down here in Savannah," I lied.

"You still coming over for Friday night's get-together? Trust me, you're gonna want to be here. I throw the finest parties in South Carolina."

"That's what I've heard."

"You in?"

"I'm planning on it."

"I need you there. We gotta meet Edgar Winter." He sometimes called cocaine Edgar Winter, after the albino musician.

"The same night?"

"Yeah, some things changed with the delivery. We'll just leave the party for a little while. Won't take long."

"All right. Count me in."

"If you want to come up tomorrow, we're gonna head over to Tela's set at Magnolia Plantation. She said we could come watch them film. Could be fun."

LOWCOUNTRY PUNCH

I told him I'd be there and bid farewell. I had other business to attend to at the moment.

It definitely didn't sound like Jack was behind my attack. He wouldn't have played it that cool. And if he knew nothing, Ronnie didn't know anything, either. They shared their secrets. Kado was still a possibility. After pulling off the lie of the century apropos Liz and me, he was capable of anything. I decided to go see him.

Kado lived downtown on Limestone Street in an old Charleston mansion that had been converted into apartments. He had the whole third floor. The building was too old to have an elevator, so I climbed the worn-out stairs. At the top of the stairwell was a window. I pulled it up and climbed out. I stepped onto the ledge and shimmied along the side of the building toward his balcony. I would enter a world of pain if I fell. Last time I'd been there, I noticed a corner of Kado's balcony screen was torn. I stepped off the ledge onto the balcony, bent down under the screen, and snuck in. Then I opened the unlocked balcony door leading into his apartment.

I found him in bed, snoring. Didn't even bother waking him. Went out the front door, satisfied he hadn't tried to kill me. If he'd been behind it, he wouldn't be sleeping right now.

Still fueled by fury, I tried to rationalize who it might be. Eliminating Jack, Ronnie, and Kado had been necessary. Now that I had, only one person really made sense. He'd already tried for me once. Any man with some sense of deduction would have made the same assumption.

Tux Clinton was a dead man.

CHAPTER 29

What had given Tux the idea that he could mess with me again? You know, I get it. He's gotta be a man. Stand up for his cousin. Look good in front of his people. But bad idea, Tux. I wasn't taking this lightly. Don't make things personal. Don't come attack me in my own neighborhood.

I was fuming as I climbed into my Jeep with my nine. Headed straight to the highway. I really hoped he was going to be home. Nothing was on my mind but hitting him. I didn't care if I went to jail for this. Didn't care if I lost my job. Liz had gone running on that road with me. What if she had been with me? Tux needed to pay.

I pulled into his driveway. Seeing his BMW made it more real. I went up the steps and kicked the door open, the lock shredding the wood. I heard a voice and went in that direction. There was a faint smell of something cooking in the microwave. His whole house seemed to be green inside. The walls. The furniture. There was a sculpture of a shark's head on the mantle.

Tux came around the corner. I didn't care that he was bigger than me. I didn't say a word. Breathing loudly, I went up to him and punched him in the stomach. He doubled over but didn't fall.

"You send people to my neighborhood to kill me," I said.

"What did I tell you about that?" I pushed him and he fell back onto the shag carpet.

"What are you talking about? I didn't send anybody your way." He started to stand, and I kicked him in the side. He fell back down. I was starting to piss him off. Went to kick him again, but he grabbed my leg. Twisted it. I fell down on top of him. He got to his knees and elbowed me in the face. My head cocked back.

Somehow, he took the advantage. The guy could throw down. I tried to sit up. He punched me in the temple. Then punched me again, harder, with the force of his body behind it. I blacked out for a second. Long enough for him to stand. He took my arm and dragged me across the room toward the front door. I was still dizzy and couldn't break free. He dragged me out the door and onto the porch. Pulled me down the first couple steps, and then I rolled down the rest, landing at the bottom on the cement. As I get older, those kinds of things hurt.

He did all the talking, standing there above me. "I don't know what happened with you, but you messed up. I haven't even thought about you in a while. You need to learn who your enemies are. If I had come after you, you wouldn't be here. Bet your ass, that. Now get the hell off my property. You brought this on yourself."

He left me there at the bottom of the steps. I didn't have enough in me to retaliate. Not that I could have. I really didn't want to get back in my car and run away like a man defeated, either. But I had been beat and needed to respect it. He'd bested me. Grabbing my gun would have been a pansy's move.

Besides, I didn't think he was lying. I've been interrogating people for a long time, and I can read innocence, from a person's tone to their mannerisms to their eye movements. I didn't know who else it could be, but Tux hadn't been behind it. I'd attacked him for no reason and probably deserved to get my ass kicked.

Still, it didn't feel good. It wasn't the first time and it

wouldn't be the last, but I didn't like it at all. I moved slowly to my feet and started walking to the Jeep. I climbed inside and as I put her in reverse I looked up at his house. He was holding back a curtain, looking at me. I gave him a look that said we'd meet again. He let go of the curtain and I backed out of his driveway.

I scrolled through a list of other possibilities. It couldn't be Stephanie. Baroni didn't like me but I doubted he was out to get me. Diego Vasquez? Hell, any person I'd put behind bars could be after me.

***

Chester finally called me back on my way to Savannah. I'd given up finding my attacker for the moment. No way I was sleeping in my Charleston house tonight, and I needed a good night's sleep. Getting chased and shot at and beat all in the span of a few hours takes its toll.

No, I didn't tell him about my attack and what happened with Tux. I'd changed my mind. I needed more information before blabbing about that. Didn't want word getting out and someone deciding to pull the Jack Riley case from me. I told him a shipment was coming in Friday night. We'd checked Jack's container orders with the importing company he used. He didn't have one coming in for another two weeks. So we ruled that possibility out. I'd already told Chester about Jack's party. He said he'd get word to Steve. I got off the phone, excited about our opportunity. We were about to hook onto a new source, but I had no idea how.

Steve called an hour later as I crossed the Georgia line. "We're rounding everybody up Friday night."

"What?"

"You say there's a meet?"

"That's what Jack told me."

"Why's he doing it during the party?"

"Said something changed and that's just how it has to happen. Probably something to do with the hurricane."

"Then we're gonna bust the meet and his party at the same time."

"I'm not on board with that."

"Tough. I'm under pressure, Reddick. No better way to sweep this Chad Rourke fiasco under the table than to make a widespread public arrest that includes this new source, Tela Davies and the Hollywood crew, and Jack Riley, James King, and most of their network. Everybody's gonna be there. It's too good of an opportunity to pass up."

"No way. Half of them won't even spend a week in jail. I'm not here to pin some waste-of-time possessions on people. We need to take it further."

"If you get this last source and he's as big as we think, we don't need to go any further."

"You're telling me this is all coming down to media coverage?"

"Doesn't it always? You can imagine the headlines."

"There's always a bigger fish, Steve."

"Yes, there is. But we're stopping here. We've made major progress. Tracked the Atlanta source all the way to Houston. You did good, Reddick. Atlanta. New Orleans. Houston. We didn't waste our time." He paused to let me say something but I was at a loss for words. Boneheaded bureaucracy strikes again.

"I've already informed the other offices," Steve said. "Coastal Snow ends Friday night. Arrests will be made across the country simultaneously. Don't fight it. You've impressed people. Don't cloud your new reputation. If you wanna work one last miracle, make sure this hurricane doesn't come our way."

"That shouldn't be too hard."

The other headache in my life was this hurricane running up the coast, and we were monitoring it closely. We'd been hearing about Hurricane Henrietta for a week now, ever since it had moved off the coast of Africa as a tropical storm and torn through the Caribbean, leaving millions of dollars in damage from Guadeloupe to Puerto Rico. Henrietta had run into a low-pressure system, and as a result, had taken a more northward track and was now two hundred miles off the coast of Fort Lauderdale. They expected the category 2 hurricane to scrape by Charleston in two days and make landfall near Cape Hatteras, North Carolina on the third day. But you never know with those things.

    I bitched to Steve for another few minutes, knowing it was pointless. He listened, letting me blow off some steam. We hung up as I pulled into a little motel outside of Savannah. I checked in and, taking no chances, spent the evening with my Beretta in my hand. I wouldn't let myself be caught off guard again.

CHAPTER 30

I'd accepted Jack's invitation to visit Tela on the set the next day, and as bad as I felt, I knew I still had to go. I didn't want to start backing out of invitations and losing ground with him. Nothing was over yet.

I arrived at the plantation in the late morning. Looking at the place made me remember how a guide described it when I was on a family carriage tour back when Will and I were kids. *Magnolia Plantation, built in 1676 by the Drayton family, is a key landmark of Charleston heritage.* That's about all I remembered. It was a long time ago.

"Here to see Tela Davies," I said to the guard as I pulled up to the plantation gate. He didn't bother standing up from his chair. I could have fit a week's worth of groceries in the bags under his eyes.

"We all are, aren't we?"

"It's not like that," I assured him.

"Uh-huh. I need to see your license."

I gave the guard my fake ID, and he scrolled down the clipboard. "Moody, Moody...Here it is." He handed me a laminated pass on a lanyard. "Hang that around your neck."

"Security is tight over here today."

"Try walking around without that thing and see what happens.

You'd think the president was in there."

"I don't think I'll test it." I put the lanyard around my neck.

"You're a lucky man. What I'd do to—"

"You don't have any sort of history on the plantation, do you? A pamphlet or something?" He dug one up and handed it to me. I pulled away.

Oak trees stood on either side of the dirt road and hanging moss brushed the top of my truck as I passed. I had my window down and my arm out. Fall had cooled the air, and it was the kind of day you just want to kick back on the porch and listen to Amos Milburn. Tap your feet. Let the breeze blow. Leave it all behind for a little while.

Eventually the woods opened up into a large field with old slave houses still standing and a saltwater river running in the background. With the help of a stranger dressed in Confederate garb, I found Tela's trailer.

She peeked through the window to the left of the door and then opened it. She wore a white robe, her hair was in curlers, and her eyes were the kind of blue that had been chipped off a glacier.

"Hi, sugar. Please come in." I started to enter and she said, "Uh, I can't get enough of you. I could just devour you...like a piece of salted caramel."

I cocked my eyebrow. It was a good thing I'd showered.

"You're the first one here, darling." She kissed me on the cheek. "Sorry I'm not dressed. I'm waiting for makeup."

"That's fine. You look good in sort of a housewife kind of way."

"At it again, are we? You do like your games."

I laughed. "I have no idea what you're talking about. You really do have an imagination."

"I'm an actor. That tends to be part of the gig." There was a bouquet of fresh flowers and a tray of fruit on the table. She reached into the fridge, saying, "Have a seat." I sat on one end of the ultrasuede couch. She tossed me a bottle of Evian. As I opened it, she plopped down next to me, very close.

Her energy filled the trailer, and I felt vulnerable. She undressed me with her eyes.

"I really thought you would break down and call me."

"Sorry, I don't have your number."

"I'll change that right now." She fished out her phone.

"You've got it bad, don't you?"

"You're going to get slapped again if you're not careful."

"I'm really glad I came."

"Hush. Now what's the number?" I gave it to her, and she mentioned they were going to Savannah soon to film a few scenes.

She pulled a tray from under the couch. There was a pile of white powder on it. "Would you care for some?"

"No, thanks."

She took a little bump using the edge of a credit card and then slid the tray back under the couch.

A knock on the door. Tela stood to answer it. As she did, the belt of her robe came undone, and she turned toward me, revealing a glimpse of her fully nude front—her large breasts and the dark pelt of brown hair below her waist. I tried to divert my eyes, but it wasn't easy. She reached over and touched my face and slowly covered back up, cinching the belt tight. As she went for the door, I downed the bottle of water and adjusted in my seat, saying over and over to myself, *Liz, Liz, Liz, Liz, Liz...* I still missed her.

The makeup artist came in with a toolbox. She wore some kind of wild Hollywood hairstylist hairdo and big dangly earrings.

As she went to work with hairspray and a brush, Tela said to her, "He's a handsome one, isn't he, Shari? I told you so."

Shari studied me as if I was a sculpture on display. "He sure is."

"I haven't quite been able to sink my teeth into him, but I

think I'm getting somewhere. He likes to think he's hard to get."

I asked Shari, "Have you ever met a man she doesn't flirt with?"

"Honey, she flirts with everybody, but I can tell when she really likes someone. I think you're it. And she gets what she wants. I wouldn't fight it."

Tela looked at me. *"See."*

I put my palms up. "What am I supposed to do about it?"

That ended up being the wrong question.

Tela hopped up out of her seat and walked over to me. Right in front of Shari, she untied her belt and opened her robe to show me the goods again. She sat on my lap, facing me, her robe flapping loosely to her sides. "You're a big boy. I think you know what you're supposed to do."

"I don't want to mess up your hair." I looked over at Shari. Tela snapped my head back with her hands. "Don't worry about her. She's seen it all. Haven't you?"

"All of it," Shari responded. "I'll be outside."

Tela held my head in her hands and put those blue eyes to use. "See."

"It's not her I'm worried about." Shari was the least of my worries at that moment. Are you kidding me? I barely heard her walk out.

Tela ran her hand along my stubble. "I kind of wish you were playing Chad Rourke's role. You'd be wonderful in front of a camera. So charming. We could make a great movie together. You can't fake energy like this. Let me take you back to Hollywood, show you what I mean."

"I don't think so, honey. I'm flattered but I don't know if I could handle it."

She lowered her voice and whispered, "Well, you're mine until I say otherwise. You understand me?"

Well, I understood, but it was complicated. I tried to summon all the good in me, all the lessons I'd learned in church growing up, and I tried to say, "Tela, get off. I'm not interested." But damn if it wasn't difficult. I couldn't say it. I dug deeper, and just as some words like that started to leave my mouth, she had her lips to mine and...

Another knock. She gave me a peck on the cheek and stood up. Once she had collected herself, she went to the door. When Jack walked in, I hadn't quite pulled it together.

"You're here early," he accused, glaring at me.

"The drive was shorter than I remembered."

"Uh-huh."

I probably looked like I had just climbed out of a clothes dryer. I crossed my legs.

"Where's Ronnie?" I asked.

"Couldn't make it. He's hanging out with that new girl. A schoolteacher. He says he's falling in love."

"That won't last," I said.

"I guess it happens to everybody eventually." Jack turned to Tela. "How are you doing, sweetheart?"

"A little hot and bothered. If you'd come ten minutes later, I might have gotten lucky." I pretended like I didn't hear that, and Jack didn't say anything, either.

She asked, "Are you still having your soirée tomorrow night?"

"Of course we are. I don't run from hurricanes." He sat on the other side of the couch and said, "I have a favor to ask of you. I brought someone. He's at the gate. Wanted to see if you would call his name in."

"Sure. Who is it?"

"Kado."

"That grimy little bastard! There's no way."

"Do this for me, please. He feels terrible and wants to apologize. He's a good friend. He made a mistake." Of course, they were referring to the incident in the pool. I didn't know whose side to take on that one. Tela could certainly stir up trouble.

She wasn't happy about it but made a phone call, and Kado

came in the door several minutes later. Jack had been quite persuasive. I didn't like it at all. Jack had gone out of his way for Kado, and something like that would make him feel bad about ratting. It might make him crack. Tela kind of accepted Kado's apology. Shari came back in and finished her makeup, and then we followed them to the set.

Ten cameras, fifty-something members of cast and crew, and a group of spectators. We spoke with her agent and Jason Corey. Tela introduced us to the director. The movies I'd seen of his weren't bad, but he was a strange dude and as artsy-fartsy as I'd ever seen. An Afghan shawl was wrapped around his neck, which looked odd with his cargo shorts. Not to mention the heat.

Tela went over toward the river in front of the cameras. She wore an old frock, still looking spectacular. Shari did some last-minute touch-ups to her hair. Someone let her sip from a drink. From his stance near one of the cameras, the director told everyone to be quiet.

We stood next to Jason, who explained what was going on. He whispered like we were waiting for a golfer to hit his ball. "Tela's just traveled back in time and is trying to figure out where she is. A ghost that they'll draw in later will come off the river and begin to chase her. In a second, you'll hear a scream blast out of those speakers." He pointed up into a tree. "It's all she has to work with. It's supposed to help her find her fear."

The director raised his hand and called action. Tela walked to the water, looking out across the marshland. She turned around, as if trying to find her bearings. The scream came and made us all jump. It sounded like an alien screaming through a tube compressor with a hint of reverb.

Tela jerked around toward the sound and took off in the opposite direction. The director cut the take, and with a strong English accent yelled, "1852, Tela, *1852*! You just traveled 150 years back in time. You did more than go down the freaking mountain, which is what you're impressing upon me now. Where are you today?"

Tela glanced at me and headed back out in front of the cameras. I felt like everyone saw her look my way. The director certainly did and twisted his head toward me.

"Do we have a distraction?" he asked. "I don't have time for this today. I don't have time for your little love things."

"Hardly," Tela said. "Calm down!"

He glared at us. "I'm sure you're fine chaps, but I have to ask you to leave. We have a great deal to do today, and I need Tela's full attention. I'm sorry, gentlemen."

We looked at each other and then back at the director. I waved my hand. "Sorry to trouble you."

"No need to apologize. Come 'round another day."

"Sorry, boys." Tela came across the grass. Everyone on the set watched her move. "He thinks he has to babysit me. Can we do it another day?"

"If it's all right with bossman," I said.

"That's funny." She put her hand on my waist and kissed my lips. It happened fast.

"Now, call me or I'll be furious. 'K, darling?"

"We'll see." I watched her strut back toward the cameras.

***

"You still claiming you're not sleeping with her?" Jack asked as we got back to our cars. "You sticking to that?"

"Haven't seen her since the last time you did."

"Right." Jack hopped into his Rover.

Kado and I got into my truck, and we headed back into town. As we drove off, he started saying he couldn't do this any longer. That Jack didn't deserve it. My blood was boiling as I listened to him, and it had nothing to do with my brief rendezvous with the woman from Hollywood. I had to choose my words carefully and stay away from calling Kado names and popping him in the face, which is what I really wanted to do.

"You don't want to go to jail," I said. "Jack would do the same thing to you, and so would Ronnie. You need to stay strong, buddy."

"Don't patronize me. This shit's not easy."

"No, it's not. What you're feeling right now happens. I see it all the time. Don't let it get the best of you. Don't crack at the last minute. You don't want to go to jail."

"I don't wanna be a rat. My dad didn't raise me to be this way."

I thought about a poster hanging in our office. It's a cartoon of a rat with the Superman emblem on his chest. Below him reads, *Rats are the real heroes*. Kind of a joke but it cracked us up.

I said to Kado, "Just the bad guys call 'em rats. We call 'em born-agains. You're saving your own life. Trust me, your dad would be on your side."

"My dad wouldn't want me in a body bag."

"No one's putting you in a body bag, believe me. We're all over these guys."

"I don't think so. I think he's figuring it out."

I snapped my fingers in his face. "Look at me." I snapped them again and he looked over.

"He's not figuring it out unless you tell him. You're one of the best CIs I've ever worked with, and I believe in you." I had to feed him something. "Tonight's the last time. You don't have to see them again. You can leave town until the trial."

"What do you mean 'the last time?'"

"Your work is done. I'm taking over from here. We want you to leave town, take a vacation or something." I didn't want to tell him the truth: that we were making arrests tomorrow night.

He didn't say anything and I turned up the radio. Someone was on NPR jabbering about Henrietta. I didn't know what was the bigger problem: Kado or this nasty hurricane coming our way.

CHAPTER 31

I was at Jack's condo the next evening, the night of the bust. I had to be there because he hadn't told us how the next exchange was going down. Just about our entire field office was in the area. We had two Coast Guard vessels standing by in the harbor. Six radio cars and a SWAT team were in a parking lot a half-mile down Coleman Boulevard, prepared for anything. One group would follow Jack and me to the meet, and, once we had the source, another group would raid the party. Fortunately, half the people on the guest list were already targets of the operation.

We also had people in West Ashley, North Charleston, and John's Island. Teams also stood by in Atlanta, New Orleans, Houston, and Santa Fe. We needed to make the arrests simultaneously. Otherwise, people would get wind of what was happening and disappear. You'd be amazed at how fast news of raids travels across the country.

Altogether, as Steve had designed it, the arrests would dominate the news outlets in the morning, and the upper echelon of the Drug Enforcement Administration—or "the assholes" as I also like to call them—would be up on their top floors jerking each other off with glee and glory.

It was a little after eight and the guests were trickling in: people from the movie, friends of Jack's and James King's, others completely unknown. Quite a few were customers of Jack, Ronnie, and Kado, ones we'd collected information on over the course of the summer. Everyone had been approved by the two large bodyguards in the lobby below. Maybe fifty people so far, drinking champagne, making conversation, nibbling on food. They had no idea how bad their night was about to get.

As Jack had promised, it was one hell of a scene. There were tables with bags of cocaine and pills laid out like party favors. Marijuana joints were stacked like green beans on a platter.

Some interested guests stood around the muted television and waited for the latest updates on the hurricane. James King, the future politician and owner of the Mazyck, was telling a group about the voluntary evacuation that had been put into place and how no one listens to those anymore. Not a drop of rain had fallen, but my knee hurt, so I knew something was coming. My knee forecasts better than any knucklehead on the Weather Channel.

I was standing at one of the tables, filling up on the fine food Kado's chef from Morph had prepared. The hybrid rock sounds of a Seattle-based band flowed out of the speakers, and I liked it. After eating enough caviar to depopulate an ocean, I moved over toward the large pot of Frogmore Stew. I dipped the ladle in, hauling in a broth full of corn on the cob, shrimp, sausage, and Old Bay seasoning, the aroma rising into the air with the steam.

As I scooped a serving into my bowl, I caught a glimpse of Ronnie. Then I looked at the girl next to him. The sight of her almost made me spill everything onto my shirt. It wasn't her face that I recognized first, because she had come in disguise. It was the dress she wore that made me look twice: it was the same one she had worn on our date—our *only* date—and I remember it because she'd looked...well, flaming hot in it. It was a white, bareback kind of thing, cut low and high in all the right places.

Stephanie Lewis had dyed her brown hair blonde, her brown

eyes were now blue, and she wore way more makeup than usual; but it was her.

Ronnie spotted me and came over, tugging her hand behind him.

"Trav, I want you to meet someone." I set the bowl of stew down and wiped my hands.

He said, "This is Eve."

Her conniving little smile brought out her dimples as she stuck her hand out. I took it reluctantly. It was her, all right. Stephanie was now Eve. Her gold heels could have doubled for stilts.

"It's a pleasure. I'm Travis."

"I feel like we've met before," she admitted.

Oh, really, Stephanie? It's funny that you say that. I said, "Maybe so. My memory is not my strength."

"Are you an actor, too?" she asked.

"Hardly," I started. "A friend of Jack's. So how do you and Ronnie know each other?" I couldn't wait to hear.

Ronnie stabbed a toothpick into a lobster bite. "It's kind of unbelievable. I was on the way to teach a lesson at the club, and she waved me down. She had a flat tire and needed help. Being the gentleman that I am—"

"*Gentleman?*" Stephanie interrupted. "Ha! Nothing like it. I had to walk right in front of your car. You almost hit me."

"Well, I thought you were one of the those club bunnies trying to hitch a ride. Soon as I got close enough to get a good look, though, I was happy to pull over."

"You should pull over for *anyone*, Ronniecakes. I know T.A. would."

"Who?" Ronnie asked.

"I mean, Travis." The look of surprise that had been on her face as my real name came out of her mouth told me she had not meant to say it.

"I don't know about that," I said. "I'm no gentleman." I made a mental note to never help anyone again. Not without doing a full background check, at least.

Ronnie held out a lobster bite, and she took it with her teeth, smiling at me. She was out of control. We talked and I hated it.

Ronnie excused himself to get drinks, asking if we wanted anything. Stephanie asked for a Mt. Gay and soda. I did the same. *More games.* That was my damn drink.

"What are you doing, Stephanie?" I asked, once he was out of earshot.

"It's Eve, and whatever do you mean? I can't date anybody? You're not over me yet?"

"You know *exactly* what I mean. You're looking at jail time."

"You're not going to start threatening me, are you, Travis? Or is it T.A.?"

"This ends now. You tell your friend you're not feeling well, and you get outta here." I was watching the room behind her and through the crowd I saw Jack. He was dressed like he'd been planning on what to wear for this night for three weeks. Knowing him, he probably had. He wore linen pants, pressed, and a shirt that few could pull off outside of Ibiza. He was moving our way. *Why not? Let's get everybody together.*

"I heard you've been tying loose knots," she continued. "Lost a boat, did you?"

"I want you out of here."

"C'mon, this is fun. You're not trying to put my new man in jail, are you?" Stephanie pivoted and looked back toward the room with me as we talked.

"You'll be the first behind bars," I whispered. Someone stopped Jack on his way over. Ronnie came back from the bar with drinks, and I knocked the whole thing back. I needed about six more.

Stephanie blurted out, "That's Tela Davies, isn't it?" Across the room, carried on angel's wings, Tela was making her grand entrance.

Let the games begin.

CHAPTER 32

"Yep, that's Tela," Ronnie said. "She has a little crush on Trav."

"Really?" Stephanie squeezed the lime into her drink and dropped the wedge in. "I can see why. He's cute."

"Not that cute," Ronnie came back.

Stephanie put her hand on his arm. "No need to worry, baby. He's a little too clean-cut for me." Someone tapped Ron on the shoulder. He turned and began to make conversation with them. Stephanie, standing right next to him, mouthed to me, "I miss you."

"Get out," I mouthed back.

She stepped very close to me and whispered in my ear, "I miss you soooo much." She reached for my zipper and found it quickly, pulling it down masterfully, like a pickpocket lifting a wallet. "Don't you miss us?"

"*Us?* That's funny." I pulled the zipper back up and looked around to see if anyone had noticed. No one had. It was a good, slick move. I really hoped Baroni's team outside couldn't hear the particulars of our conversation through the mic above us. Hopefully, the loudness of all the useless conversation covered up our own.

Jason Corey, the man who had replaced Chad Rourke, stood

up on a chair and began tapping a lighter against his champagne glass. Everyone gathered and shushed as he began to speak, his clenched fist in front of his face feigning a microphone. Every girl in the room was hot for him.

"I propose a toast," he said. "To Chad Rourke." Everyone raised their glass. "We'll never make this movie as good as he would have made it, but may it pay a worthy tribute to him. To Chad." We all raised our glasses.

Then everyone went back to their little conversations about the best shrimp and grits in town, their favorite spas in Europe, their new fur coat, whatever.

***

About a half an hour later, I practically bumped into Jack. He had a huge grin on his face.

"What's got you so perked up?" I asked.

"Nothing. I'm in a good mood, that's all." He'd already consumed too many drugs and too much booze. His words were slurred.

"No reason?"

"Love, Trav…love."

"Oh, yeah. Who is it this time?"

"You're getting ready to watch her walk right out of that elevator. Can't you feel it? Love is in the air. *El amor está en el aire.*"

"*Quién es la muchacha afortunada?*" I asked. I'd spent some time down in South America, too.

Before Jack replied, Tela slipped her hand under my arm. "You two look handsome tonight."

"And you look gorgeous, Ms. Davies." Jack kissed her other hand. Then she kissed me on the lips. She did look gorgeous. A light blue gown. More pearls. Looked like Shari had done a number to her hair, all tucked up intricately. Was she accepting an Oscar or what?

Jack didn't seem to care and then I found out why. He said, "Liz is on her way up."

"Oh, wonderful," Tela said sarcastically. "Shall I go hide in the shower?"

"Not funny at all," said Jack. "I do need you to steer clear of her, though. Is that possible?"

"Am I your little puppy dog?"

For a brief moment, I thought of taking Baroni's way off the balcony into the pool, but maybe headfirst. Oh yes, I had questions. Liz? Liz was coming over? Wasn't she in New York? Why was she coming? To see Jack? That thought pissed me off. My mind assaulted me with more questions. It was definitely time to go. I wasn't coming back in until I had a machine gun in my hands.

But before I could make a move, Liz came around the corner. She was underdressed in ripped jeans. Even though she was dressed casually, she owned the place and distracted several people from their conversations. I noticed Stephanie looking in her direction. I excused myself and jetted off.

Rounding a corner, I nearly slipped on the floor of the kitchen and barreled into a chubby chef slicing an avocado. *Jerry*, read the cursive on his shirt, above *Morph*. "Excuse me," I said, regaining my balance and positioning myself behind one of the walls.

"Good Lord, man," the chef said. "You look like the police are after you."

"Worse. A crazy woman."

"You want me to hit her in the head with a ham hock?" he asked, lifting one up. He seemed serious.

"It would really help me out."

"What's she look like?"

He was going to do it. "You know what? I appreciate the offer, but I better handle her myself."

"You sure? I don't mind."

"Next time."

The chef went back to chopping, and I took a peek around the corner. Liz and Jack were talking next to the couch. Tela and Stephanie were nowhere in sight. I put my back up against the wall and waited.

"Some strange game you're playing," the chef suggested, his knife hitting the cutting board repeatedly.

"You have no idea. You got anything to drink back here?" He'd been nipping on a bottle of Crown, and he poured some over ice for me.

A few minutes passed, and I looked again. Just as I turned my head around the corner, Stephanie almost knocked me down. "What on earth are you doing?" she asked. "I've never seen anything like it. Is someone out to get you? Do you want me to protect you?"

"Stephanie—"

"It's Eve, remember?"

"Eve, I don't have time for this. I thought you were taking off." I heard the chef stop chopping behind me, and part of me hoped he was reaching for that ham hock. Instead he stepped next to me and addressed Stephanie. "Hello, there. Are you one of the actors? You really look familiar. What have you been in?"

She ate up the compliment. "No, I'm just Ronnie's friend."

"Nothing *just* about it. He's a good man. Can I trouble you for a moment? I need someone to taste my guacamole. Your friend here refused. Would you, please?"

"Sure." She followed him deeper into the kitchen.

My new best friend was bailing me out. I scoped out my getaway. The elevator was on the other side of the condo, and it was my only way out.

It was crowded, and I was able to stay almost entirely unnoticed. I nodded at a couple people I knew along the way. I glanced over towards Liz; she hadn't seen me yet. I was almost sure of it. I ducked and walked briskly to the elevator.

CHAPTER 33

Tela was already waiting for the elevator. I started to turn but she saw me. "Are you leaving, too?" she asked.

"Yeah, I'm not feeling that well."

She touched my forehead. "You do have a bit of a fever. I'm sorry, darling. Is there anything I can do for you?"

Open, door, open! That's all I could think of as I stared at the elevator, wishing I could wrench the steel doors apart and jump down the shaft. *For God's sake, open!* "No thanks, Tela. I need to get home."

"All the way to Savannah?"

I nodded, stabbing my hands into my pockets.

"You're welcome to stay with me. You can ride in the limo. I've got a couch and plenty of room in the bed. I'm a healer. A bit of a medicine woman."

"No, thank you, Tela."

"You and I have unfinished business, and I don't know why you keep fighting it."

Liz called my name as the doors opened. Of course, she didn't say Trav or Travis. It was, "T.A."

I followed Tela into the elevator, refusing to turn my head. Then again, "T.A."

Close! Close! Close! The last thing I needed was the three of us in that elevator.

"Maybe she's why," Tela offered in a low voice.

That would be part of it, my little British fancy. I stood in the elevator, facing away from the doors. The walls of the elevator were made of carpet with long strips of metal. I could see the doors begin to close in the reflection, and then I accidentally saw Liz. We made eye contact.

Yes, I am an idiot.

I turned and thrust my hands in between the doors, and they opened back up. Then I stepped back into the vestibule, toward Liz.

Some things we can't control. Even the great Vincent van Gogh had his Ursula and Kay and all the other women Liz had told me about. All the women he had loved, all the heartache he had endured. My own paled in comparison, but I could empathize. The grand sorceress of them all stood only a few feet from me. I sure as hell couldn't walk away from her.

I told Tela to have a good evening. Once the elevator doors closed and she was gone, I took Liz by the arm and pulled her behind one wall, avoiding the direct line of sight into the living room.

"What are you doing?" she asked.

I squeezed her arm. It had gotten so loud in there that I had to speak into her ear. "It's going to be hard for you to believe me right now, but you have to." I squeezed her arm harder. "I'm a DEA agent, and I'm undercover right now. The cops are coming up any minute. Everybody's going to jail. I want you to get in the elevator and go home. I don't want you to get hurt. I'll call you later and explain everything." I didn't know what else to say.

She pulled away from me, her face full of doubt. She started to speak but stopped as a couple came around the corner, both wobbling, champagne glasses in their hands. Neither of us knew them. I turned one corner of my mouth into a smile, and they said hello as the man pressed the down button. Liz and I stared at each other as we waited for them to catch their ride. The couple began getting fresh with each other, and I leaned back toward Liz. "Go home. I'll call you in a while. This is not a joke."

Right then, I could see, part of her believed me. Like she knew all along that I'd been hiding something, and this revelation was the missing piece to the puzzle.

The couple stepped inside the elevator. So they could hear me, I said to Liz, "Go ahead. I'll catch up with you."

"I came here to get something," she said. "That's the only reason I'm here."

"I'll get it for you. What do you need?"

"It's a painting. I don't know where it is."

The man in the elevator asked, "You two coming?"

Liz looked at him. "We'll get the next one. Thank you."

I couldn't argue with her. I was too worried about making any more of a scene. Surely, Jack was about to round the corner, and I wouldn't have been surprised if he was getting suspicious. "Look, I don't want you to go to jail. You have to get out of here. And you can't mention this to anybody, especially Jack. If you do—"

"T.A., don't start threatening me. If that's even your name. Look, I'm going back in to get my painting, and I'm going to leave. As far as I'm concerned, I don't care what you have going on. Just leave me alone, all right?"

"Don't you breathe a word to Jack about this—"

She rolled her eyes.

"You understand me?"

"I'm not going to say anything to anybody."

In parting, I told her, "I hate seeing you under these circumstances, but it's good seeing you. I miss you. I wanted to tell you all this for a long time but I couldn't."

Without a word, Liz disappeared around the corner. She obviously wasn't in the mood to be wooed. Not that my timing had been great. I should have left when I had the chance. After a safe amount of time, I walked back into the living room. People were dancing to "Billy Jean." Liz was following Jack into his bedroom. He closed the door. *What the hell was going on?*

I took the next elevator down and sprinted three hundred yards down the street. Baroni's surveillance van read *Mike's Auto Glass Repair*. Making sure no one saw me, I climbed in. Spock and Baroni both wore headphones and were sitting on stools in front of audio receivers. A cigarette burned in an ashtray. One small screen showed the entryway to the lobby.

Baroni ripped off his headphones. "What's Liz doing up there?"

"No clue. Can you pull up the audio in Jack's bedroom?"

Baroni looked at Spock. "Do it."

"Go! Go!" I said.

"I'm on it."

He twisted some knobs, and all of a sudden I heard the two old lovers speaking. Very crisp audio.

"Let's talk for a couple minutes," Jack was saying. "Please."

"Did you hear me?" Liz asked. "I've got a flight out. I'm barely gonna make it."

"Five minutes won't kill you."

"I said no! Give me the painting, Jack."

My mind was racing. I didn't want to kill the operation but Liz's safety was more important. Was she okay? I could still go in there as Travis Moody. Maybe the op wouldn't be compromised. I was ready to dart back out the door but I listened further.

"I have to talk to you," Jack continued. "Forget your flight. Stay in Charleston with me."

"Why are you being like this? What happened to you?"

"Forget your flight," he barked. "Forget your fucking painting!"

We heard something crash against the wall. Presumably her painting.

"What is wrong with you!"

Calmer, Jack said, "Just give me a few minutes. That's all I'm asking."

"You get the hell away from me."

"You need to show me some respect—"

And that's all I heard. I was out the side door and sprinting back toward the condo as fast as I could. Nothing mattered but Liz. I ran to the stairwell first, but the door was locked. I knew that it would be but I wasn't thinking straight. The two bodyguards recognized me. I pressed the button. Waited for what felt like forever. Finally, I was on my way up.

I shot out of the elevator and pushed my way through the crowd. Stephanie waved. I went straight to Jack's door. Liz was coming out with a painting under her arm. She had a red mark above her cheek. Her shirt and hair were messed up. But worst of all, those brown eyes I'd come to know were shallow and lifeless. When she saw me, she began to bawl. Fought hard to hide it, though.

"You okay?" I asked. She kept walking. I took her arm and asked again, "Are you okay?"

"Get off me!" She pushed me away and rushed to the elevator.

I turned back toward Jack's open door. Looked inside. He was sitting up. There was a gash above his forehead. A leg of blood ran down his nose to his mouth. He was dazed. Wasn't looking my way.

The paperweight he'd shown me—the one Ava Gardner had hit Howard Hughes with—lay next to him on the rug. Liz's weapon of choice. How fitting. Thank God she'd fought him off.

I wanted to finish him off.

But I didn't. Before he saw me, I went back across the living room. Men At Work's "Overkill" was playing now. Stephanie grabbed my arm. I jerked it away from her. "I don't want to see you again." I didn't stick around to listen to her lies.

The elevator door was closing. I jabbed my hand in with only inches of space left. It opened back up. Liz was in there by herself, holding the painting to her chest. I leaned against a wall and took some deep breaths, trying to regain my composure. I didn't have many more of those sprints left in me.

"What did he do?" I asked.

Nothing.

"Did he touch you? Did he do that to your cheek?"

She shook her head, not like she was saying, "No," but more like she didn't want to talk about it. Despite her best efforts to fight it, tears ran down her face.

The elevator doors opened. I followed her out, not making a show in front of the guards. Once we were out into the parking lot, I said, "Can I get you out of here?"

"I have a flight to catch." She was trying to outwalk me. I wouldn't let her.

"Can I give you a ride?"

"No. Give me some space."

"I'm not letting you drive, Liz."

She turned and screamed at me, telling me to leave her alone.

"Let me give you a ride to the airport. I'll return your car for you. Save you a lot of time."

She was thinking about it.

"I won't say a word to you if you don't want me to. But I can't let you drive."

She turned and threw me the keys. We both climbed in and I drove the Mustang out of the lot. I called Chester. "What the hell is going on?" he asked.

"I'm taking Liz Coles to the airport. She wasn't supposed to be here."

"What's going on with Jack?"

"He's fine. I think we're still good to go. Let me drop her off and I'll call you. We're still waiting on the word."

LOWCOUNTRY PUNCH

"Lots of people waiting on you, Reddick."

"I know. Call you in fifteen."

I hung up and looked back at Liz. "Let's go to the airport." I ignited the engine.

We crossed the new bridge in silence. Once we were on the highway, I put a hand on her arm. Something told me that was all I could do. A human touch. A reassuring hand. The smallest yet only possible gesture of love that I could offer at the moment. I wanted to hold her, but I knew she didn't want that. She couldn't even look at me.

There was nothing to do now but take care of the woman I loved. Be there for her. Not feed my own anger and hatred, or my need to find savage retribution. My wanting to know what had happened up there. This wasn't about me at all. I pushed my anger away and thought only of her. Of what I could do for her. Of what she was going through.

But the silence had to break.

CHAPTER 34

What could I say to her? Should I comment on the heavy traffic? Should I ask her why she was there? Should I ask her what I could do? Or should I just drive? Both hands on the wheel, speeding towards the airport—the woman I loved to my right, a hurricane wielding its might not too many miles behind us.

As I sped up I-26, I put my hand on hers. "Do you want to call the airline? See if they've cancelled the flight?"

She tilted her head down. I didn't know what that meant. I put my eyes back on the road.

What could I do in the face of that anger? I could say I didn't have control, but what did that really mean? Was I that weak? I didn't need to talk to someone about it. I needed to deal with it. Every time the devil climbed back into my heart and soul, I needed to man up and fight the good fight. The good part of me wanted to be there for Liz, and the bad part of me wanted to be there for Jack—every step of the way, blow by blow, knocking him too far to ever climb back. The battle raged, and I fought on.

"I didn't want to lie to you," I said to her. "I didn't have a choice. It's part of being an agent. It's the way it is." I couldn't tell if she was listening. "Can you forgive me?"

"Don't bother talking. None of it really matters anymore. You're no better than he is."

"You know that's not true. I've done nothing but love you—"

"You've done nothing but *lie* to me. Don't change that story, too." She was tough, no doubt about it. Not one to forgive easily, not that that's what I deserved.

"It wasn't all lies," I said. "Nothing I said about my feelings was a lie."

"Let's not do this."

"I *am* doing this, Liz. I've waited a long time to say these things to you. That day on the porch—when I told you it was over—it was one of the worst days of my life. I didn't have a choice, though. I'd just found out about you and Jack. I was two months into an investigation that was going to put him in jail for a long time. I couldn't tell you that."

"You could have trusted me."

"I knew that and I wanted to, but I couldn't make a decision based on my love for you. Or my trust. I had to do what was right for my team. You have no idea how hard we had worked to make this operation happen. I couldn't risk it all." I suddenly realized that I was speaking too aggressively. I took a breath and calmed my tone. "I knew, Liz, that you loved me. Just as much as I loved you. That's what made it so hard. And that's what I am telling you now. I love you. All I hoped since that day was that I could eventually walk away from this case and tell you the truth. That you could look into your heart and find a way to forgive me. To love me again."

"I don't want to do this now."

"When are we going to do it, then?"

She didn't answer.

"Give me another chance."

"I could never do that. We don't even have a foundation anymore."

My phone rang. I glanced at the screen. It was Jack.

"Let's start over," I said, ignoring the call. "I will tell you the truth now and always. I am a DEA agent. My name is T.A. Reddick. I love you, Liz Coles, more than you'll ever know. I want to be with you. I will make sacrifices to be with you. What else matters? I know my timing is all wrong, but there was no other way. You have to see that."

"I don't have to see anything."

"Please consider my position. I can't let you go."

"You have to."

The airport was a mess. People were racing everywhere with luggage in their hands, worried about missing their flights. Liz had thirty-five minutes before her 10 p.m. flight, and she was out of the car before I had fully stopped. I threw it in Park and hopped out to help her with her two bags, a canvas carrier and another that said Jack Spade on the side.

She finally looked at me, but I could not decipher what I saw. To think she was even thinking of me or of us was probably absurd and selfish, considering what had happened, but I wanted to think so. I wanted to think she could see past my lies and see the difference between Jack and me. I opened my arms, and she hugged me. Not for long, but it was something that said she knew the difference.

***

I had a few choices to make on the drive back in her Mustang. I could go back to Jack's and kill him. Not good for my career or much of anything, but it would feel good. It would almost be worth life in prison. Or I could go back and find Steve and Chester, see what I could do to help. A few years ago, the decision might have been harder. Though nothing had been proven, it appeared I might be growing up.

There was still a hell of a storm on the way. Most of the cars on the road were headed out of town, but some brave souls drove toward the coast like I did. Maybe they had some unfinished business to attend to as well.

I've seen a few hurricanes in my day, from living down in Miami. Looking through the darkness to the heavens, seeing the long, thin clouds that looked like rooster tails, I knew Hurricane Henrietta was on her way.

Chester's call pulled me out of the mire. "Baroni filled me in. Did you get her to the airport?"

"Yeah, she's gone. I'm on my way back."

"Jack, Kado, and Ronnie just hopped into Ronnie's truck and are riding toward the marina. The buy might be going down."

"Jack tried to call me. Let me call him back."

I dialed Jack. Hearing his voice made what happened to Liz so much more real.

"Where'd you go?" he demanded.

"Had to run out for a bit. Who are you, my mom? I'm headed back now."

"All right. Meet us at the boat. It's time. Make sure you're packing."

"I'll be there in ten."

I called Chester back and told him the plan. "Wear your wire. Say the word and we're there."

"Got it."

"How's Liz?" Chester's always thinking about other people.

"She's waiting for her plane now. Wasn't talking much."

"I can only imagine what's going on in your head. You sure you're up for this? Maybe you don't need to see Jack right now. We can probably take them without you. We just gotta figure out where the meet is."

"I got it under control, podna. If I don't show up, he might scare and call it off. I appreciate you looking out for me, though. You're a good friend."

"Don't get all sappy on me, Reddick. I don't like you that much."

"As long as you got my back, I'm cool."
"I got your back. Let's wrap this thing up."
"I'm on it."
How could it get any worse?

IV

"The heart beats in its cage."

- Julian Casablancas

CHAPTER 35

I left the Mustang hidden in the far corner of the parking lot and jogged toward the docks. The marina where Jack kept his boat was about a mile away from his condo. The black clouds in the Southeast moved across the sky like a battalion of men on horseback on their way to war. Looking around, I realized there were no animals. No birds. No squirrels. No dogs or cats. It was a strange feeling, being that alone.

The first drops of rain fell as I reached the A-dock, and I followed the lights to the middle. A few boaters were preparing their vessels, doubling up dock lines and fenders and making sure everything was tied down.

At the last minute, I decided I couldn't go in wired. I said into the mic, "I'm taking this off. They'll search me. I'm not taking the chance." I ripped the wire off my chest and the transmitter off my waist and tossed it into the water.

Jack, Ronnie, and Kado were on the *Taggin' Wagon* waiting on me. Jack was on the bridge. He had removed his Ibiza shirt and had no shoes on. His pants were rolled up. When he saw me coming, he started up the twin Cummins engines and they roared to life.

The rain picked up as Jack weaved us through the marina and into the black, swelling harbor. I climbed the ladder and joined him. It took everything I had not to throw punches. I couldn't get the images of him and Liz out of my mind. How he'd gone after her. How he'd tried to force himself on her.

"Where the hell you been?" Jack asked. He had a deep gash in his forehead from where Liz had hit him.

"Tela and I went for a walk."

"I had a feeling. I know everything, Trav. Get used to it."

"I've got nothing to hide. You wanna fill me in on what we're doing?"

"We're meeting some guys I know down South. Over near John's Island. I don't expect problems but you never know."

"You ever worked with them before?"

"Never. That's why I'm bringing the three of you. I met the one guy down in Cartagena a couple years ago. He's legit. It'll be the cleanest coke that's ever hit Charleston. People will be begging for it. Mark my words."

Jack steered us right, moving close to the Battery. The water crashed violently against the sea wall and the wind blew hard against the trees. We rode nearly the same path that Liz and I had traveled when we'd gone to see the fireworks show, under the James Island Bridge and through the Wappoo Cut. We lowered the outriggers—thick poles that are used for trolling—and barely squeezed under the Wappoo Cut bridge. We couldn't have done it if it hadn't been low tide. Then we passed by my house. I'd completely forgotten to get someone to board up the windows. Too late now. We came out at the Stono River, near where I'd met Liz.

"There he is," Jack said, pulling back on the throttle. The *Taggin' Wagon* settled down into the water as it slowed. I looked out over the bow. Through the sheets of rain, I could make out the outline of a Hatteras motor yacht, about fifty feet long, waiting for us. An eerie feeling came over me.

"Ronnie!" Jack yelled. "Get up here. You're steering."

Ronnie took over, and Jack and I threw on rain jackets and

went down to tie up the boats. The older Hatteras looked like it had been built in the 1970s. It was in good shape but it didn't have the sleek design of anything built in the last twenty years. There was one man at the helm and another tossing out fenders.

Once we were ten feet away, I threw a line over. The man who caught it was Latino and had an unkempt beard and big, round eyes. Probably mid-forties. He didn't have a shirt on, but he wore a piece in a shoulder holster. He tied the other end of the line to a bow cleat. We did the same with the stern. That's when I noticed the boat's name painted in blue: *Blackbird*.

Jack jumped aboard *Blackbird*, and the captain, covered by a poncho, climbed down from the bridge and met him in the cockpit. They embraced and talked for a moment. The screams of the wind and rain covered up their voices. They stepped inside the salon.

I negotiated my way to the bow, the wind now blowing the rain sideways, stinging my face. I looked forward. We weren't that far from a patch of marshland. I could see the oyster beds. The marsh reeds were swirling back and forth and fronds were ripping off palm trees and flying violently through the air. How far was my backup? There was a GPS transmitter on the boat, so they knew where I was. Why weren't they moving yet?

Jack emerged moments later and stepped back on board the *Taggin' Wagon*. He went inside, I assumed to get the cash.

A third man appeared on the *Blackbird's* deck. No shoes. A submachine gun dangling from his shoulder. I held an arm over my eyes, trying to make out his face.

Under the hood pulled over his head, I saw the pockmarked face of a Cuban man I used to know. The eyes of an old friend. A ghost from my past. I'd been anticipating this moment, but not in this way. Not this way at all.

It was Diego Vasquez.

Guess it wasn't him that had tried to snipe me. We wouldn't have been caught in this situation if it had. Our eyes met and locked, the recognition taking longer than you might think.

He swung the machine gun around and pointed it right at me. "He's a Fed!"

CHAPTER 36

I hit the deck and barely missed the spray of Diego's gun as the bullets ripped into the fiberglass. I rolled onto my stomach and carefully aimed. Put his chest into my sights and fired. I'd missed him in Miami and didn't plan on making that mistake again. The bullet smacked him backwards, his finger clinging to the trigger, the submachine gun still firing.

The captain was scurrying up the ladder toward the helm. We exchanged fire, but my best shots missed him by inches. I crouched down low and scurried to the port side of the *Taggin' Wagon,* hiding behind the main cabin. A continuous stream of bullets blazed by me.

I heard *Blackbird* start up and the engines whine as the throttle was pushed down. The boats were still tied together, and *Blackbird* began to drag us. The *Taggin' Wagon* tilted starboard, and I grabbed onto the deck railing with my free hand. My body slid forward. Someone was still firing. I didn't know which way it was coming from. Once I got my footing, I looked to the stern, making sure it wasn't from Jack or Ronnie. I had no idea what they had made of Diego's accusation. I didn't see them.

I crawled forward and tried to get another good shot in at the captain, but the line holding the two boats' bows together suddenly snapped, leaving only the sterns connected. The massive sixty-one-foot hunk of fiberglass underneath me whipped around so quickly that the bow popped up into the air, and I tumbled back and smashed into the window, hearing it crack. Upon impact, I lost the grip of my gun and watched it splash into the water. Another jolt sent me rolling back to the railing. I barely grabbed the outrigger, saving myself from falling overboard.

Now *Blackbird* was pulling us backward at full throttle, one very taught line holding the boats together. The stern dug in, and the *Taggin' Wagon* started taking on water. With all the strength I had left in me, I pulled up and got onto my knees. Took a couple breaths, still holding onto the outrigger with both hands.

I started working my way toward the stern. I needed to cut that line. I slid down into the cockpit. Ronnie, Jack, and Kado were all there. Jack was hitting the cleat with a fish club, trying to break us free. If the line snapped, it could whip back and kill someone. A bolt of lightning zapped the water, and thunder erupted around us.

With a loud rip, the cleat gave way. I grabbed the ladder just in time. *Blackbird* sped off with tremendous propulsion, and the *Taggin' Wagon* completely stopped and sat upright. We were all thrown forward. Kado slammed into the bulkhead and yelled liked he'd broken something. His hand went to his head. The water on board washed away like liquid dumping out of a bucket, and we all finally found our balance.

Jesus, where the hell was my backup? I didn't want to jump overboard. Even if it was going to save my life, I couldn't let these guys get away. I had to assume the GPS transmitter Baroni had installed weeks earlier had failed on me.

"Get up!" Ronnie said, pointing a Glock at me. "You too, Kado."

"Me?"

"Shut up. Both of you get inside the cabin. Now. And put your hands in the air. Jack, you should have listened to me, man."

"Yeah, you're right."

"Get up!"

Kado and I both stood. Blood was running down the side of his head. Ronnie followed us in. The TV had been ripped off the wall, and wires dangled everywhere. The floor was wet. Everything was scattered all over the place.

"Take a seat on the couch," Ronnie said, shoving us forward with the gun against our backs.

We both collapsed onto the L-shaped ostrich-skin couch. Despite the gun on me, I welcomed getting out of the elements and wiped the water from my eyes.

"Who the fuck are you?" Jack asked me, his teeth gritted in fury.

"You know who I am."

"Kado, who is he? You're the one who brought him in. Is he a cop?"

No response.

Jack fired a shot into the couch, inches from him. "Who the fuck is he!"

"Please," Kado pleaded. "Please. Don't kill me, Jack."

"I will not ask again. Who is he?"

"His name's T.A. Reddick. He's DEA." Kado looked at me with tears in his eyes. I glared back at him.

Jack aimed the gun at Kado's head. "You flipped on us!"

Kado crumbled before our eyes. *Rats are rats are rats.* A soft hum at first, and then the tears and wailing. "I had to! They didn't give me a choice. They busted me. They were onto us anyway. Please don't shoot me. I'm begging you."

I could see Jack's mind spinning with questions. He had decisions to make. Was he really going to pull that trigger? He pulled the slide back and tightened his aim on Kado. "I hope it was worth it."

"Wait, wait, wait! I can get you out of it. I can help you."

Jack pulled the gun back. "How's that?"

"You gonna let me go?"

Jack fired another shot. "Talk!"

"I'll refuse to testify. And I've got something else, too. Travis—I mean T.A.—is the one that's been seeing Liz. The one you've been looking for."

No, he didn't.

Lightning flashed around us, and the thunder cracked like someone was breaking boards in the sky.

"What are you talking about?" Jack asked.

"I swear to you. He was seeing her before I met him. Before he went undercover."

"Is this true?" Jack asked me.

"No idea what he's talking about. Look at him. The guy's losing it."

Kado could see he was getting somewhere with Jack and his optimism was borderline pitiful. "Look on my phone. It's in the drawer there. I've got a picture of them together. Took it at the Blind Tiger." With his gun still on us, Jack moved around the counter of the galley and opened up the drawer. He pulled out Kado's phone and went to the picture gallery. Started flipping through with Ronnie looking over his shoulder.

Kado kept talking. "This could help you, Jack. If they catch you. You can say he set you up as some sort of payback for leaving Liz, or cheating on her or whatever. See what I mean?"

"Kado…Shut. The. Fuck. Up." Jack kept clicking through the pictures until he found something. His eyes filled with rage. Whatever he was looking at wasn't good. He set down his gun and glared at me with eyes that could kill.

CHAPTER 37

"Keep your gun on them," Jack said to Ronnie. He came around the corner fast.

What kind of fight do you put up when there's a gun pointed at you? I soon found out. Jack's first swing had the power of a damn jackhammer. Even blocking it with my forearm, it hurt like hell. It's amazing what a little hate will do; how much extra strength you're able to tap into.

I had some hate, too, and came back hard with a left to his chin. He backhanded me and bloodied my mouth. We were on display for Ronnie and Kado, but it wouldn't last long. I got a good one into his stomach and decided I liked my odds better on the ground. I slammed him up against the wall and knocked him to the floor. He took the advantage first, getting his arm around my neck and squeezing. I'd never seen Jack fight, and it was becoming clear that he knew what he was doing. I didn't have time to wonder how this little daddy's boy had learned how to throw down.

There are no rules in fighting when you're fighting for your life. That's another Quantico tidbit, one that had been circling around dojos and kwoons since the beginning. Go for the balls, the nose, the eyes, the throat, the ears. I took a good hold of his left lobe and tried to rip it off. He let go of me. I struggled to my feet.

"Get back on the ground!" Ronnie yelled.

Taking a gamble, I went for Ronnie. I pushed the gun away and went at his face with a left. Then I locked his arm down and tried to pry the gun from him. My gamble didn't pay off. Just as I got my hand on the barrel, Jack slammed into me and tackled me into the cabinet. The wood split.

I slung and kicked at anything and everything until Ronnie fired the gun. The bullet lodged into the ceiling.

Jack pushed himself up. "You just put a hole in my boat, asshole!"

"You put two into the couch a minute ago. Does it really matter now?"

Ronnie said to me, "Put your face on the floor."

I collapsed, knees to hands to chest to the ground, gasping for air. Almost thankful that it was over. Jack fell onto my back with his knee and jerked my arms behind me. He unclasped my father's IWC watch from my left wrist and yanked it off.

I didn't appreciate that.

"Don't make it personal," I said. "You don't wanna do that."

"It's already personal." I could hear him snap the watch around his wrist. "Ronnie, I need some rope." Ronnie found some in a closet and handed it to him. Jack tied my hands together.

A good beating followed. This great, strong man found it much easier to get to me with my hands bound. First, he brought me to my knees and hit my face. Two big blows that nearly broke my jaw and knocked me out for a second or so. I fell and tried to fight him off with my legs. I got a few knees into his stomach. Stomach blows don't seem as bad as head shots, but if you get a few true ones in, they can cause some very real damage. I failed to do so. Jack caught my feet and pinned my legs down.

Staying at a safe distance, Ronnie tossed Jack more rope, and he tied it around my ankles. Another unfortunate thing was

Jack's gift with knots, something that comes with years on the water. He wound me up with care. I wasn't going anywhere.

Standing up, he began kicking me. I rolled, trying to avoid the blows, but he just kicked whatever was available: my back, my head, my legs. "Tell me about Liz. How do you know her?"

He didn't give me a chance to answer. More big, hateful kicks that knocked the wind out of me and left me writhing. "How long has this been going on?"

I'm not one to beg, but I did feel an explanation was necessary, especially if it could prolong my survival. "When I met her, I had no idea you knew her. It was months ago. Soon as I found out—"

Another kick.

I choked a couple times before I could get more words out. "Soon as I found out you had been with her, we stopped talking."

Another kick, this time in the head. I didn't have much time left. I could barely see or breathe and had at least a couple broken ribs. I was too tired to be angry. Ronnie noticed my condition, and came from behind Jack and put a bear hug on him. "You're killing him. We gotta get out of here."

I curled in a ball on the floor, nearly losing consciousness.

Jack said to Ronnie, "Give me the gun. I'm ending this now." He reached for it.

"No. I'm not letting you dig any deeper."

"*Give me the fucking gun!*"

"Don't you think the DEA knows where their agent is? We need to get the hell out of here. If we get caught, do you really want a murder rap on top of whatever it is they have on us?"

"He's making sense," I mumbled from the fetal position on the floor, spitting blood.

"I'll give you the gun, but you kill him and you're on your own," Ronnie said. "I'm not a murderer. I don't wanna fry."

"Fine."

Ronnie handed him the gun and said, "You know we can't go home."

"Yeah. I know it. Can you handle that?"

"We signed up for it a long time ago."

"That we did." Jack turned back to Kado. "What else do you know? Are they close by? Do they know where we are?"

"I think so. He told me I was done yesterday, so I guess they were planning an arrest soon. Tonight, maybe."

Jack turned back to Ronnie. "Let's get out of here. I'll be up there in a minute."

"Don't kill them."

"I won't."

Ronnie opened the door and stepped back out into the elements. We were alone with Captain Insano. Through the window, I watched Ronnie climb the ladder to the bridge. I said to Jack, "Where the hell are you gonna go?"

"Sweden." He leaned against the cabinet on the other side of the salon.

"Every move you make from this point forward is adding years to your sentence. You let me take you in now and I'll be your friend—"

"I don't believe that."

"We're even now. You could say I deserved that. Let me put you on the stand against a few people. Testify for us. You'll be out of jail in no time. All I care about is this case. I have nothing against you. You're a target in this investigation. Nothing more."

He thought about it but wasn't biting.

The boat cranked up and we started moving. Jack tapped the barrel of the gun on the cabinet several times. "I'm not going to jail."

"You don't know how to run. I've chased men across the earth for years, and none of 'em make it...and I'm talking men with global connections. Endless finances."

"We'll see. I'm betting we don't see a soul from here to North

Carolina. And they won't find your bodies for a week. Long after the crabs get to you. Ronnie's a softie. You think I give a shit what he thinks? You both betrayed me. You both die. End of story. If I have to run, so be it."

Jack retrieved a bottle of Ketel One vodka that had fallen onto the floor. He took a swig and his back arched. It looked like it had done him some good. I knew he was mustering up the courage to kill us. It's easy to talk about, but pulling that trigger for the first time on another human is anything but easy. It's not natural. I've killed three men in my life, and they all still haunt me.

"Can I get a shot of that?" I asked.

"How'd you meet Liz?"

"Who cares?"

"I care, damn it!"

"I ran into her wakeboarding, right around here. I had no idea who you were at the time."

He slowly nodded. "I don't know that I believe that."

"Does it even matter?"

"You have no idea. How'd you get Kado to flip?"

"Like he said. I didn't give him a choice."

"How'd he get you, Kado?"

"I got pulled over. It was the night we got in that fight. I was pissed at you after you hit me and took Tela's side. I wasn't thinking straight."

"Damn right, you weren't thinking straight."

Jack asked Kado more questions; I ignored them. I closed my eyes and fell into a relaxed state, hoping it might give my body some strength.

Joni Mitchell recorded an album in the early seventies called *Blue*. My dad would play "A Case of You" over and over on an antique phonograph, and he'd take my mother's hand and they would dance around the house, staring into each other's eyes. He'd even dip her from time to time, and my brother and I would run around them and make throw-up sounds, so embarrassed.

There was nothing embarrassing about it now, as it played in my head, and I awaited fate. I felt Liz take my hand as Joni's words danced along the melody.

Oh, I am a lonely painter
I live in a box of paints
I'm frightened by the devil
And I'm drawn to those ones that ain't afraid
I remember that time that you told me, you said
Love is touching souls
Surely you touched mine
Cause part of you pours out of me
In these lines from time to time.

I didn't want to leave Liz alone. It was more important than leaving my mother and brother by themselves to deal with my death. I hate to say that, but it's true. And Liz was so alone now. She had touched my soul, and if I ever saw her again, I would make sure she knew that. I'd let her know that she was in my blood like holy wine. Yeah, I could drink a case of her and still be on my feet.

At least I would die with love in my heart.

I peeled my eyes open. Through the back window, I saw the hatch leading to the engine room open up. A second later, someone climbed out. A woman.

Then I saw her face.

CHAPTER 38

My eyes opened wide. Knew it couldn't be true. *Stephanie was climbing out of the engine room.* Was she on board or was I really losing it? Had Jack given me something? I hadn't had enough water to drink, so maybe that was it. Dehydration can definitely get you.

We were back into the rougher water of the harbor. The ocean juggled swells that shook the boat violently, and the seasickness was hitting me. My body wanted to throw up, but I fought it. Told myself seasickness wasn't an option. Tried to suppress it.

It was definitely Stephanie I had seen. Now she was pressing her face to the window and peering inside. I moved my eyes back down to the floor so Jack wouldn't see me looking. His back was to her. When I looked again, she was gone. Next thing I saw was her going up the ladder.

Kado was a wreck. His whole body trembled as he answered Jack's questions. I was too beat and defeated to even try to stop him. Unless Stephanie had brought the DEA with her, we were all going to die. What was the point?

Jack turned back to me. "Did Liz know about the investigation?"

"She had nothing to do with it. Never knew any of it."

"I'll find that out later. She's got some explaining to do. I'll beat it out of her if I have to. You'd like that, wouldn't you?"

Our eyes locked.

"Can't wait to tell her what it felt like to put a bullet in your head. I wonder if she'll care."

"You know, I even felt bad about it," I said, sitting up against the couch. "There you were thinking I was with Tela. I could have had her, too, but I had my fingers in the other pie." I felt filthy talking like that, especially about the one that I loved, but I was trying to get to him a bit. Tweak him. Not that I wanted another beating. Just wanted to make him make a mistake. Since no one had come to the rescue, I had to assume I was on my own. Well, except for Stephanie. *What the hell was she doing anyway?*

I pissed Jack off, all right. He raised the gun.

"No turning back now," I said. "Pull the goddamn trigger!"

"No, Jack!" Kado yelled.

The boat turned right unexpectedly. More severe than something intentional. I looked out the back window where I'd seen Stephanie. Someone fell from the bridge, which had to hurt. I couldn't make out if it was a man or woman. The boat changed course again. Jack went outside to figure out what was happening. Rain poured in as the door opened. "Ronnie!" He looked down where the person had fallen. "What are you doing?"

I couldn't hear a reply. Jack looked up toward the bridge, then hopped onto the ladder and pulled himself up, screaming.

How the heck did Stephanie get onto the boat? And what was she doing there anyway?

"I'm gonna get us out of here," I said to Kado, maneuvering myself into the center of the salon. Probably not all that convincing with a face covered in blood. "Hang in there." There was no sense being mean to the guy, even though he'd dug this grave. I kicked my bound legs up and tried to bring my hands around my feet, but it wasn't happening. I wasn't as agile as I used to be.

The boat tilted into an even bigger turn. The bottle of vodka slid along the counter and fell. The engines roared. Full throttle. Something felt dreadfully wrong.

We crashed hard.

We hit land at full speed. Land, or something large and stationary. I got that falling feeling, where your stomach is in your chest. As the yacht turned sideways, we were thrown against the opposite wall. Can't do much with your hands tied up. My shoulder hit the wall with my full weight behind it. I felt the pop when it dislocated, but it didn't touch the pain from my ribs, which splintered further. The sharp sting ran right up my chest and into my temples.

The boat landed hard on its side, the fiberglass cracking and glass shattering. The stereo equipment fell, magazines, cups. Anything loose. I tried to protect my face. The boat settled at about a thirty-degree angle, and I slid down to where the floor met the wall.

Gusts of wind and torrents of rain slashed through the broken windows on the port side, stirring up debris. Above the roar of the wind and thunder, horrifying noises from the storm—screams and creaks—echoed through the salon. I let the rain pour into my mouth. I was so thirsty. I took some breaths and tried to gather myself. Diesel fumes filled my lungs. Thank God diesel isn't as combustible as gasoline.

A bolt of lightning struck nearby. I could feel the electricity. More snaps and cracks of thunder.

"Kado," I said. He was out cold. Then louder, "Kado!" I saw that a piece of glass had nearly severed his leg. It stuck into his upper left thigh, and the blood had covered his lap. I got to my knees and moved toward him. My shoulder started aching like hell, so I slammed it against the wall, trying to knock it back into place. I hit it hard and yelled at the pain. My eyes watered. It stayed dislocated. The second time, it locked back in.

I moved quickly to him, one knee to the next. I didn't think I should take the glass out without free hands. "Kado, wake up. You gotta wake up."

His eyes opened to lifeless slits.

"You gotta stay awake, my friend. They'll be here soon. Keep your eyes open. Think of a good movie—and popcorn, with lots of butter. A little white cheddar powder. A girl dipping her hand in the bucket with you." I don't know where that came from, but it did sound like a damn fine place to be. His pupils kept trying to force themselves to roll backwards. "Kado!"

Jack appeared in the doorway. The continuous lightning lit up his face. He'd survived the crash. The guy had the devil's luck. My eyes went to the watch on his wrist first. Then, seeing the steel in his hand, I knew I was breathing my last breaths. *What a way to go.*

"We need to help Kado," I yelled over the madness. "He's bleeding out."

He ignored me as he negotiated the slippery, crooked floor and made his way in my direction. "Looks like we've hit the end of the line, huh?" He raised the gun.

"You don't need to do this."

He laughed. "Save your breath. You're not getting out of this one."

"Looks like we're in the same boat then—if you know what I mean."

Jack straightened his arm further and started to pull the trigger. I forced my eyes to stay open, embracing death.

CHAPTER 39

Jack and I shared a similar kind of hate.

His was an uncontrollable rage, a desire to watch my blood run cold. Seeking vengeance for betraying him, but more than anything, seeking vengeance for my relationship with Liz, though he didn't even know the full story. Nothing I could have said would have made a difference. He had decided my death was a necessity. Merely the idea of my relationship with Liz had been enough.

My anger and fury came from many sources. Ultimately, it was Liz, though. He had attacked the woman I loved. He would pay for that, even if I had to chase him down in hell.

It was the cocaine I hated, too. It's what had made him this way. It's what had brought me into the position of staring at the wrong end of his Glock, waiting for the trigger to be pulled. It's what had eaten his soul and wrenched him from reality. It's what had numbed his human side. Cocaine destroys lives and that's why I was in the business.

I'd seen it happen so many times, and the first was with Shawn Philips, my father's murderer. Imagine a man shooting someone and barely remembering it. I can hate both the drug and the man, for it's the drug that became the seducer, but it's the man who had been weak enough to let it happen. It was the man there before me who'd let evil creep into him and blind his morality.

Jack's eyes widened some, and I knew I was a goner.

Charleston was a good place to die, though, and it's where I had intended on meeting my fate. The great Holy City, the greatest place on earth. I had a couple last words for Jack.

"I'll be waiting for you." I didn't even blink. Didn't want to give him the satisfaction of thinking he'd won.

"On the other side," Jack said.

"*En el otro lado.*"

Aiming at my left cheek, he pulled the trigger.

***

Now, I'd seen and done some things in my day, and when you're about to die, they zip right through your brain, playing like an old movie reel spinning out of control.

I'd surfed the sunrise from Folly Beach to Indonesia, and I'd caught my perfect barrel. I'd seen St. Basil's in the falling snow, and had ridden a scooter to the end of the world in Sagres. Of course I wish it had been a motorcycle, and I had planned on going back and doing it right, but time wasn't abundant. My story had been written and closed, and now was the time to question it all. Did you take the world by its tail, Reddick?

Had I? Well, I'd danced with a Colombian woman on the walls of the Cafe del Mar in Cartagena. I'd stood at the end of the Isle of Skye and yelled out to my ancestors who'd been living and dying there since the beginning of time. I'd even scuba dived the Galapagos. And I'd seen Pat Metheny and Diana Krall and George Benson live in Montreaux.

It sounds like my deathbed was a soapbox—and maybe it was—but it's my right when I die. No, it was my duty and obligation to revisit the life I'd led. The one I'd spend eternity thinking about, knowing that I had or I hadn't lived it to the fullest. It's there on that deathbed that you first can make that decision, because that's when you know you're out of time. And only then.

I never caught Tom Waits or Miles, and I never made it to Black Rock City, and I'd never played the Grand Old Opry, and I sure as hell hadn't done enough for other people. Maybe working for the World Food Program would have been a better way for me to give back than a few short years chasing the devil. Oh, and I hadn't written the book I'd always talked about, and I'd never been to space, and I'd never circumnavigated the globe, and I'd never planted a vineyard...

But I had drunk some great bottles in my time, and I'd sipped the perfect Guinness in a pub in Ireland, and I'd played banjo in a bar in Carcasonne, and I'd Spey-casted the River Tay, and though the salmon weren't biting, the single malt certainly was. I'd even met Chevy Chase and Ronald Reagan. And I'd met some great women, too. Even fallen in love. Most importantly, I'd been blessed with the greatest family and friends a man could ask for, folks who had put up with me long after they should have.

But nothing compared to the look on that son of a bitch's face when the trigger clicked and nothing came out. There wasn't even a report.

He pulled the slide back. There was no bullet in the chamber. He checked and the magazine was empty.

I nodded my head. "Empty promises, you stupid fuck. That's all you are."

Maybe the wrong choice of words. He struck the side of my face with the butt of his gun. Now, that's pain. I'd almost rather have been shot and accepted oblivion. If you've ever been there, you know what I mean.

He would have finished me off right then, but as he started to strike me again, we heard the sirens of a Coast Guard boat. Through bloody and blurry vision, I watched him take his phone from a drawer and then disappear into the night. I sighed, finally having a moment of relief.

I hoped Stephanie had survived the crash. She'd saved our lives, and I had so many questions for her. A bellow of thunder shook the boat, and the rain came down even harder. It was the worst I'd seen yet. We must have been north of the eye.

I went back to Kado. Unable to pull him from consciousness, I tried to figure out a way to stop the bleeding without removing the glass. While I tried to apply pressure in the right places, I spoke to him, quietly and calmly, letting him know I wasn't giving up on him. And I wasn't.

CHAPTER 40

Sometimes the person you least want to see one day is exactly the person you want to see the next. Stephanie came in through the door calling my name. Her dress had completely soaked through, and I could see it all. Not that my mind could even go there.

"Hey," I said. Nothing too dramatic.

"You're alive. Thank God." She crouched low to move across the floor.

"I'm glad to see you are, too. Where'd they go?"

"They took off."

"Where are we?"

"Fort Sumter." She touched my cheek. "You look awful."

"I bet."

"But I'm so happy you're alive."

"Me, too."

She let out a cry when she saw Kado. "Oh, my God! Is he breathing?"

I guess we did need to focus on him at the moment. "I think so. Help me find something to stop the bleeding."

Stephanie nodded. Her body shook in fear at the sight of his blood. She crawled to the kitchen and found a knife.

"Take care of him first," I said, watching helplessly. I told her what to do. She began to saw off the rope binding his feet. Once she had enough length, she spread his legs, pushed up his shorts, and wrapped the rope around his thigh above the laceration and tightened it. The blood slowed significantly.

"I'm glad you're here, Stephanie," I said.

She cut me free. I sat up and tightened the rope even more around his leg.

"I'm...I'm sorry," she said. "I thought I could help…"

"You did. No idea how, but I owe you a beer."

"It's a date then."

I couldn't help but smile. The sirens got louder. "You wanna tell me what happened up there? How did you get on board?"

"When I saw you at the condo, I knew something was wrong. I saw Jack coming out of his room with a gash on his head. He grabbed Ronnie and said they needed to go down to the boat. I beat them to the elevator while they were looking for Kado and drove over. I thought you'd be there, but you weren't. So I decided to hide in the engine room. I think it's just a woman's protective instinct. I knew you were in danger."

"Then what?"

She sat back on her ankles. "I heard everyone come aboard. I kept my ear to the hatch, trying to figure out what was going on. When the engine turned on, it was so loud in there. Luckily there were some earmuffs hanging on the wall. The engine cut off finally, and I tried to figure out what was going on. I couldn't hear anything over the sounds of the hurricane, though. Not until the gunfire. Then all of a sudden I was getting thrown around."

"I bet it was bad down there."

"Yeah. But I didn't want to climb out. I didn't know who was shooting."

"I don't blame you."

"Then, once we were moving again and things were back to normal, I decided to get out of there. I saw you and Kado tied up and saw Jack with the gun. And Ronnie on the bridge. Didn't know what else to do. I went up and tried to talk to him. As you can imagine, he was shocked to see me. I told him I'd hopped on at the last minute. While he was trying to figure it all out, I took that empty white cooler up there by the handle and slung it at him. It knocked him off the bridge. When Jack came after me, I didn't know what to do. So I jerked the wheel toward land."

"I guess that was the best option."

"Well, I didn't have many."

I grinned a little. "You're crazy."

She looked at me like I'd insulted her.

"Not *crazy*... you know what I mean. How'd you know how to get into the engine room?"

"An ex used to have something like this."

"How fortuitous. You undoubtedly saved my life. Thank you, Stephanie. Really. You risked your life for me."

***

Two men from the Coast Guard carefully carried Kado out on a stretcher. I tossed back a bottle of water they'd given me and sat back against the wall. I'd be damned if I too was going to be carried away. I just needed a few minutes to get my strength back.

Ches, my trusty partner, came in next and looked at me with Samwise Gangee eyes. Rainwater dripped from the brim of his DEA rain jacket. I mumbled, "Am I dead?"

"Could be." He grinned. "I can't believe you made me come out in this. I hate hurricanes."

"You look good wet."

"I'm sure I do. You know you almost cleared a wall of Fort Sumter?"

"No shit?"

"Didn't make it, though. You're going to piss off every historian in the country."

"These things happen. What happened to y'all? I could have used some help."

"Your transmitter went down. We lost your signal."

"I figured. We met the source. I was ten feet away from their boat. We could have gotten them."

"The Hatteras? They didn't get away. We got 'em. Three of them. Twenty kilos, Reddick. Biggest bust in Charleston in a long time."

I was elated. "Did one have a bullet in him?"

"I wasn't there, but yeah. I heard the Coast Guard say one was dead."

"That was Diego Vasquez. The guy from Miami whose brother I shot."

"Really? That's hard to believe."

"If I hadn't seen him, I wouldn't believe it myself. The drug world spins on a tiny axis, Ches."

"Yes, it does."

Finally, closure. I didn't have to worry about Diego anymore. No more phone calls to the US Marshall. Not as many sleepless nights. There would always be people out to get me, but he'd always been different. He was a true enemy.

"How about the party?" I asked.

"As we speak, they're booking everybody. Couldn't have gone any smoother. They even picked up Tela Davies back at the Mazyck."

"Good." I started to push to my feet. Nearly fell back down but held strong. "Let's quit talking and go get these boys."

"You're going to the hospital, my friend."

"The hell I am. Don't even try. What kind of boat do they have?"

"A twenty-five-foot Defender, twin 225 Hondas on the back."

"Do you know the draft?"

"Probably three feet."

"She's perfect."

Chester helped me up and we moved to the door. Spock was coming in. "You look like shit, Reddick."

"At least I have an excuse, rookie."

"Oh, snap."

"I think Jack had his money in one of the cabins. You wanna do the honors?"

"I'd be glad to." He moved his way through the salon.

I hobbled out into the hurricane. Had to see what we'd hit with my own eyes. We really were at Fort Sumter, a pentagon-shaped fort built on an island in the Charleston harbor many years earlier. It's where the first shots of the Civil War were fired, where Beauregard's rebels won their first battle against the Union. The boat had crushed one of the walls. Stephanie had steered us right into it. I carefully stepped over the broken bricks, and we made our way toward the water.

It took some convincing, but after I let one of the Coast Guard guys set my nose, Chester came around. And as I told him, there was no freaking way I wasn't going after them. I'd do it alone if I had to. We'd destroyed the dock on the island, so we had to wade out a few feet before climbing into one of the two Defenders. The Coast Guard was taking Kado and Stephanie back to the mainland in the other one.

As we pulled away, Spock came out dragging a bag. He set it down and reached inside. Pulling up a stack of cash, he raised it high in the air. "Jackpot!"

***

There's a rule Beau Tate taught me when I was a kid about leaving the harbor by boat. Never go right of Fort Sumter. It's too shallow. At low tide, like it was now, you could almost walk across. Because of the hurricane, it wouldn't be easy, but with a little luck and some swimming, Jack and Ronnie could make it to James Island and get a chance at escaping.

LOWCOUNTRY PUNCH

The captain of the Defender steered us around some of the shallow parts, trying to cut Jack and Ronnie off. The waves were rabid with white foam and juggled us in every direction, repeatedly slamming the boat down and sending shocks up our spines. Debris blew by so quickly that you couldn't tell what it was or even what direction it came from.

We moved back toward land after a few hundred feet. With our draft, we got pretty far. The captain sent a man to the bow to look for obstructions with a spotlight, and we slowed and made way into the shallow water. The reeds were bent down to the water by the wind. The sound of the storm was almost like holding the end of a vacuum cleaner up to your ear.

Forcing our way through the marshland in the hurricane, the absurdity of our chase became all too real.

CHAPTER 41

I was losing faith that we'd find them. There was so much marsh out there, and I could barely see a damn thing. They could have gone a number of ways, toward the lighthouse on Morris Island; to the middle of the marsh to hide under one of the old sailboats that had been left there to die; or closer to James Island, toward the DNR (Department of Natural Resources) site and, past that, to the many neighborhoods.

I hoped Steve had gotten their faces on the news, because Jack and Ronnie had a great chance of getting out of that marsh without us catching them. We could only hope that someone who hadn't evacuated the storm would see them running along the street and call it in.

Chester and I knelt near the spotter on the bow, searching and listening for any signs of life. All three of us gripped the bow rail with everything we had, knowing some of these gusts could easily lift us off the deck. The black clouds were much closer now, like the whole ceiling had lowered. The dank smell of pluff mud—the typical wet mud found in and around the marshes in the lowcountry—spun around us.

A board flew by in the air and nearly knocked Chester in the head. "That was close," he said. My ribs wouldn't let me laugh.

We hit another sandbar and all flew forward. We'd gone just

about as far as the Defender was going to take us. I had a banged-up shoulder, a broken nose, broken ribs, and a broken heart, but I was starting to catch my second wind.

"I got something!" the spotter yelled. Chester and I nearly knocked each other over in our eagerness to see what he was talking about. I squinted; there it was. *There were prints.* In between a patch of blown-down reeds, there was a path of footprints a foot deep in the brown mud. My heart started pounding.

"Good eyes," I said, patting the spotter on the back. "That's all I need." I hopped off and started following the prints with my light, staying low to keep my balance in the wind. My feet sank deep into the mud with each step. I was wearing Italian loafers, which weren't ideal, but what the hell. I guess I should have known to dress for a chase. When one loafer didn't come back up with my foot, I decided to leave both of them there.

My team wasn't too far behind me, but I wasn't waiting. Off in front of me, something reflected off my flashlight. "I got one!" Forty feet away, somebody came out of the weeds. Holding my light on him, I charged. Jesus can walk on water, but T.A. Reddick can run in mud. Leaves and debris flew past me as I tore through the hurricane.

My flashlight lit up Jack's back. It was my watch on his wrist that had caused the reflection. *Serendipity, asshole.*

I screamed back to the others, "I got Jack! No sign of the other one!" As fast as I ran, I couldn't catch up with him. Forty feet is too much of a head start, and Lord knows he had as much motivation to haul ass as I did.

The lights of several DNR buildings came into view. Mostly brick structures. I was yelling my heart out. Jack tripped and went down hard. I was able to gain some on him, but he was on his feet in no time.

A man appeared in front of us, shining his light on Jack. "Police!" He was standing up the hill from the marsh. Jack was running right for him. The officer yelled, "Stop or I'll put one in your knee!" Another few feet and I recognized him. Darby Long, Kado's arresting officer.

"Don't shoot him!" I yelled back. "He's mine!"

Jack turned a hard right along the shore and one of his feet stuck deep in the mud. It was all I needed to catch up. Making a good dive, I hit him in the kidneys with my shoulder and took him to the ground. We splashed into the wet slope and slid down into the muddy oyster bed about ten feet below. Shells tore through my shirt and cut my bare feet, but I didn't care. It was my time for revenge. My prey had no chance.

At least I didn't think so. He came on strong, going for my ribs, then my nose. I don't know how either of us were still moving. It was our second fight of the night.

Once again, it wasn't going to be easy. I tried to ignore the screams of pain from my body. We scrapped in the mud, wrestling to gain the upper hand. We both went to our knees. I slipped onto my back trying to stand. Grabbed onto his shirt, and he fell next to me. I rolled on top of him.

Flashes of Jack under me began to mix with images of Shawn Philips, the man who killed my father. Those lost eyes again, staring back at me. It felt like someone was trying to climb out of my flesh to kill Jack, like some phantom devil being exorcised. I put my hand around his neck and pressed hard, cutting off his air flow. I raised my fist, ready to drop a right that would send this demon back to hell. I'd had enough.

He spat some blood and said, "You may have fucked up the little vacation I'd planned for Liz and me, but I'll always know she never made her flight tonight. You should have been worried about her, instead of chasing me through this goddamn storm." He spat some more blood and smiled. "Good luck putting her back together again."

I had no idea what he was talking about. I squeezed and pressed his neck harder. He kicked with his legs and reached for my hands, trying to free himself. I tightened the hold around his neck, ignoring the pleas from Officer Long and Chester begging me to let him go. Jack's arms fell to his side. He was dying.

Generations of men, some great, some not, danced around me, waking up the animal. I looked up. The storm screamed and roared down, feeding my rage. I roared out into the night and my heart pumped adrenaline through seething veins.

Then it stopped.

The rain and wind came to a halt—like we were in the eye— and we became the only two people in the universe. The hate I felt for the man below me began to drift away like a cloud. A calmness I've never known descended upon me. I took in great breaths of air. At that moment, I found peace with Jack and with myself. I'm not quite sure where it came from, but perhaps Liz had something to do with it. She'd healed me in some way.

I let go of him and he gasped for air. Once he'd gotten control and his eyes opened, I patted his cheek a couple times and said, "Don't let the hag ride ya." I smiled with my eyes. Yet another wonderful look on his face, one that I would never forget.

As quickly as it had come, my moment of clarity passed. We were back in the storm, back under the mighty strength of Hurricane Henrietta. I flipped Jack onto his stomach and reclaimed my father's watch.

Officer Long cuffed him and jerked him up out of the mud, saying, "I already got Ronnie Downs. Plucked him out of a mud pit. He was hiding in there like Saddam Hussein."

I patted Darby on the back. "I've gotta borrow your cruiser and cell phone."

Darby nodded and handed me his keys. "All yours."

CHAPTER 42

I had to find out what Jack was saying about Liz, and I wasn't about to underestimate him again. With both prisoners in the back and Chester sitting shotgun, we tore across town in Officer Long's patrol car. We were the only ones on the road, and I drove like Earnhardt was trying to cut around me on the next turn. The wind had calmed but the rain still came.

As I waited on hold with Delta, I listened to Ches on the police radio. He was putting some people to work, including getting a unit of cops to the airport and initiating a search. Finally, after a round of robotic voices and some unbearable muzak, a human came on the line. I explained who I was and asked her if Liz had made the flight. The woman verified my credentials, and after an agonizing wait, she came back. "No, sir. Elizabeth Coles did not check in."

I screeched to a halt on the side of the road near MUSC, just over the bridge to downtown. I got out of the car with a Colt Chester had brought me. Opening the backdoor, I grabbed Jack by the arm and dragged him out. He fell into a puddle collecting on the pavement. I knelt and put the barrel of the Colt to his temple. "Where is she? Who has her, Jack?"

He looked up at me and didn't say a word. I thrust my hand into his pockets, looking for his phone. It wasn't there. I remembered seeing him take it from the boat. Now, it was probably somewhere out in the marsh. Even if we did find it, I couldn't imagine it was still operational. Nevertheless, that phone could have all the answers.

With the barrel still on his temple, I called Officer Long. I still had his number from the first time we met. I asked him to round up help and search every inch of that marsh. He said he was on it.

I hung up and put my eyes back on Jack. "Start talking."

Nothing.

I clocked him on the side of the head. "Where is she?"

Chester put his hand on my shoulder, stopping me. "This is not how you wanna do it."

I stood and faced Chester. "I want you to take a walk. You don't want to be a part of this. He's the only one who knows where she is."

He grabbed my shirt. "Doesn't work like that. We'll find her, but we're gonna do it the right way."

He was right. I knew it. I took a few breaths to calm down. "He was going to pick her up somewhere. He said something about a vacation. I think he had someone grab her at the airport and then that person was going to drop her off with Jack. He mentioned heading to North Carolina." I looked down at Jack and stepped on his leg. He grimaced. "Am I right? Where are you meeting them? Somewhere up the Intracoastal?"

Ches looked down at Jack. "You're gonna want us on your side. Tell us where she is and we'll help you out." He looked back into the car. "You, too, Ronnie. You're welcome to say something. Buy yourself a few years."

Jack grinned. "You're wasting your time. Ron doesn't know anything about it."

I wanted to kick Jack but didn't. Instead, I lifted him up and pushed him back into the police car next to Ronnie. "Let's go," I said to Ches. "I have an idea."

Once we were moving again, driving through the flooded streets, I said, "There are only a few places that would make sense. I know it's a big leap, Ches, but we gotta do something. If I'm right, then McClellanville and Georgetown are plausible since they're stops on the way north. We're going to McClellanville. That's where his cabin is. That's his turf."

Jack opened his big mouth from the backseat. "You got it all figured out, don't you?"

Chester looked through the glass at Jack. "One more word and I'll let him beat it out of you. Count on it."

Jack wisely chose not to reply.

I dialed Steve's number and told him what I was thinking. He said he'd get a couple teams together. One would meet us in McClellanville and the other would head into Georgetown.

There wasn't much else up that way. Most of it was government property without any access. The private docks in between Charleston and McClellanville would be hard to find in the black of the storm. And if Jack had to give directions to someone on the fly, that lowered the number of possibilities yet again.

The crosstown highway was buried in two or three feet of water. I was sure the cruiser was going to drown, but she made it through, and we lifted up onto the new bridge. I hit the gas, and we sped up Highway 17, chasing the hurricane up the coast.

During the twenty-minute drive, we tried several more times to get some information, to give Jack and Ronnie a chance to help, but it became evident we were wasting our time. I tried Officer Long again. He still hadn't found the phone. Ches and I ran through every scenario we could think of and nothing else made sense. If I was wrong, we had no other way to turn. I knew it wasn't right, but torture was heavy on my mind.

As we came close to town, I didn't bother turning toward Jack's cabin. He didn't have deepwater access. If he'd had someone pick her up, he would have had them bring her somewhere highly accessible, somewhere that Jack could pull up to in his boat, grab her, and keep on going. He had a much better chance on the water. Also, it made sense to run *with* the hurricane, not away from it. It was his shelter against everyone pursuing him. It's what I would have done.

But our moves were based on assumptions. Was he even picking her up? I think he was just crazy enough to think he could take her with him. In fact, I don't think he would leave town without her.

***

I turned off the highway onto South Pinckney Street. There were no cars on the road. Though the elements weren't as bad as they had been back on the harbor, we still couldn't roll down the windows without inviting all sorts of hell. Following a feeling, I cut right toward the south side of Jeremy Creek, the main creek off the Intracoastal. I lost the pavement under the tires and had to slow down some. I drove toward the houses along the water, the car bouncing over gravel.

I turned back to the prisoners. "How we doin'? You're still welcome to help out."

Jack turned up one side of his mouth and shook his head. But he wasn't quite as confident as he had been. *Were we doing something right?* We drove up and down driveways for a while, looking for cars out of place, anything that didn't look right. With no luck, we decided to move on.

We got back on the main road and followed it around to the other side of the creek where the actual town is. McClellanville is really just a one bank, one hardware store, and one mechanic kind of municipality.

I took another right, heading back toward the creek. As it came into view, I saw a line of shrimp boats tied to the docks. Only a few streetlights lit our way, surely run by a generator, as the town had clearly lost its power earlier in the storm.

Right as I started to doubt myself, a pair of headlights appeared. A car came our way. Once the driver saw us, it stopped. *Was this our guy?* I continued on and waited for him to make a move. He shut his lights and hit the gas, peeling away from us. Relief overcame me. I couldn't believe we could get that lucky. I floored it, not bothering to turn on the siren or lights. Chester radioed it in. We had our guy.

As the car came into the glare of my headlights, I saw that it was an older model BMW. It bounced over a curb into a parking lot. "That looks like Tux Clinton's car."

"Sure does." I only saw one head through the back window, though. "I don't see Liz." I drove up over the same curb, and we bounced into the parking lot after him. He drove over another curb and onto South Pinckney, making a run back for the highway.

Chasing him, we gained ground quickly. As I drove the cruiser to the left of him, Ches rolled down his window and fired a shot at the tire. I kept my eyes on the road. We were going close to ninety. We came even with the BMW and confirmed that it was Tux Clinton. He rolled down his own window and raised a gun. I braked when he pointed it toward us.

Chester's next shot hit the tire and it lost its air quickly. The BMW began to drag on its one side. "One more!" I yelled. "Don't hit the trunk! She might be in there." Ches kept firing until the other tire collapsed, and the BMW lost its speed. Tux brought the car to a stop in the middle of the road. I pulled up behind him and stepped onto the wet pavement.

"He's gonna run!" Chester yelled, already halfway to the BMW. The passenger side door opened. Tux rolled out and started to run along the shoulder. But Ches didn't let him get far. "Stop, Tux! I'm not chasing you." Ches fired a warning shot. Tux stopped running and put his hands up.

I ran to his car and looked inside. There was a body in the backseat. My heart stopped. "No!" Blood flooded my cheeks. I tried the backdoor but it was locked. I opened the front door and scrambled for the unlock button. Finally found it, finally got to her.

Liz was on her back, her head turned toward the side. Her eyes were closed. A strip of Duct tape covered her mouth. Her feet and hands were also taped. I whispered, "Tell me you're alive, baby." I looked up and down her body looking for bullet wounds. I didn't see any. "Liz." I choked up. "Liz!"

As I reached for a wrist to check the pulse, she mumbled something through the tape. Then she lifted her bound hands. I will never experience a finer moment in my life than knowing then that she was alive. "It's okay, baby," I whispered. I put my cheek to hers and felt the warmth of life. "Everything's gonna be okay."

I stood up and looked over the top of the car. Ches was walking Tux back up the hill. I winked at him, beat on the hood twice, and smiled. He may have bested me the last time, but he was the one going to jail. We'd finally gotten Tux.

I tore the tape around Liz's hands. "I'm gonna let you get the tape off your face, all right?"

She nodded and jerked at the tape, making a deep gasp as it came off.

"How do you feel?" I asked. "Did he hurt you?"

She shook her head and knelt forward, ripping the binding off her legs. I gave her a hand as she stepped out into the drizzle from the last of the storm. One of the holes in her jeans near the knee had been ripped wide open. We watched Chester push Tux into the back of the patrol car.

I tried to hug her, but she resisted, waving me off. She'd had enough. Saving her wasn't going to make a difference.

All the pain I'd ignored came rushing back, the last of my adrenaline depleted. I fell backwards.

CHAPTER 43

All right, Eddie Rabbit, you're right…you can't run from love. I landed at LaGuardia around lunchtime three days later. I hadn't checked a bag, so I went straight to the cab line. I'd gotten the address of Liz's studio from someone at the School of the Arts at the College of Charleston. Would it be as easy as walking in there and telling her I loved her? I hoped so. She'd had time to digest everything and had hopefully come to some new decisions. This was it for me: my last chance to redeem the greatest thing that had ever happened to me.

Before I left for New York that morning, Ronnie told me during an interrogation that he had taken the bullets out of Jack's gun while we were on the boat. That's why I was still alive. He didn't want anyone to die. That's the kind of thing that I appreciate.

I handed the cabbie sixty bucks and stepped onto the sidewalk on Little West 12th Street. The cobblestone had Charleston written all over it, and I could see Liz had found a little of home in the big wheel of confusion. Late September in Manhattan is a fine time to be there, especially when you're chasing love. But I knew my chances weren't good.

As the cab turned down Charles and disappeared, I saw Liz through the window of the second floor. She was painting. I found a small pebble and drew back my arm to throw it, but paused.

I could feel the passion radiating from her body into the brush as she moved up and down on the canvas, putting every damn thing she had into it. She must have felt me watching, because she stopped and looked down. I waved to her. She put down her brush and headed my way. A moment later, she walked down the steps to the sidewalk. She still had her apron on, and there was paint on her jeans and in her hair. "You look terrible," she said.

"Yeah, I've heard." I touched my bruised face.

"Why'd you come?" she asked, and we were off to a great start.

"Did you think for one minute I wouldn't?"

"I didn't think about it."

"I wanted to check on you. You wouldn't return my calls. I was worried."

"I'm a big girl."

"You know that's not the only reason I came. I had to see you. We can't let this go, Liz. Come back to me."

"I thought I'd made myself clear."

"I hoped you might have reconsidered."

"Look, T.A., I'm sorry you came here. I really am. And I am thankful for what you did, but I have nothing more to say to you."

I read anger and pain in the tightness of her cheeks, and I saw exhaustion in her eyes. "I'm sorry I lied," I said.

"You're forgiven."

Last shot. "C'mon, Liz. Can you hear me out? I feel like you're not even seeing me right now. Can you please give me a couple minutes?"

"Don't talk to me like I owe you something. I've already heard all this, and I'm over it."

"You're right. You don't owe me anything." I took her hand

and held it for a moment. "You have every reason to hate me, and I know I'm one big lie to you, but I love you. You have to know that. And if you would look at all this from a different perspective, you might understand that I handled everything the best I could—the only way I could. I was always looking out for you."

She wiped her fingers on her apron. "I hear what you're saying, loud and clear. You have to understand, though. It's over. I'm back to work. I don't love you anymore."

"I don't believe it."

"Believe it. You got in the way of what I do and what matters most, T.A. You and everything back home makes it hurt. We don't want the same things."

As a single tear dropped from her eye, my heart fell along with it.

Just like that, I'd lost her and it couldn't have been any clearer. Sometimes destiny fails to deliver, and I wanted to appeal, but to who? It was her decision, and I was gone.

"Sorry you came all this way," she said, backing toward the door.

"It was worth a shot." I began to walk away, too. "Any good places to eat around here?"

"Pastis on the corner there. Make sure you get the fries."

That's how it went. Our last words were about fucking potatoes. Not exactly the exchange I had hoped for.

CHAPTER 44

I moped around for a couple weeks feeling sorry for myself, drinking too much and not eating enough, but eventually it was time to get out of the house and move on. Liz was never coming back and looking at the phone wasn't going to make her call me. Staring at the door wasn't going to make her knock.

The men and women we arrested had made the front page again, this time below the fold. Their story had already begun to fade into history. Even though Kado had broken down, it was Diego that had ultimately blown my cover. So I fought for Kado, and now he was back at his restaurant, Morph, living the life of a free man.

Despite many setbacks, Operation Coastal Snow had been deemed a success. Twenty kilograms of cocaine, a half-million dollars in cash, and one dead Cuban. Ninety-seven people in four states had been arrested, and many indictments would follow. People say that we don't make a difference, that the war on drugs is a waste of time and money, but I'd like to think that Operation Coastal Snow saved at least one life, maybe prevented one kid from growing up without a father or mother.

Tux finally started talking. It's funny how a few days behind bars loosen your lips like alcohol. Especially when you start dangling lighter sentences in front of them. He admitted that he and Jack had met at one of James King's parties at the Mazyck a year back. Tux was with one of his friends who played professional football. He and Jack hit it off and Jack started kicking him some powder. Tux had been dealing a long time but hadn't been able to get anything so pure. Their relationship grew from there.

The night of the arrests (I assume right after Liz had hit him with the paperweight), Jack called Tux and offered him fifty grand to keep Liz from getting on that plane. That's that. Tux had been so smart for so long, but eventually, greed got him. Hard to turn down fifty grand for a night's work. I also asked Tux how he had found out it was me who beat up his cousin. He said he had a cop on the payroll. I passed the cop's name down the line. One more turncoat we didn't have to worry about anymore.

Then he threw another nugget my way, something that had really been puzzling me. Tux said the day after I showed up at his house throwing punches, he'd found out who had come after me with that rifle. True to his word, Tux had told his cousin, Jesse, that he was cancelling the hit on me. This was right after Chester and I had left Tux's house the first time. Well, Jesse didn't listen and went out and hired someone else to kill me. When Tux heard, he paid him a visit. Tux assured me that I wouldn't have to worry about his stupid cousin again. I didn't tell Tux at the time, but *I* was going to make sure I wouldn't have to worry about Jesse anymore. He and his rifleman would hear from me shortly.

I'd thought long and hard over what to do with Stephanie. We could have put her in jail, but I knew that wasn't right. I finally decided to call her mother in Fort Lauderdale, and I told her nearly everything. From what I'd heard from Stephanie, her mother was a commanding force in her life and the person she most respected. Her mother took it well and there were no hints of skepticism; I got the feeling she knew what I was talking about. She said she would bring Stephanie down to Florida and find her help. I hoped it would work out.

Speaking of hope: I kept playing at The Children's Hospital. I'd started going for Liz, but I kept going for the kids. There couldn't be many better things in my world than watching a group of unfortunate and brave children dancing to the sound of the banjo, wielding smiles that could melt icecaps.

But I was alone. And chances were I'd be sleeping with a gun by my side until someone finally got me. Or, more optimistically, until I was old and gray.

CHAPTER 45

One day in November, Beau Tate had a heart attack.
He was on his riding lawnmower when it happened. (Only in the Southeast do you still have to cut grass in November.) His wife called me at work to tell me the news. I rushed over to the hospital and he was up and talking by the time I got there. It had only been a mild heart attack, but I spent the night in a chair watching him sleep and listening to the chirp of the EKG. I couldn't handle losing him. Not for a long time. It was like losing my father all over again.

That next morning, still wearing the same clothes, I left the hospital and drove toward the airport to pick up Anna. It would be the first time I had seen her since December the year before. She came out from baggage claim, and the emptiness inside of me lit up and burned. She'd grown her blonde hair back out, like it was part of the new "California" Anna. But she still fit the image I'd held in my mind. A tomboy kind of beauty. I'd always remember her as the little girl playing with me in the marsh.

We embraced and she broke into tears on my shoulder. We spoke of her father on the way back. Then spent the day playing cards and entertaining him as best we could.

That night, Anna and I went out to get a bite to eat at Shi Ki, an unassuming little sushi establishment tucked into a building with a Blockbuster on East Bay Street. We talked and drank Nigori and ate various sashimi: yellowtail, fluke, salmon roe, sea urchin, and surf clam. I liked that she had some sushi eating flexibility. I'd forgotten about that.

She was giving me a hard time about how OCD I was over cleaning, and I caught myself getting defensive. I shook my head. "You're good at this, aren't you?"

"At what?"

"Getting under my skin."

She reached across the table with them and pinched my ring finger. "I'm the best."

We left my Jeep in the parking lot and started walking. Walked for more than an hour, talking about old times, and about life and death. In the end, as we meet death, is there anything more important than relationships? Loved ones? Family and friends? I didn't think so, and we agreed on that.

I didn't know where Anna fit in. Did I love her? You're damn right. I'd loved her since the first summer I'd spent down in Charleston. Before our first kiss.

What kind of love was it, though? Was is right that we almost married? Had she made a mistake by leaving me? Or had she saved us from a much more painful heartache down the line?

She took my hand and led me up the steps to Waterfront Park. We passed by several children playing in the fountain and took a seat in the grass not to far from the seawall. Waves were splashing up over the railing. A lone cloud pushed its way across the evening sky.

"What's wrong?" she asked, picking up on the fact that I'd gone silent.

"It's been a long year, Anna. That's all."

She nodded. "For me, too." A breeze brought a wave of silence between us. We both had things to say but neither one of us wanted to go first. I didn't know what she was thinking. There she was, one of my best friends on earth *and* the woman who'd left me a note ending our engagement, now sitting next to me, wanting to pour her heart out. I could feel it, but I didn't know if I wanted her to.

She was the first one to speak. We faced each other.

"I know you're wondering why I left. After I heard what happened with Robert that night, I hated myself for abandoning you. But it had been so hard to leave. I knew that even calling you would have broken me. For whatever reason, we weren't right then. I still had some things I had to work out."

"Why are you telling me this?"

"Because I love you, T.A. Seeing you today made me sure of it. I want us back. I want to marry you. Ask me." She choked up. "Let me say yes to you again. Let me have the honor."

Some of you know what it's like. Those words coming out of a lost lover's mouth. So many times, people lose someone and hope and pray and beg that they'll come back. The truth is that they usually don't. Probably for good reason. So I'd gone on and found a life without her, accepting that it wasn't meant to be. Now, she was trying to change all that.

I'm reminded of the blessings of unanswered prayers. I wished she had forgotten about me. For the first time in a year, I wished she had gotten married or fallen in love with someone else. But she hadn't. She'd done what she had to do and was back.

Minutes passed. I ripped some blades of grass out of the dirt and rubbed them in my fingers. Stared out over the water.

"There's a woman in my life. Her name is Liz."

"My dad mentioned her. I thought she left you."

"She did."

"So..."

"I still love her."

"I don't understand. If she left you, why does it matter?"

"I can't stop loving her just because she doesn't feel the same. Anna, we have a friendship to repair. That's where we belong."

I put a hand on her shoulder. "You are important to me, and I want you back in my life, but it has to stop at friends. You know that, too."

"I don't know that or agree. I wouldn't tell you I want to marry you if I thought otherwise."

"I'm telling you how it has to be. I want you in my life. No. More than that. I *need* you in my life. But it's only gonna work one way."

She took in a deep breath. A pause.

Minutes of nothing but the salt air blowing by.

"Well," she finally said, "I'll take you any way I can get you, T.A. You're right. We do have a friendship to repair."

"Yes, we do." I stood and helped her up. "Let's go check on your dad."

"All right."

Before we walked back to reality, we hugged. An embrace I wouldn't soon forget. Life is too short to hold grudges and unsorted feelings. We'd put it all on the table and knew where each of us stood. I don't have enough friends in this life, and I wasn't about to let her go. We both felt good about things as we went back down the steps with our arms around each other.

CHAPTER 46

That weekend, I motored the *Pretender* over to the marina next to Salty Mike's and walked into town. It couldn't have felt any better outside. Weather to make San Diego drool. Charleston just blooms in late fall. I perused several galleries near the market and saw some really great stuff. None of it had the impact that Liz's art did, though. I listened to a sidewalk saxophonist for a while, and after a couple hours, I started back.

I strolled along the uneven sidewalks of King toward the Battery. Reaching Battery Park, I crossed over the soft green grass. The branches of the live oaks surrounding me drooped down to the ground as if they were growing back into the earth, limb by limb. It was from those limbs that they'd hung the pirate, Stede Bonnet, and twenty of his men, back in 1718. As a warning to all the Atlantic pirates, they let the bodies swing from the oaks for four days before they took them down. I could feel their presence.

I stopped near a cannon and gazed out over Fort Sumter. Those walls had stood the test of time, only to be taken down by a sixty-one-foot Viking captained by a woman named Stephanie Lewis. I've known many women over the years that are stronger than cannons, women who could break down walls, and she had proven to be one of them. Ain't no denyin' that.

***

Back on the boat, I went down to the galley and took a Kalik beer out of the cooler. I found the shuffle on my iPod, and climbed back to the deck. I sat down in the cockpit, looking out over the ocean. The Thievery Corporation's remix of "Can I Get a Witness?" came on, and their signature beat, the one my own life beats to, led me to a wonderful place. I'd finally gotten used to being alone, and life was grand.

A dragonfly landed on the wheel in front of me, like the dream I kept having. *It couldn't be...*

I watched it flutter in place for a moment, its purple wings flapping in rhythm, shimmering in the sunlight. It took flight again and flew out over the water with grace. I looked down at the blue and white label wrapped around the beer in my hand, and a warmth came over me, like I'd come in from the cold.

I knew she'd be there. I looked to my left.

Liz wasn't there. Of course. How stupid could I be, to think she would be walking down the dock, coming back to me, manifesting the dream I kept having? That idea suddenly seemed so absurd. *Who am I to live such a poetic existence?* It was okay, though. I'd made peace with being single. It's a fine thing to love a woman, even if she doesn't love you. Lord Tennyson isn't such an asshole after all. It is better to have loved. There was someone out there waiting for me. I just knew it.

I removed the sail covers and tossed them down the hatch.

Then I heard her voice. "You got room for one more?"

I didn't look up. I closed my eyes and took in a deep breath. I let the feeling run all over me. I lifted my head and looked at Liz. She stood right in front of me on the dock, utterly angelic. She wore a light green top and a white skirt with turquoise flowers along the bottom. Her brown hair was pulled back, and her eyes said so much.

I looked to my right and left. "We can squeeze one more on, but I don't know that I can assure your safety."

"I'll take a chance."

I smiled, and I mean a real smile, from deep, deep down.

"So I heard you've been going back to the Children's Hospital."

I nodded. "I told them not to tell you."

"Well, they did."

As I started the motor, she pulled the lines and tossed them onto the deck. I reached out my hand and helped her aboard. Her touch made me feel whole.

I put my arms around her and we kissed in a way that made us forget about the past, like we'd just met. Then we squeezed each other tight. There was a faint scent of orchids in her hair.

"You knew I'd come for you, didn't you?"

"I could have guessed the day." There I was lying again. Last one, I promise.

I got behind the wheel and began to work my way out of the marina. "What changed your mind?"

"I spoke to a friend of yours the other day. She said you were still thinking about me."

"What friend?"

"Anna called me."

"Anna? How'd *she* get your number?"

"You're not the only one who's Googled me over the years."

"So you just changed your mind all of a sudden?"

"I never stopped thinking about you, T.A. It just took some time."

When we reached the channel in the middle of the harbor, Liz took the helm. I raised the jib and main, and the wind began to push us. She shut the engine, and we took on a fantastic tilt starboard, gliding across the water, the settling of the boat the only sound.

LOWCOUNTRY PUNCH

Fort Sumter came about and Liz read my mind. "I can't believe they haven't fixed the wall yet."

"Walls take longer to build than tear down."

"Thank you, Socrates. Do you have any other little tidbits for me?" She buried a smile.

"I'd almost forgotten why I love you."

"I almost forgot that I did."

Stingy...and I liked it.

The open ocean welcomed us, and the Holy City began to fade away in the distance. The bow performed with finesse through the waves, and the seabirds circled above. Standing next to Liz at the helm, I closed my eyes and let the breeze roll across my face. Sometimes you can taste how good you feel. Like the salt in the air. I had no idea what would become of us, but I was optimistic.

And that's all you can be. Optimistic.

With a woman like Liz in my life, that was not too hard to do. I put my hand on the wheel to join hers, and the *Pretender* sailed across the Atlantic like so many ships had done before her.

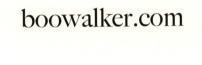

Acknowledgments

I could not have written this book without the help of some amazing family and friends. *Lowcountry Punch* was my first book, and as your first book should, it took many years and many drafts to write. I originally wrote it in first person, then rewrote it in third person and included several other points of view, then went back to first person, eliminating all but one character's point of view again. For the first four or five drafts, the second part of the novel took place in Bolivia! Those pages are long gone. In the first few years of learning how to write, I did my best to mangle the English language, and I am so grateful to those brave souls who dared put their time and energy into reading the early drafts and leading me in the right direction.

Charlie, Drew, Steven, and Scott—my bandmates and brothers—thank you for showing me how to tap into the creative consciousness. I miss our days together; it was a good ride.

Shayna and Travis Howell, among the many hours you put into helping me with my book, my most vivid memory is the day we read dialogue out loud at my place in James Island and ate Andolini's Pizza (still my favorite in Charleston). Not many people on this planet are that selfless and encouraging. You two were there from the beginning, and probably the only ones who remember the Bolivia parts. Thank you.

LOWCOUNTRY PUNCH

My mother, Jo Walker, passed down her love of books to me, something even the required reading in school couldn't break. Mom, your contributions to this book were countless and crucial, and I will be forever thankful.

Aunt Linda, thank you so much for all you have done. You are a great English teacher and even better person.

Mikella Walker, my words will always be for you. I am one lucky son of a gun!

Thanks to all of you who were there from early on. It warms my heart thinking about all the good souls in my life.

Made in the USA
Charleston, SC
12 March 2014